COURAGE
RISES
FROM THE
ASHES

HANNAH LYNN GRACE

ISBN 978-1-64140-292-7 (Paperback)
ISBN 978-1-64140-293-4 (Digital)

Christian Faith Publishing, Inc.
296 Chestnut Street
Meadville, PA 16335
www.christianfaithpublishing.com

Printed in the United States of America

DEDICATION

To my loving family and those who inspired it. Thank you for telling me to stop talking about writing a book and saying that I needed to put pen to paper and actually write it. I love you. End.

CONTENTS

1

A Story

The sun was not quite up yet, though the rooster was crowing as if he were not diligent enough in his endeavors that the sun would refuse to rise. It was apparent that his efforts were not in vain as soft twilight glowed through the window curtains. It was the first of May, and the promise of summer vacation was a not-so-distant glimmer on the horizon. It was not that Abigail did not like school; in fact, she was an excellent student. It was just that summer is a special time of mixed laziness and chaos rolled together. This year, Abigail was finally old enough to attend the church summer camp. She anticipated spending an entire week there, along with her friends Miriam and Sarah. What fun it was going to be for the girls as they participated together in all the camp activities. In the evenings, when they all gathered around the huge campfire, they would sing and have Bible studies. This was a personal landmark for Abigail; what she felt was her first step into adulthood. Suddenly, she was feeling very grown up and responsible. It was a very nice feeling.

At her mother's call, she got dressed in her blue gingham dress and her sturdy plain shoes. She spent a few moments braiding her hair and wrapping it in a bun at the nap of her neck. She was compelled to do this task because of Jimmy Ware. He had taken to pulling her pigtails at regular intervals, causing no end to the snickering and teasing. It was common knowledge that he was sweet on her, and even though she had advised him on numerous occasions that she did not return the sentiments, he prevailed in his despicable behavior. Instead of being put off by her protests, he was somehow convinced that if he just kept trying, she would magically change her mind and accept and even return his romantic overtures. It was so very annoying, but Abigail was at a loss as to how to change the situation.

As she exited her bedroom, she could hear her brothers as they awakened and made their preparations for school. Jeremiah seemed to be having problems finding socks, and he was jabbering like a magpie. Abigail smiled to herself and skipped down the stairs. As she entered the kitchen, her nose did a dance when it was assailed with the odor of sizzling sausage. Breakfast was her favorite meal of the day, and today was a prime example of why. As her mother was frying the French toast, which also was Abigail's personal favorite, she proceeded to set the table. She lined the table with plates, silverware, and glasses. She then turned to the pantry and brought out the maple syrup and the blueberry jelly. She pulled the butter and milk from the icebox, pouring the rich milk into each glass. They lived on the very edge of town and were almost the last stop on the ice delivery man's route. His home was a mile up the road, and his horse always seemed in a hurry to get back to the stable where it knew that a measure of grain waited.

Abigail turned to her mother and announced that she had finished with the table. Her mother's smile, quick hug, and peck on the cheek signaled a job well done and that her efforts were very much appreciated. Grabbing a basket by the door, she headed out to do the next task, which was collecting the hen's treasures and feeding them. Her brothers ran nosily past her toward the barn as she crossed the yard toward the chicken coop.

"Hey! You don't need to run me over!" Abigail yelled out to their retreating backs. The only response she got was loud whoops and laughter.

After she gathered the eggs, she took the feed bucket and scattered the grain on the ground. The chickens hurried to harvest the feast, and Abigail stooped to pet one of the largest red-brown hens. She had raised this chicken from the egg, and as a chick, it had bonded with her. Now Abigail saved some of choicest grains for the hen who delicately ate the morsels from her right hand as Abigail petted her with her left hand.

"I know that the biggest brown egg was from you, Harriet. You are a very good girl, therefore only you get a special treat. The money I got from the sale of your eggs is what paid my way to go to summer camp this year. Thank you, my dear feathered friend, for all of your hard work. Eat well." Abigail crooned. Harriet showed her appreciation by strutting and clucking importantly, seeking the special rubbing that Abigail gave her. It was as if she understood everything that Abigail had said and that it gave her crowing rights as queen of the roost.

Next, Abigail did a quick check of the garden to see what was ready to harvest. Hiding under a large broad leaf was an acorn squash, Mother's favorite vegetable. Its dark-green skin blended in with the leaves of the plant and the dark earth it grew in. "Hum, trying to hide from me, will you? Well, it just won't work," Abigail announced with a small laugh. She also plucked a number of tomatoes and cucumbers, along with some lettuce, radishes, and young spinach. Mixed together, this would make a wonderful salad. With her basket filled, she stood and went back to the house. The children had finished their chores at the same time and were boisterous as they entered the house. Grandmother was up and sitting at the breakfast table, and they all gladly greeted the elderly lady. Each one planted a loving kiss on her withered cheek with Jeremiahs being more exuberant than the other two.

"My, this makes me remember the days when all of my children were young. The house always seemed to be filled with joy and laughter too. I'm sure some of this happiness is because school will be out for the summer soon."

"Oh yes, Grandmother, it is only a few weeks more before we are off for the whole summer," Jeremiah stated with happy enthusiasm. He was not fond of school, as it required sitting still and being quiet for extended lengths of time, a pure trial for him. To his credit, he did show sufficient restraint much of the time. He adored his teacher, Miss Plummer, so he went to great lengths to please her. One way that he did that was to exhibit good behavior in the classroom.

Some days, it was harder as he had to ignore the spit balls hurled at him by his friend, Tucker Ware, Jimmy's little brother. The Ware boys were always getting into trouble at school as neither of them seemed to be able to follow any rules.

"Is Father taking you and Miriam's grandmother to visit Mrs. Rogers today?" Abigail inquired.

"Yes, he is in need of feed again too, so it works out well for all of us. We ladies need to keep in touch with each other even more now than ever before," Grandmother said with a sigh. She seemed about to say something more but just turned quiet and introspective instead.

With the chores done and breakfast finished, the children gathered their school supplies and headed for the door when Grandmother called out to Abigail.

"Abigail, I need you to do something for me," Grandmother said as she pulled Abigail aside.

"Yes, Grandmother?" Abigail queried.

"This may sound strange, but I would like you to keep an eye out for Miriam. There may be some hard changes in her life soon, and she will be in need of a good strong friend. I do not like to be so cryptic, but it is a feeling that I have, and if it goes the way that I think that it will, you will soon understand," Grandmother said.

"All right, Grandmother, she is one of my best friends, and I see her nearly every day. I will watch her and be there if she needs me."

Her grandmother gave her a gentle pat on her hand. "I knew that you would say that, my dear. Do have a good day at school today."

"Come home right after school so that all of you can weed the garden. The rain seems to have given the weeds great hope, and they threaten to overgrow the vegetables. I have not ever had to serve a plate of weeds for a meal, and I don't wish to start now," Mother said with a laugh. She had once received a letter from some cousins from down Louisiana way who had informed her that they gathered weeds to make something called poke salad. Abigail and her brothers did not know for sure just what exactly poke was, but they had no desire to find out. Dear Mother threatened to research this if the weeding chore was not done in a timely fashion.

The children all laughed as they exited the door and called out with hardy assurances that that garden would be weeded before sunset.

They didn't live too far from the school, and they enjoyed the walk. Sarah and Randy joined them and then Miriam and Jerald also as they passed by their respective houses. The boys raced out ahead as the girls walked at a more leisurely pace.

"Father is taking Grandmother to visit Mrs. Rogers today. Is your Grandmother going too?" Abigail queried.

"Oh yes, she has had her breakfast and is gathering a few things to take for Mrs. Rogers. She and Mother made some sauerkraut, and Father made some venison sausage. She is taking that and her Bible, of course. I don't know why Grandmother goes to visit with her. She is just so strange, and we get worried because Grandmother always seems so tired now and especially so when she gets back from an outing," Miriam shared.

"My grandmother told me about what happened to Mrs. Rogers that made her the way she is now. Would you like to hear the story? It may answer your questions about your grandmother's continued friendship with her," Abigail asked quietly.

Miriam looked quizzically at her friend. "Yes, please tell me."

Mrs. Rogers's odd behavior had begun some ten years before after she had been in a carriage accident. She had been a very independent type of person, and she had needed to buy some supplies for a church social engagement as she was the hostess for the event. It was early in the winter and bitterly cold, but there had not been snow as of yet. Her son, Zachariah, had become ill after breakfast with a violent upset stomach, so he was unable to drive her to the mercantile. Mrs. Rogers insisted that she was perfectly capable of driving herself, so she hitched the horse to the carriage and set out. After she made her purchases, she had started home. The heavy-laden clouds finally decided to open up, and the snow began falling, slowly at first but soon reaching epic proportions. As Mrs. Rogers came to a bridge, the wheels of the carriage began slipping on an icy patch when one of the wheels fell into a hole, causing the carriage to lurch violently. Mrs. Rogers was thrown from the carriage, bumping her head on the wheel rendering her unconscious. She ended up rolling down the embankment and was half lying in the icy water. No one knows how long she had laid there, but she was found around noontime by Reverend Arden. He pulled her from the icy water and hurriedly brought her into town to Dr. Holliday's office. The doctor did what he could, but he could not revive her. He sadly pronounced her dead and took on the task of taking her body back home to her son. Reverend Arden would make the rounds to advise the family and church members of her demise so the community could prepare for the wake and burial.

Within a short time, Mrs. Roger's sister and some of the neighbors arrived at the farm. With soft tear-filled voices, they washed and dressed Mrs. Roger's body in her best clothing. As was the custom, sawhorses topped with some stout boards had been set up in the parlor, and her body was reverently positioned on them. Throughout the remainder of the day, more friends arrived, many bringing food, sharing their grief, and comforting one another. As the early winter sun began to set, they gathered in the parlor for the wake. Zachariah and a number of the men had just returned from digging the grave. The frozen ground had made the task difficult, and they all were thoroughly chilled. As they were revived with hot beverages and hearty plates of food, they discussed who would take turns for the overnight vigil. The rest of the folks would go home to return in the morning for the service and interment. These arrangements were discussed in soft, hushed tones as if raising their voices would disturb the deceased woman. Then to their everlasting amazement, that is exactly what happened. Mrs. Rogers sat bolt upright, looked around the room at all her friends, and then asked if someone would bring her a glass of water as she was very thirsty. Since that time, Mrs. Rogers was subject to strange outbursts, and folks couldn't agree on what exactly caused it. Some thought that it was from the blow to the head, some blamed it on her being almost frozen by the time she was found, and still others said that it was from her having no signs of life for such a long time. In any event, the community at large kept a distance from her as they did not want her to become focused on them. Her wild talk about angels and demons and asking folks if they knew Jesus was just too unsettling for them. Her last outburst on Easter Sunday when she spied Mr. Ware was just the latest incident. To his dismay, she had focused on him and, in strident tones, kept asking him if he knew Jesus, that he just had to know Jesus. He had been completely traumatized, and he had rushed from the church as fast as his inebriated legs could carry him. After that outburst, some less-than-charitable folks had concluded that she was just plumb crazy.

"That is quite a story. I had heard bits and pieces of it, and I've seen her when she starts acting funny like. She is just lucky to be alive after being frozen like that," Samuel stated as he shook his head. "I still plan to steer clear of her when I see her. I'm just not sure about that angel and demon stuff."

"Well, Samuel, the Bible does say that it was an angel that spoke to Mary and told her that she was going to give birth to Jesus. I can't imagine an angel talking to me especially about something like that, but I do believe that it is all true. And in all of the stories about Jesus, he just told those old demons to be gone and they had to leave. Just because we don't want to hear about these things, Mrs. Roger's talking about them is firmly based on the Bible." Abigail felt that she needed to defend the older woman. Besides that, it moved her to think more deeply about the Bible in new and different ways and like now just how the teachings did and could relate to her more personally.

Samuel looked at his sister in wonder, realizing that in a simple way she had just shared concepts that were deeply profound. He tucked this new realization firmly away, promising himself that he would look up these stories in his Bible study time and perhaps he too would come to a new and better understanding of the Bible and how this information applied to him. He looked at his sister with a new awareness, suddenly becoming conscious of how she had grown and matured and how he had missed it until just now.

They had walked steadily and reached the school yard entering the gate. "Hey, there's Bobby over by the well." With that, Samuel took off running toward his friend, hailing him from across the school yard. Bobby looked up at the call but didn't answer back. He just stood there quietly as Samuel raced up to him.

The girls had wandered over to the benches that had been placed under the trees, and Sarah had pulled out her math papers. Mulling over the problems, she finally just let out a heavy dramatic sigh. "I'm just never going to understand this math. You have tried to explain it to me so many times, but I just don't get it. I'm afraid that I'm not going to pass it," she said in despair.

"Let me think about it, and together we will find someone to help you. I'm not giving up on you. And you are so good with all of the other subjects that I just know that you will be able to do this too. We both plan to study to become teachers, so you'll have to know the math. Don't worry, I will put my thinking cap on and come up with something." Abigail was concerned and was determined to find a tutor to help her friend.

Samuel and Bobby crossed the yard and sat down on the next bench. Abigail had looked up as the boys had approached, and she saw that Bobby had a somewhat dejected expression on his face. "Hi, Bobby, are you all right?"

"He just found out that his Father died," Samuel blurted out.

"Oh my, I'm so sorry, Bobby." Abigail was flustered that her brother was such an unfeeling brute. Couldn't he see that Bobby was really hurting? She moved over and took Bobby's hand in sympathy. "Is there anything that we can do?"

"No, my mother and I are going to be all right. Friday afternoon, Mr. Huffmeister called my mother into the bank, and he gave her the news. Some friend of my father's had sent money to us, along with a letter. Well, for the last five years, my father had been living in New York City. He had a steady job, but it didn't pay very much, so he started boxing at the matches they have out there. He was a really good boxer, and he was saving his winnings so he could come back here and buy a farm for us. I guess that's not going to happen now." A frown pulled at the corners of his mouth, and his brow wrinkled. "After his last fight, he got back to his boarding house with the prize money, and he was set on by some thugs. They got that night's prize money, but they figured that he should have more somewhere. They got mad at him because he wouldn't tell him where his stash was hidden, so one of the robbers hit him in the head with a board. His friend found him there in his room just before he died. My father asked him to send the rest of the money he had hidden back home to us. He also told him to tell us that he was sorry that things didn't turn out the way that he had planned and that he loved us."

"Oh, Bobby, that is just so sad. I'm so very sorry." Abigail, Miriam, and Sarah had flanked their friend and offered him their comfort.

"Aw, it's not so bad really. My father had been gone for a long time, since I was really little. I barely remember him. But he did send letters and some money sometimes, so Mother always had hope that he would come back someday. I think that she really knew that he had a wanderlust in him and that he would never settle down for long. One other good thing came out of this too. It seems that Mrs. Huffmeister made a point of being in the bank that day so she could comfort my mother. Then she totally surprised my mother by asking her if she would come to work for her. It seems that she has needed a housekeeper for a while, and she had asked folks in town if they could recommend someone. So many people suggested Mother for the position, and after meeting Mother for herself, she hired her on the spot. And we're going to be moving into the Huffmeisters' carriage house in a couple of days. Since Mother isn't going to be doing laundry anymore, she recommended her customers to Mrs. Hensley, who also has a good reputation as a laundry/seamstress."

"Oh, Bobby, that really is good news. I think that your mother is going to be so happy working for the Huffmeisters. Mother and Father have said numerous times that they think so highly of them." Abigail was glad that things were changing for the good for her friend.

"Yes, I have heard that about them too. Even Rolf is a good guy most of the time." Sarah was quick to shed a good light on the banker and his family.

"And there is something else. I don't have to work out anymore, and if I do work, I get to keep what I've earned. I still want to keep working for the Larsons. They are really great people, and they have been so nice to me. We do have some money in the bank now, and my mother is going to be making a good wage. Plus since we will be living in the carriage house, we won't have the apartment, so we won't have to pay rent anymore." But Bobby still had a forlorn expression on his face. "Before I always kind of watched down the road thinking that one day I would look up and see my father coming. I guess now that just isn't going to happen."

The group had a lot to think about as the bell rang for classes to begin. After school, Abigail, Samuel, and Jeremiah walked slowly home, talking about their friend and all of the changes he was dealing with. They were concerned for him, and they wanted to do something to help. Mother met the group at the door as she had heard the news, and she knew that the children would need to talk. They discussed some possibilities, and they realized that the best thing that they could do was to just be there for him for support and of course to lift him in prayer. Just talking things out had given the children a measure of relief, and after they had put their school supplies away, they headed for the garden.

"We'll have the garden weeded and our other chores done in time for supper," Samuel assured their mother.

Abigail and the boys worked steadily and had the garden in tip-top shape in no time. They had pulled all of the weeds, picked potato bugs and squashed them, and tied up the runners of the beans and peas to keep them off the ground. They had also harvested the ripe vegetables, so Mother could can them. It was going to be great to have them ready to serve up in the winter when the snow covered the ground.

As they finished the chores and rounded the barn, they saw that their father had come home from work and that he was talking with Mr. Larson. Both men smiled as the group walked up.

"Well, hello there! It looks as though you all have been busy. Those are mighty fine-looking vegetables that you have in that basket there. The missus has been busy canning the last two weeks, and she has put up some of those marvelous farmer's pickles that she does so well. Yes, siree, I sure am looking forward to having some of those soon, along with the fried chicken and potato salad that she whips up." Mr. Larson smiled as he bragged on his wife and her cooking.

"We are both blessed to have wives that are so talented in the kitchen." Father was quick to agree and to praise his wife also. "Mr. Larson has some business that he would like to discuss with Samuel and Abigail. I will say in advance that I like the idea, so listen to what he has to say, and then you can decide if it is something that you would like to do."

Mr. Larson cleared his throat and began. "I have a sister who is very ill and has asked for me and the missus to come for a visit. We would be traveling to Minneapolis and would need to be gone for an entire week. We need someone to take care of the farm while we are gone, and though Bobby knows everything about the milking, he just can't do all of the work by himself. If you two are interested, I would be willing to pay you a fair wage for the entire week. I am sure that the three of you are capable of doing the work and that you are responsible enough to do it. What do you think? Are you willing to do this?"

Abigail and Samuel looked at their father in surprise, but they also basked in the praise. "Sure, we would be more than happy to do it. When would you be leaving?" Samuel asked.

"Great! We plan to leave the first week in June the Monday after your last day of school. I am talking to Bobby about it in just a bit here. I just wanted to check with your father and the two of you before I said anything to him. We'll iron out all of the details later. I am off for now. Thank you for doing this for me." Mr. Larson left Abigail and Samuel with huge smiles on their faces as he drove out of the yard. The two hurried off to tell their mother the good news.

"Hey, what about me? Can't I work too? Golly, first, I can't go to Bible camp, and now I can't work for Mr. Larson either." Jeremiah's feelings of dejection were plainly written on his face.

Mr. Eckhardt put his arm around Jeremiah's shoulders. "Well, son, I have thinking about that. I considered that you might be feeling a tad left out of things that prompted me to put my thinking cap on and come up with something different for you this summer. I have devised a plan, and I am pretty sure that it will be a real adventure."

Jeremiah's face lit up with a huge smile as his father began sharing with him just what the wonderful plan entailed.

2

Randy

Randy Bernhardt was a special child. The day he was born, he was very ill and was not expected to live. Almost from the moment that he exited the womb, he had a very high fever. His tiny body just would not cool down, and at times, he would bend backward with convulsions so hard that Mrs. Bernhardt feared that he would not straighten out again. When he was three days old, the fever finally broke, but he was so weak and listless that he could not even be enticed to suckle. Mrs. Bernhardt would take a small piece of cloth soaked in her breast milk and patiently squeeze it drop by drop into his mouth, praying fervently the entire time. After about a week had passed, he finally grew strong enough to suckle on his own. As he grew and finally thrived, the young parents noticed that he was not developing as he should. He was slow to roll over on his own; then he was late to crawl. His problems were especially apparent when it came to the art of walking. With an unsteady gait, he gallantly struggled to maintain his balance. His general movements were fraught with twitches and jerks, and when he tried to focus on any object, his eyes would roll to the side. He was also late to begin talking, and when he did, his speech was guttural and slurred. His family could understand his labored speech, and later his friends learned that if they listened carefully, they could also understand him. Despite these problems, he was a happy child. His smile was lopsided but frequent, and his laugh was infectious. He was a very loving, giving boy. Dr.

Holliday told the Bernhardt's that the medical diagnosis was called cerebral palsy caused by the fever at birth. The young parents decided that they would not treat him as having disabilities. Instead, they helped him find things that he could do and even excel at. As their other children were born hale and hearty, the couple was grateful, but the love that they had for Randy was ever present.

Randy had a difficult time concentrating, and to that end, the school teacher, Ms. Plummer, was given permission to let Randy leave school when he became too restless from being frustrated. His grasp of rudimentary math was good, and when handling money, he could accurately make change without mistakes, but he just couldn't grasp reading and writing. Oh, he could read simple words, and he could even sign his name, but reading a book was beyond him. He was a good boy, very polite, and obedient; and most of the time, he spent the entire day in the classroom. But on warm days, when the sun was shining brightly, it drew him out into nature where he was the most comfortable. All animals, even a number of the wild ones, recognized that he was a gentle person and weren't afraid of him. Some of the wild animals would even go so far as to let him touch them, and they would accept treats from him as well.

Today was such a fine day that Randy did become restless, and he set out from school for an adventure. In town, there were a number of places that he was welcome, and the folks would even find tasks for him to do. At the mercantile, he could sweep the front porch, wash the windows, straighten stock in the back room, and even assist customers to find items. Through repetition, he had learned the location of most of the merchandise and could retrieve items from the storeroom. At the smithy, he could work the bellows, feed wood to the fire, and tend the horses that were left to be shod. But today as he wandered down the road from the school, he found Mrs. Acres out tending her bees. He waved to her, and she beckoned to him.

"Good morning, Randy. It is a fine day, is it not? It is much better to be outside today than to be cooped up in a schoolhouse, right?" Mrs. Acres asked laughingly.

"Oh yes! Can I please help you?" asked Randy. Randy had spent a lot of time with Mrs. Acres, and she had no problem understanding his slurred speech. Plus Randy's gift with animals even extended to the bees, so she was glad to have his assistance. They worked quietly side by side, pulling the wooden frames out of the hives and placing them in the waiting washtub. Later, they would take the laden trays to the shed and use a heated knife to scape open the wax so the honey would drain out. It was a process that they were both very familiar with and truly enjoyed doing.

"Look! There is the queen bee. She is so pretty no wonder the bees want to make honey for her."

Randy's observations were so quaint and sometimes so insightful that Mrs. Acres thoroughly enjoyed having Randy assist her. Randy had come to understand the art of beekeeping to the point that she was certain that he would be capable of keeping hives of his own. Soon she was planning on broaching the subject with Mr. Bernhardt. There would be startup costs, but if Randy was successful, he would make the investment back in no time, and it could be a good way for him to become self-sufficient. Physically, he was a large boy, and he was already fifteen years old. This could be a big step into the adult world for him.

"Well, Randy, I certainly do thank you. Once again, you have been a tremendous help to me. Do you need to go back to school for any lessons this afternoon?"

"Yes, my lunch pail is at school, and Ms. Plummer will be sure to have some numbers for me to do. I better go now. Bye!"

As he arrived at the school, he saw that some of the students were playing ball in the front of the building. When he entered the gate of the school yard, he was greeted by his sister, Sarah. "Randy, I put your lunch pail on the bench under the tree. If you hurry and eat, we will still have time to play for a while. Where did you go this morning?"

"I saw Mrs. Acres, and we got the honey out of the hives. I saw the queen bee today!" Randy said excitedly. "She is really pretty."

He settled on the bench and ate the sandwich and apple tart that had been packed for him. He followed this with a long drink of cool water he got from the well. As he drank his fill, he felt something wet and cold touch his hand. Startled, he looked to see what had caused this sensation. He looked down into large golden-brown eyes set in brownish-gray fur touched with black and accompanied with a lolling pink tongue and a fiercely wagging tail.

"Who are you? You kind of look like a wolf. Are you thirsty?" He got the pan that they used to give animals a drink from and filled it for the friendly dog. The dog lapped up the water appreciatively; then he followed when Randy went back to his lunch pail. Randy had a crust of bread left from his lunch, and when he offered it, the dog it took it very gently from his hand, and then he swiftly gobbled it down. The dog looked up at him adoringly, and Randy began scratching him behind his ears. He snuffled Randy's hand again; then he lay down quietly at his feet. Both were contented to sit side by side in the shade and watch the others as they played in the school yard.

The town's elderly banker was hoping to retire, so he had put out an advertisement offering a partnership in his bank. Mr. Huffmeister, a banker from Connecticut, answered the ad and bought the partnership. Mrs. Huffmeister had health problems, and they were hoping that the clean air and slow, gentle lifestyle would prove beneficial to her. Their son, Rolf, was seventeen years old and was full grown at six feet tall and 140 pounds. His father had ambitious plans for him to go back east to attend college, so he had Ms. Plummer tutoring him in the higher subjects, including calculus and world literature. She had even found someone to teach him Latin. Mr. Huffmeister wanted Rolf to get a college degree, then to join him in the banking business.

Rolf was an intelligent young man, but he could be somewhat arrogant. He felt that not only should he be privileged because of his father's status but also after having lived in the fast-paced life back east, he railed at being stuck in what he felt was a backwater community. He was critical and could sometimes be cruel in his dealings with his fellow school chums. To Sarah's chagrin, he decided to focus on Randy today, and he began to ask him about the dog.

"Hey, kid, where did that dog come from?" Rolf taunted.

Randy sat quietly and continued to scratch the dog's ears. "Don't know where he's from, but he can stay with me if he wants to."

"What's his name? You could just call him ugly, and I'm sure that he would come right to you!" Rolf gave out a wicked laugh.

"Not so bad looking, and he has really nice eyes." Randy defended his newfound friend.

"Well, I think that you need to take another good look. He's all dirty and scruffy looking like he could be diseased or something. Maybe we need to run him off before he hurts somebody," Rolf said with a sneer. He had been hitting a ball, and he still had the bat in his hand. He swung the bat slowly back and forth as he approached Randy.

The dog jumped up from Randy's side, bared his teeth, and began to growl menacingly. Randy quickly grabbed him around his neck. "You just stay away from my dog!' Randy yelled at Rolf.

Rolf stopped up short, lowered the bat, and backed away. "All right. I didn't mean anything. You just better keep him away from me." Rolf stated as he ambled back across the school yard.

The dog quieted down and snuffled Randy's hand; then they both lay back down in the shade. Sarah came over to them, and the dog greeted her with a gentle head butt and a lick with a very wet tongue. "Well, Randy, I think that you've got yourself a dog, but you'll need to ask Father's permission to keep him first. He sure stood up for you against Rolf. Maybe that will teach him a lesson on how he should treat people."

"Yup." Randy laughed. "He sure made Rolf back up quick! Do you think Father will let me have him? I want to call him Jack. I think it's a really good name."

"You will have to ask Father tonight at supper. He does seem like a smart dog, and except when it comes to Rolf, he sure seems to be friendly enough."

Just then Ms. Plummer came walking from the direction of town and entered the school yard. Jack stood at Randy's side as she approached. "Who do we have here?" she asked as she reached out a hand toward the dog. The dog's tail began beating Randy's leg like it was a drum, and his pink tongue slathered the proffered hand, giving it a good drenching. She laughed heartily and gave the dog a good scratch behind the ears.

"His name is Jack. Can he stay here and wait for me? He'll be good, I promise," Randy asked worriedly.

"Of course he can, as long as he does not cause any problems. He seems well-mannered enough. I'm glad that you're here, Randy. Will you work with little Jenny today? She is still having problems with addition, and you have a way of explaining it to the little ones so they finally understand how to do it. Would that be all right with you?"

"Yes, Ms. Plummer. I know addition real good. I'll help little Jenny." Randy beamed. He liked to help out, and he especially liked to please Ms. Plummer.

The schoolroom was filled with the soft buzz of children's voices as they recited their multiplication tables. Randy was in the corner with Jenny, patiently explaining the addition problems to her until she grasped the concepts. She was radiant when she finally got the problem correct. With a flash of insight, Randy had changed the apples and oranges in the problem to Betty's dresses and Molly's dresses. Now Betty and Molly were Jenny's dolls and her constant companions. Each had to have the same amount of just everything, so Jenny spent much time keeping the dolls' wardrobes straight. Using the dolls' dresses for the example caused the whole concept of math to suddenly become startling clear to Jenny.

Jenny ran to Ms. Plummer, who was at her desk, and excitedly told her how she now knew how to do addition and subtraction. As Ms. Plummer was praising her for her efforts, the quiet tranquility of the room was shattered by the shrill blasts of the mill whistle. The entire room instantly became motionless, all frozen in the last task they had been engaged in before the whistle had sounded. Everyone knew that the whistle meant that there had been an accident at the mill. Since a large number of the students' relatives were employed at the mill, they were all concerned, wondering what had happened and who was involved.

"Children, everyone needs to remain calm. I am sure that Mr. Hooper is calling to see if he can get any information about the mill. I want you all to remain at your desks and try to concentrate on your math problems."

There was soon a steady buzz of children's hushed voices as they speculated about what may have happened at the mill. In any event, no matter what kind of accident there had been or whoever had been hurt, it would affect the town as a whole. They were a tight-knit community with everyone knowing everyone else, and they were quick to step in and help anyone who had a crisis.

Suddenly, Mr. Hooper was at the door. Ms. Plummer walked up to him, and they began speaking in hushed voices. She then turned to face the room full of children, her eyes settling on Jenny. "Jenny, gather up your things. Your brothers are here to take you home."

As young as she was, Jenny knew that something bad had happened, and it probably involved her father. Like many men in the town, he had worked at the mill for many years. Though it was a good job sawing the trees into lumber, it could be dangerous. The saws themselves were large and very sharp, and the blades whirled at frightening speeds that were necessary to cut the huge trees into usable lumber. The owner of the mill did her best to keep the equipment in the best working order so that accidents would not occur. Despite these efforts, there was still equipment fatigue and human error.

As Jenny walked to the door, her eyes were huge with fear. Her oldest brother, Jimmy, reached down and took her hand into his. "Hey, Jenny, it's going to be all right. Dad's leg is broken, but he is going to heal up fine. Let's go on home and get the chores done so he and Ma will have one less thing to worry about when they get there."

As Jenny walked away, the others called out to her. "Bye, Jenny! See you tomorrow. I'm sure everything will be all right."

And her best friend, Viola, said, "I will pray for you tonight before I go to sleep." Jenny looked back at her friend and gave her a watery smile.

Ms. Plummer turned back to the classroom. "The news from the mill is that Mr. Ware does have a broken leg from an accident today. As far as we know, he is the only one who got hurt. As Viola has said, we all do need to remember the Ware family in our prayers. Since it is so close to dismissal time, Mr. Hooper has decided to let everyone leave early. We will see you all in the morning."

Jack had waited patiently under the tree for Randy to emerge and hurried to his side, snuffling his hand in greeting.

"Come on, Jack. We gotta go home and see if I can keep you. I'll ask Father real nice 'cuz I really like you and you like me too." Randy gave a heavy sigh. He was sure that Father would see right out that Jack was a really good dog, and he was pretty sure that he could talk his father into letting him stay.

"Um, Randy, tonight may not be a good time to talk to Father about the dog. He is one of the people in charge of safety at the mill, and he is certain to be upset about the accident." Sarah was already thinking ahead about what she could do to help the Ware family. She was sure that her mother, along with a group of church ladies, had begun organizing meals, chores, and childcare.

When Sarah and Randy got home, their mother had indeed been cooking. Mrs. James was just leaving the house with a large pot of stew and a basket filled with buttermilk biscuits and a jar of blueberry jam. As the group stood talking on the porch, Mother was distraught, stating that the cow had gotten out again and that Mr. Bernhardt would now have to deal with that also when he got home. Randy immediately volunteered that he and Jack would go and search for the cow.

"Who's Jack?" Mother was puzzled. It was only then that she noticed the dog sitting next to Randy.

"This is Jack," Randy said as he rested his hand on the dog's head. "He found me at school today. He's a really good dog, and I know that he will help me find the cow. Come on, Jack, we got to go find Bossy."

Before Mother could protest, the boy and the dog disappeared around the side of the house, heading for the barn. "Well, I guess it will be a big help to have the cow back before Mr. Bernhardt gets home."

Mrs. James thanked Mother for all of the fine food and said that she had better be on her way. The Ware children were sure to be worried about having something to eat for supper. She planned to stay with the children until one or both of their parents returned home.

To Mrs. Bernhardt's surprise within less than half an hour, Randy had returned home with the wayward cow in tow, and he began to shore up the broken fence.

"My, how did you find Bossy so quickly? She usually finds such a good hiding spot that you really have to search for her."

"She was about half a mile away hiding down in a gully, but Jack left out of the barn and went almost straight to her. So he's a good tracker too!" Randy said with pride. "Do you think that Father will let me keep him? I really want him, and I'm sure that he wants me too!"

"Well, we will have to see what Father says about it. I know that he will be relieved that he didn't have to go cow hunting tonight." Then Mother got a worried look on her face. "He's going to have a lot on his mind, so we may not bring up the subject until in the morning. Do you think that if we let Jack stay here tonight that he can behave himself?"

"Uh, huh, he's found a spot under the porch that he likes, so I think it will be all right."

Suddenly, they heard the dog barking down by the barn.

"Oh my, that's what I was afraid of, that he would make a ruckus. Father will not put up with that at all. Let's go see what he is barking at." Mother gave a sigh as she knew that Randy was already very attached to the dog, and it would be hard to have to send the dog away.

Randy ran out ahead as they approached the barn. They could hear the dog's loud barking coming from behind the structure, and as Mrs. Bernhardt rounded the corner, she discovered what the problem was. The persistent cow had rebroken the fence area that Randy had just repaired and had gotten out once again. The dog was doing its level best to get the cow back into the corral or at least to keep it from running off again.

Randy and his mother coaxed the cow back through the opening and were trying to figure out how to block up the hole again when Mr. Bernhardt arrived on the scene.

"Has that errant beast broken out again? I had meant to make more permanent repairs but just got sidetracked. Here, Randy, we'll get some boards from inside the barn and shore it up again for now. I will fix it for good on Saturday." Father shook his head with a smile. "I'm sorry that you had to deal with this again, my dear."

"This is the second time today that old Bossy has broken out. Randy and Jack had retrieved her once from her earlier ramblings. She was going to make a break for it again, but Jack persuaded her that it would not be a good idea." Mother's grin was mischievous.

"Jack, huh? And just where did this talented dog come from?" Father was petting the dog, looking him over, and the dog gave his hand a thorough drenching with his tongue as was his way.

"He found me at school. I want to keep him, and he wants to keep me! Oh, can we please keep him, Father? He's a really good dog, and he already helped with the cow and everything!"

Father and Mother shared a look over their son's head. A small smile began playing at Father's lips. "Well, seeing that I didn't have to go chase down a cow tonight is a point in Jack's favor. He does seem to be smart and well-behaved." Father put his hand to his chin as if he was thinking very deeply. "Hum. If he does not cause any problems, I guess that he can stay."

Randy gave out a whoop and hugged Jack fiercely around his neck. As if the dog understood the decision that had been made, he wriggled his body and gave Randy's face numerous sloppy wet licks.

"All right, son, we need to get some boards and shore up this fence."

As Randy and the dog sped off to find the boards that were needed, Mr. and Mrs. Bernhardt shared an embrace. Mrs. Bernhardt looked up into her husband's face, glad to note that some of the tension that had been there earlier had eased and that color was slowly returning to his cheeks. She did not push him but instead calmly waited for him to share his day with her.

"It's not as bad as it could have been. Mr. Ware's leg is broken very badly, but the load could have easily crushed him completely. Early speculation that the accident was caused by alcohol consumption were proven false. Investigation found that one of the hooks fastening the chains around the load showed metal fatigue, causing it to break from the pressure. It will take him a good while to heal, but the doctors feel that he will recover completely."

"Well, that is certainly very good news," Mother said with relief. "We have already sent food and arranged for childcare so Mrs. Ware can focus on her husband."

Mr. Bernhardt took his wife's hand, and he became very still. "The strangest thing happened." Mr. Bernhardt shook his head as if to clear it. "When those logs fell, not only was Mr. Ware's leg trapped, but other logs had his upper body pinned beneath them. One was so close that the bark had scrapped his face. We had to use pry bars to lift the heavy logs so we could pull him out, and just as we got him free, the log that had been above his head slammed into the ground. It was as if something had been holding it back, and suddenly it let loose." He turned and looked in his wife's face. "As we were strapping Mr. Ware to the gurney to put him in the ambulance, he reached out and touched my hand. He looked up at me and asked me if I had seen the angel too. When I asked him what angel, he reached up and touched the bruised scrape on his face. Then he answered back that it was the angel that had held back that log, the one that would have crushed his head." Mr. Bernhardt gently shook his head again. "I certainly didn't see any angel, but I can't explain why those logs didn't fall and crush the man."

"Perhaps you witnessed a miracle today. Just because you didn't see the angel doesn't mean that one wasn't there." Mrs. Bernhardt looked at her husband and smiled gently.

As the two smiled and embraced again, Randy was heard hollering from inside the barn. "Hey, Father, what boards do you want to use? There are a lot of them here."

Laughing together, the two adults hugged again. "I guess I had better go help my young man so we can get this job done."

"Don't take too long." Mrs. Bernhardt gave her husband a quick peck on his cheek. "I have supper ready to put on the table." Then with an introspective expression, she said, "It seems that we have a lot to give thanks for when we say our prayers tonight."

And that was how Jack came to live with Bernhardts.

3

The Honey Tree

Randy was running through the town with his legs pumping so fast that he could barely keep his balance. Mr. Heimlich, the owner of the mercantile, was out sweeping his front porch when Randy sailed past him.

"Why, I wonder who lit a fire under that young man?" he puzzled out loud.

Randy didn't pause until he reached Mrs. Acres's house. She had just finished working the hives and had put the honeycombs to draining in the shed. She was heading for the house to eat lunch when Randy reached her. He was so out of breath that he was gasping and wheezing. He was attempting to talk, but all he could manage was to say her name over and over.

"Son, come up here on the porch, and have some lemonade, and you can catch your breath." Mrs. Acres smiled as she pulled Randy up the steps. "Then you can tell me what has got you so worked up."

Randy sat down in one of the wide chairs that Mrs. Acres had there, and she handed him a glass of lemonade. He took a large drink, and then he blurted out "A tree. A big tree. And bees, lots and lots of bees." He was still so excited that he could barely talk. "The tree, it was humming like the hives." He was talking so fast that Mrs. Acres could barely understand him.

"All right, now you slow down so you make some sense. Start from the beginning, and tell me everything." Mrs. Acres smiled as this man-child excitedly gulped his lemonade. His gentleness, curiosity, and giving nature had always warmed her heart. But something had sure got him riled up so much that she thought he would burst. "By the way, aren't you supposed to be in school?"

"Yes, Mrs. Acres, but it was so pretty outside that I just had to go to the woods. Miss Plummer said that I could go, so I lit out. Then I went out by the dam because I was looking for the big fish. I walked on down the creek where I could see the Indian burial grounds on the other side. Father always warns us not to go near it. Then I saw some lady's slippers off up by a big tree, so's I went to look at them. Mother loves them, but she tells us not to pick them. I'm going to tell her about them so's she can get some for her flower garden. Then I got tired, so I sat down on a tree root. The tree was hit by a lightning, so it is dead, and the top of it looks like a fork, and that made me hungry for lunch."

"Have you eaten yet? No? You wait right here, and I'll be right back." Mrs. Acres went into the house, and she returned a few minutes later with sandwiches, cookies, and some more lemonade. She gave him a sandwich and refilled his glass. "All right, son, you can finish talking while you eat."

His face lit up with a smile. "Thank you, Mrs. Acres, I am mighty hungry." He took a huge bite of the sandwich, so it was a few moments before he could speak again.

"That's when I heard the humming. And I looked up, and I saw a bee go into a crack in the bark. Then I saw a bunch of bees all going in and out of the crack. Then I heard the tree, and it was humming just like the hives do. Is it a honey hive?" he questioned.

Mrs. Acres looked thoughtful for a moment. "You could have found a wild hive. Usually, they are not very big, but you say that it is a big tree? Well, I guess that we will just have to go and have a look at it after we finish up our lunch. We'll bring along the smoker can and the washtub too. Then we will go and have a look at this humming tree of yours."

"Yes, Mrs. Acres," agreed Randy.

They followed the road until they found a deer trail leading off from it. Randy led the way through the woods, and they broke out into a small meadow. They could hear the creek gurgling up ahead and could just make out the top of a dead tree peeking over a rise. "There it is, just like I said," Randy declared. "See, there's the lady's slippers too!"

When they got to the tree, it was definitely a honey tree, and the bees were indeed busy. Mrs. Acres was surprised at how many bees there were. She lit her smoker can and put it up to the hole in the bark. "It won't take long, and the bees will calm down. Then we can look and see just what you have found here." Mrs. Acres donned her cap with the veils and put her gloves on. She had brought a hammer and a chisel, and she began carefully tapping at the bark to pry it loose. A large piece came clear, and she stopped to smoke the hole again. When she peered into the tree, she saw that the tree was filled with honeycomb. "Why there must be at least fifty pounds of honey in here, maybe even more if the tree is hollow. I'll begin to cut it out. Then we will be able to tell more. Careful now, Randy, and hand the saw to me. I will do the cutting, and you hold the wash pan."

The basin was soon full of sticky honeycombs. They had stopped from time to time to smoke the hive again so the bees would stay cooperative.

"All right, the pan is full, so we need to stop and come back. We are going to need more washtubs, and we really need some help. I've never seen such a large hive before. Why, I can't even say how much honey there is, because the tree is so large. We should be able to harvest a quite a bit of honey. You have a real find here, Randy. You will have a lot of honey to process and sell," Mrs. Acres said proudly.

"Me? Sell the honey? But you sell the honey," Randy stammered in genuine surprise.

Mrs. Acres let out a merry laugh. "Not just me anymore, my boy. This hive is your find, so it is your honey. Just like you have helped me so many times, now it's my turn to help you. Let's go and talk to your parents. We are going to need more help to get all of this honey out of the woods." They carefully positioned the chunk of wood back over the hole again, so it was covered from the elements. The bees were again using the hole that they left to enter and exit the hive.

The washbasin was heavy as they carried it between them, and it took them a while to get it to Randy's house. Mrs. Bernhardt was surprised when the two arrived with the large tub full of honey. Randy began talking excitedly. "Mother, I found a big honey tree, and Mrs. Acres says that I am going to sell it. And I found a bunch of lady's slippers too. We can get them for your flower garden."

Both Mrs. Acres and Mrs. Bernhardt smiled at Randy's excitement and enthusiasm. "All right, Randy, calm down while Mrs. Acres and I discuss this. I think a cup of tea and some cookies are in order. Do come in and sit for a spell, and we can talk."

"A cup of tea does sound really good right now. Thank you so much." Mrs. Acres was grateful for the respite as it gave her a chance to rest and gather her thoughts. "For my part, I am sure that Randy will be able to do this. He has been helping me for quite some time now, so I'm sure that he can handle it just fine," Mrs. Acres said reassuringly.

"You really do think that Randy is capable of processing the honey?" Mrs. Bernhardt turned to Randy. "Well, Randy, we will have to talk to your father about this, but I have a feeling that he will also agree that this is a good idea." She turned back to Mrs. Acres. "Why don't you come and have supper with us this evening? Then we can discuss this with Mr. Bernhardt and consider all that needs to be done. Randy, are you sure that you can do this?" Mrs. Bernhardt questioned him once again.

"Yes, Mother, yes, yes, yes! Do we have some jars? I need jars for sure!"

Both of the ladies just began laughing. "Don't worry, Randy, I'm sure your father will help you to get everything that you will need."

Mrs. Acres came back to have supper with the family that evening, and of course the main topic of discussion was the wild honey tree. But Mrs. Acres also assured Mr. Bernhardt that Randy had learned enough about beekeeping and honey processing that she was sure that he could do the task on his own with little or no supervision.

"Well, son, according to this fine woman, it has become apparent that you will soon become a man of means as you are going into the honey business. Your mother and I will assist you in every way possible to make this adventure a success. How do you feel about all of this?"

"I'm sure that I can do it, Father. I have been helping Mrs. Acres with her bees. I paid real good attention, and she taught me a whole lot." Randy was very solemn when he answered his father as he wanted very much to do this.

"All right, son, we will go in the morning and have a look at this tree, and then we will take it from there. Mrs. Acres has said that the tree may have to be cut down in order to get all of the honey out. I think that I will get Mr. Eckhardt to come with us in case we have to fell it."

"I will be up early and come with you to assist with the bees. They will not appreciate having their home chopped down, but they will soon move on and start new hives elsewhere. What time do you want to get started?" Mrs. Acres was happy to offer her assistance with the endeavor.

"Let me give Mr. Eckhardt a call, and we can set a time. It will probably be an early rise."

"Oh, I am always up with the chickens, and an early morning in the woods is always refreshing," Mrs. Acres assured him.

The next day was Saturday; so in the morning, Mrs. Acres, Randy, and his father went to pick up Mr. Eckhardt. Not wanting to be left out of adventure, both Samuel and Jeremiah tagged along. It was a short drive to the trail that led to the tree. Mr. Bernhardt parked his truck under a tree for shade, and everyone piled out of it and began the trek back toward the creek.

"I've been on this trail before." Samuel was the hunter of the family, and he had been over much of the woods at one time or another. "I don't come this way very often because the Indian burial ground is just on the other side of the creek, and I don't want the Indians to think that I would go on their sacred ground."

"That is very wise, son. I'm glad that even though we do not practice their traditions, you still honor theirs. Mr. Eckhardt and I have met the chief on a number of occasions, and he did mention that boys have been observed hunting in the area and that all of you always give the burial grounds a wide berth. He knows how curious young men can be, and he was grateful for you honoring their burial ground."

The boys took long looks at one another as the mystery of the burial ground was always a strong pull, but they had not desecrated the grounds by going on them. Now they were especially grateful that they had resisted the desire to explore the forbidden grounds. They never knew that they had been watched or what would have happened if they had crossed the line.

"There is an old Indian who comes around a lot of the time. We always talk when I see him. He said that he had watched me and saw that I was real careful to not walk onto the sacred ground. So he walked around the whole burial ground with me one time and showed me how they mark it. He said that way I won't make a mistake and go in it. He said that he knows you, Father." The other boys were totally surprised at Randy's revelation. In all of their outings, they had never seen the old man.

"Did he tell you his name?" Mr. Bernhardt was curious as to which Indian had talked to his son.

"He said his name was Lone Wolf. He really liked Jack too and said that Jack looks a lot like a wolf. He could see right off that Jack was really smart, 'cuz he never barked or growled at him. He just looked at him really hard. See, Jack knew right away that he wasn't going to hurt us. Then once the old man talked to him and reached out to pet Jack well, Jack gave his hand a real good licking." Mr. Bernhardt smiled at the thought, though he was surprised that the old Indian would reveal himself to his son. He was also puzzled as to why the old chief would take the time to show the boy the boundaries of the burial ground. With a flash of insight, he realized that it was a way the old man could take the measure of the boy in a nonthreatening way.

In the end, they harvested over three hundred pounds of honey from the tree. It was the largest wild hive that anyone had ever heard of. Because there was so much honey all at once, all of the Bernhardts became active participants in the honey processing. Randy and Mrs. Acres taught them what needed to be done as they went along. When they had filled all of the jars that they had available, Randy and his father took the honey to Brainerd and sold it to the mercantile there. That store owner told Randy that he would take all the honey that he could bring in as he had buyers from the cities who wanted wild honey. Randy paid his father back for the jars and things he had used so far, and then he bought more jars and other equipment that he needed. In addition, he also sold the wax from the honeycombs. He was so proud to be making money, and he was happy that he would be making even more when he got the rest of the honey processed.

They finished their business in Brainerd and headed back home. "Randy, you have a goodly amount of money here, and you are going to be making quite a bit more. What do you think about putting it in the bank? I'm sure that Mr. Huffmeister would be glad to help you open an account."

"All right. It is an awful lot of money," Randy agreed.

"I am so proud of you, son. Except for a little help from us, you have been processing the honey all on your own. Mrs. Acres was right about you. She said that you had learned about beekeeping, and she thinks that you are ready to have hives of your own. You have shown all of us what a responsible young man you have become, so when we get back home, I would like to help you build two hives right away."

"Yes, Father, I want some hives. I can do it. I can do the honey all by myself." Randy was all smiles because his father trusted him and was proud of him. "I will figure out how much it will cost and everything. I'm good with figures. And I need to give the tithe too. I have to give back to God because he gave the honey tree to me. Right, Father?"

"Yes, Randy. That's right. That is what I taught you, and I am so proud that you remembered."

He put his arm around Randy and gave him a mighty hug. Yes, he was very proud of this son of his.

Randy had a new status with the townspeople and especially with his peers at school. Everyone knew about the honey tree and that he was selling the honey. He no longer had to just do odd jobs to earn money; he now had a real business. The two new hives that he built were already thriving and promised a good crop of honey.

Randy was a kindhearted and generous person. At Sunday school, he approached his teacher with an idea he had. He wanted to use some of the money he had made to provide a treat for his friends. After hearing his idea, the teacher was in full support, agreeing that it was a wonderful teaching incentive, and she was appreciative of his generosity. The next Sunday, his idea was put into play. He brought peppermint sticks that he had purchased at the mercantile, and everyone who memorized and recited a Bible scripture would receive one. Of course, everyone, even the youngest of the children, was able to do this, so all received a treat. But Randy knew that they really received two prizes. One was the candy, and the other was the everlasting prize of writing God's word on their heart.

Randy ate his dinner after church and then asked permission to hike back out to the honey tree and to do some fishing at the dam. His father bussed him playfully on the head. "Sure, Randy, go ahead and check it out. You have worked hard to get that honey processed, and you deserve a break. Just be home in time to do your chores."

"Yes, Father!" Randy gave his father a big smile as he disappeared out the door. Of course, Jack was at his side as they headed for the woods.

The day was bright with sunshine as Randy traversed down the road. He turned onto the small trail that had been made by his father's truck when they had cut down the tree to get the honey. As he walked through the meadow toward the creek, he looked at the crest of the hill where the top of the tree used to be. It was strange, but he missed seeing the bare branches of the tree reaching up into the sky. As Mrs. Acres surmised, they'd had to cut down the entire tree so they could get all of the honey. Then Mr. Bernhardt had brought the rest of the tree back home and was still in the process of chopping it into firewood. As Randy reached the top of the crest, he looked down to see the stump with its roots. To his surprise, he saw that someone was sitting on his favorite root, and Jack was lying on the ground next to the person.

As he got closer to the tree, he saw that it was the Indian, Lone Wolf. The old man intently watched Randy as he drew closer, and though he appeared stern, Randy knew that he had nothing to fear.

Jack had immediately recognized his friend and had sat quietly as the old man gave him a thorough scratching.

"Hello. Jack didn't even bark, 'cuz he knows you." Randy greeted the man with a smile.

"Yes. The dog knows a friend. So you found the beehive that was in this tree."

"Yes, sir. I sat down on the root, and then I heard that the tree was humming. Then I saw the bees going in and out of a crack in the bark."

"Humph. It was a very good find. I saw you and your father cutting down the tree, and that was when I saw that it had a very big hive in it." Randy had sat down on the ground next to the old man, and he waited quietly for the man to continue speaking. "As you know, I often come to the burial grounds to check on it and to commune with the ones who have passed on. I don't often come to this side of the creek, as for me it is a long walk to go up to the dam to cross. I am going fishing now. Do you want to come with me?"

"Yes, sir, I was going to visit the tree. Then I was going to see if the fish were hungry today."

The old man nodded his head. "Then we will fish together."

The old man, the boy, and the dog ambled along the creek with the old Indian pointing out the squirrels, birds, and rabbits to the boy. Of course, the dog saw everything and sometimes would take off on a run following critter trails. While he was off on a quest, the old man quietly pointed out a very large buck that was on the other side of the creek. It watched the humans for a bit; then it slowly disappeared into the underbrush.

Just at that moment, Jack came running up from the creek. A few yards away, a rabbit had popped its head up and remained frozen watching the dog. The old man raised his rifle and took the shot.

"We will have to start a fire to roast this rabbit. Do you know how to skin it?" When Randy shook his head no, the old man nodded his. "We will gather wood for the fire. Then I will teach you. Do you know how to cure the pelt? No? That will have to wait for another day. We will gather wood as we walk to the dam."

As the rabbit was roasting on a spit, the old man had fashioned the two prepared to get their fishing lines ready. The Indian had cut two switches to use as poles. Randy opened the leather pouch he was carrying and took out a small fabric packet. When he unfolded the packet, it contained new fishing hooks, some line, and four new cork bobbers. He had purchased these with his honey money. When he attached his line to the pole, he noticed that Lone Wolf had line and an old hook that had been well used. He also noticed that he did not have any bobbers.

"Sir, that was so nice of you to show me how to skin that rabbit. You can have two of these fishhooks and bobbers if you'd like. They are brand-new, so they should work real good. I want you to have them." Randy offered the gifts to his friend.

"Hum. I do not have any bobbers, and my hook is old. Thank you, my friend. I will take them in trade for teaching you about the rabbit." The old man smiled at the boy. "I will have to have my woman make me a fine pouch like yours to carry them in."

The two threaded worms onto the hooks and threw the lines into the water. Jack had gotten worn out chasing critters, so he curled up next to Randy and took a nap. By the time the rabbit was done, both had a number of fish on their stringers. Randy was happy as he not only had a number of perch; he had also hooked two rainbow trout.

"We will eat the rabbit now. Then I will show you some secrets of the fish."

"Secrets? What secrets?" Randy asked.

"We eat first. Then I will show you." The old man had walked over to the cook fire and started pulling the rabbit apart. It smelled delicious, so Randy was not inclined to argue. The old man had gathered some plants and stuffed the leaves from them into the cavity of the rabbit before he put it on to cook, and now the meat was wonderfully smoked and fragrant. Jack had been very well-behaved, and he had not bothered the rabbit as it had cooked.

"Did you pay attention to the leaves that I used for the rabbit? They have flavored the meat as it cooked. Eat."

"Yes, sir. I watched real close." Randy took a bite of the rabbit, and a huge smile crossed his face. "Um, this is really good. I'm going to take my mother some of those plants so she can use them in her rabbits. I know she will like it."

After the rabbit was consumed with Jack getting his fair share, the old man had Randy build up the fire again. Then he cleaned a few of his fish and skewered them onto some sticks.

"These will smoke, so I will have them for my journey home. Come, I will show you the secrets now."

The old man showed Randy where the larger fish hid in pools that had formed under trees that had fallen into the water. He showed him how to work the line to entice the fish to bite and then how to set the hook well. He also used a piece of wood to hit the fish to stun them, which made it easier to pull them in.

"Do this, and you will not break the line and lose your hooks."

They were successful in catching two good-sized northern pike when the old man looked up at the sky. "I must start my journey home before the sun sets. We will break camp."

The two friends made sure that the fire was thoroughly out and then gathered their belongings.

"It was a good day, my friend. We will meet again soon, and I will teach you how to tan a rabbit hide."

Randy smiled up into the old man's face. "Yes, sir, thank you for everything that you have taught me today." Then Randy had another thought. "Sir, the next time you come to the tree, look inside the stump. I will leave a jar of honey in it for you."

"I would like that very much. Your bees have started another hive in a tree on the other side of the dam. It will take them a while to get it built up. I will show it to you the next time we meet."

With that, the old man nodded his head and headed off toward the crossing at the top of the dam.

Randy picked up his bag and patted Jack on the head.

"Time to go home and do the chores, Jack." The two turned and started down the trail to the road. When Randy looked back so he could wave good-bye to his friend, the old man was nowhere to be seen. He had disappeared into the foliage.

Graduation

Memorial Day marked the official end of the school year. This year was going to be extra special as there was going to be a huge party for the graduates after the ceremony. For the past month, for an hour every afternoon, the students had been learning to dance. Mrs. Huffmeister had donated her Victrola with its records so that the students would have music to practice with. The youngsters enjoyed the music itself, but the dancing was another story. Some of the students, especially the boys, were prone to stepping on their partner's toes. The music for the polka was punctuated with periodic yelps from one of the girls, with a hurriedly mumbled sorry from the offending boy. But as a whole, the school gymnasium was filled with the sounds of merriment and laughter.

Mrs. Huffmeister had requested to further contribute to the party festivities in another unusual way. She had arranged delivery of three very large crates to the school, along with a full-length mirror. There was much speculation as to what was contained in the crates, but what was even more surprising was the arrival of Mrs. Finney, who had brought a large sewing basket with her.

After the dance lesson, Miss Plummer asked for two of the boys to assist her in opening the crates. When they were fully opened, it was apparent that they all contained clothing. Her eyes danced with merriment as she clapped her hands together, stating that she had an exciting announcement to make.

"Mrs. Huffmeister had these crates shipped from out east. She had requested a favor from her friends there to donate clothing that they no longer had a use for. Some of the articles have never even been worn, and all of the rest are like new. She wanted you young folks to be able to dress up for graduation, to have what is referred to as a prom. I have received permission from your parents for all of you to look through the clothing, and if you find something that you like, you will be able to keep it. Mrs. Finney here is an excellent seamstress and will help you with any alterations that are needed. Two of the crates are filled with girls' clothing, and the third has clothing for the boys. We will empty the crates, and everyone will make their selections. Then the boys will leave, while the girls will stay and try on the dresses." With that, they all began taking the clothing out of the crates and draping the items across the desks and chairs.

"Oh my! These dresses are all so pretty. How will I be able to choose?" Sarah gushed.

"Me too! I think that I will look for colors that I like and then choose one from that," Abigail stated. "Oh, look, this one has a cape, and this one has beautiful appliqués on it. They are just so wonderful!"

The room was filled with excited ohs and ahs from the girls and hoots of discovery from the boys. It seemed that everyone had happily found some kind of finery that they wanted or needed to have for the dance. The boys had not only found some suits with vests, but there had also been belts, ties, and even some shoes.

Miriam jibed Billy, "Yes, Billy, take the shoes, and make sure that you wear them to the dance. I would rather you have them on when you step on my toes than your work boots! But don't despair, my friend. I will still dance with you. It would take more than the fear of a foot trouncing to keep me from going to the dance." Then she smiled at him to take the sting out of her jest.

Poor Billy, it seemed that no matter how hard he tried, he just could not catch the rhythm of the music, and he had decimated the feet of every dancing partner whom he'd had. Miriam was the only girl who had not given up on him.

"Well, if you're still game, then I will do my best. Maybe with the new shoes, it will all magically sink in, and I will be able to dance on my own feet instead of using yours." The two friends shared a good laugh and then continued digging through the treasures.

Ms. Plummer clapped her hands to get the group's attention. "It is time for the boys to leave so the girls can start with the fittings. The dance is only two weeks away, and Mrs. Finney will need time to make alterations. I am very pleased with the dance lessons. I see the great improvements that all of you have been making. We will see you boys tomorrow."

The boys picked up their goods and yelled their good-byes as they exited. Some of the girls were still traversing about the room, wanting to see all of the dresses one more time before they made their final choices.

"Now, Brianna, that pink dress is truly beautiful, but I fear that it fights with your red hair. Oh, now just look at this dress," exclaimed Mrs. Finney. "Why, this emerald green will not only compliment your green eyes, but will also flatter your creamy Irish complexion. And, look, it has a matching cape with beautiful black braiding. Do go and try it on so we can see what kind of adjustments that it may be needing."

Brianna's eyes widened in disbelief. She had never thought to have a dress as fine as this. She tentatively took the dress and stepped behind the makeshift curtain that had been hung to make a dressing area and began changing.

Sarah had chosen a dress of cornflower blue. Its sleeves and over bodice were made of sheer white chiffon that was puffed at the shoulders and tapered to the wrists. The blue under bodice was sculpted and strapless as it peeked out through the sheer material. The waist was nipped in and had a belt fashioned of white ribbon, and the blue skirt flared out from it. When she held the dress up to her and swayed back and forth, the material made a soft shushing sound. She was anxious to try it on, but Brianna seemed to be taking a lot of time. "Brianna, do you need some help with the dress?" Sarah asked.

"Yes, I do. There seems to be quite a few buttons that I can't quite reach," Brianna answered.

Sarah stepped behind the curtain, and her breath caught in her throat at the sight of her friend. "Why, Brianna, you are just beautiful. That dress is perfect for you. Here, let's get you buttoned up so you can go and see for yourself."

Brianna stepped out into the room and started to walk up to the mirror. She was certain that Sarah was just being kind and trying to make her feel good. She stood in front of the mirror with her eyes downcast, afraid to look up at her own image.

"Look at me, Brianna." Brianna obediently turned her head toward Mrs. Finney. "Aye, it is as I thought it would be. That green has made your eyes turn an even darker shade. And it is as if the dress was made for you. It will only require some small adjustments in the waist and the bodice. Well, Brianna, how does it feel on you? Are you satisfied with it?" asked Mrs. Finney.

When Brianna slowly raised her eyes and saw herself in the mirror, she gasped in surprise. She could hardly believe that it was her own image that was staring back at her. She had always viewed herself as being plain, cursed with a pale washed-out complexion that burnt to a crisp in the summer sun, and this was accompanied with wild red wiry hair. Well, the hair was still a bit wild, but the green color of the dress did make her skin appear creamy. Her eyes mirrored the green of the dress, and they appeared huge and glowed softly.

"Oh my, is that me? It is me but not as I have ever looked before," she stated softly.

"Why, that's not true at all, Brianna. You are as pretty as you always have been. That dress is certainly fancier, but that is all that is different." Sarah assured her friend.

"Aye, girl, she is right. You have the fairness of a true Irish lass. That is why you look so good wearing the green. It is the right color for one whose roots are in the Emerald Isle. Now let's get the dress marked with the changes that I need to make," Mrs. Finney said through a mouthful of dressing pins.

All of the girls had soon made their selections, and Mrs. Finney was busy marking and pinning. Some of the dresses just needed a bit of hemming or a small tuck taken or just decorated with small embellishments such as ribbons or bows. Some of the girls opted to do the simple sewing themselves so that Mrs. Finney could concentrate on the more complicated alterations. All were certain that they would be done and ready for the dance.

Ms. Plummer was pleased with the selections that the girls had made from the offerings contained in the boxes. The clothing was remarkable as to colors and styles. Some of the items had never even been worn. The dress that Brianna had chosen was a prime example. Its classic elegance was exquisite and the embellishments as in the choice of buttons and the braiding on the cape were a true fashion statement. Ms. Plummer suddenly realized that it was one of the dresses that had been created by Mrs. Huffmeister's dear friend's daughter. Ms. Plummer approached Brianna as Mrs. Finney was marking and pinning the dress on her. Brianna's smile was shy but radiant as she gazed at her reflection in the mirror.

"Oh, look, Ms. Plummer, isn't this dress just divine? I've never had such a beautiful dress before. I want to thank Mrs. Huffmeister for getting this clothing for us. But I am doubly excited because now I will have a fine dress not only for this dance but to take off to college too. I know that there will be social engagements there also, and I can now be suitably attired."

"Yes, Brianna, you will have a chance to thank Mrs. Huffmeister in person soon." She turned to the room and clapped her hands to get the attention of all of the girls. "I would like to share with you the story behind some of the clothing contained in these crates. Please take a seat as this story is somewhat involved and may take a while in the telling of it." As the girls settled in their seats, she began the tale.

"Mrs. Huffmeister has a dear friend back east who had a daughter who was born frail and sickly. Despite her illnesses, she was a joyful girl, intelligent, and creative. The family owns a textile mill, and at a very young age, the girl became fascinated with the fine materials that the mill produced. Confined to the house and usually settled on a settee, she began drawing dresses and then actually produced patterns for her creations. Her father saw how much she enjoyed her pastime, so he began supplying her with the materials to actually bring her creations to fruition. Family and friends saw that she had a real gift, and they began commissioning her to create dresses for them not only for everyday wear but also for social events, including cotillions, bridesmaid dresses, and even a few wedding dresses. Some of the dresses here are the end product of her creative imagination. She always said that she did not make a dress that she could not picture a person wearing it. Brianna, your dress is one of her unique creations. She had told her mother that she pictured this particular dress being worn by a willowy redhead. Mrs. Huffmeister will be thrilled to convey to her friend that her daughter's vision was fulfilled. The sweet young woman has succumbed to her illness, but she left behind a wonderful legacy in her custom creations."

Brianna was deeply touched by the story of the young woman. It made her feel so special to think that this dress could have been designed with her in mind. She tentatively approached Ms. Plummer. "Do you think that I could get the name and address of the lady who sent this dress?"

"I'm sure that we could get that information from Mrs. Huffmeister. Can I ask what you have in mind?"

"Um, well, I thought that I would like to have a picture taken of me wearing the dress and send it to her along with a thank-you note. Do you think that would be appropriate?"

"Why, I think that is a marvelous idea. Let me speak with Mrs. Huffmeister about this. There are a number of dresses here that the girl designed." Ms. Plummer smiled and lightly touched Brianna's arm. "I will get back with you soon with an answer. You were very sweet to think of such a thing."

"All right, girls, we need to finish this up for the night. Mrs. Finney, I hope that you will not be working your fingers to the bone making all of the alterations. It is very kind of you and Mrs. Huffmeister to do this for us." Ms. Plummer was so appreciative of the kind gestures on behalf of both of the benefactresses.

"Oh yes!" "Thank you so much!" "It is so very kind of you to do this." The girls' voices rang out in gratitude.

"Aye, it will not be that much work as far as the alterations go. For the most part, the dresses fit perfectly, and I only have to make minor changes here and there. The girls are going to look spectacular for the dance, but that is easy for them because they are all so beautiful to begin with. Mrs. Huffmeister is going to be so pleased when she sees these sweet things looking so very much like flowers in a garden."

"Those of you who are going to do your own alterations need to take your dress home and have them back within a week. Mrs. Finney has promised to have the other dresses ready to be picked up at that time. If things have not worked out as you thought, bring it on in, and we will work on it with you. Our wish is that everyone be pleased with their choices. Off you go now so you can return for classes in the morning." With that, Ms. Plummer dismissed the group who were excitedly chatting about the clothing and the dance to follow.

"Oh my, I am afraid that minds are not going to be focused on spelling, grammar, or mathematical problems from now to the end of the year." Ms. Plummer laughed merrily. "I believe that if I would have had such an opportunity, I too would have had a hard time concentrating on schoolwork."

"Ms. Plummer, I would like to speak to you about something, and I pray that you will not be offended." Mrs. Finney looked a little uncomfortable as she addressed the teacher.

Ms. Plummer put her hand gently on Mrs. Finney's arm. "Please, Mrs. Finney, I hope that we have become good enough friends that you should have no fear to approach me about anything. What is troubling you?"

"It's just this. Mrs. Huffmeister had held out a good number of the dresses for my use also. I would like very much if you would look them over and take a few for yourself. There are really too many for me alone. Please, I would be very upset if I have affronted you with this offer."

Ms. Plummer's mouth made a perfect *O* in surprise, and her eyes were shining as she graced the other woman with a smile. "Really, you would share the bounty with me? I would be thrilled to have a new dress. I had been wondering just what new doodad I could use to sprig up my tired old gray suit with. I only have one thing that I absolutely insist on, though, and that is that you pick out those dresses that you want first. I will make my selection from what is left."

Mrs. Finney was extremely relieved that not only was the woman not offended but was even happy at the prospect of getting a new dress or two. "All right, I can agree with that. I have them at my apartment. Even though it is rather late, do you have time to come with me right now? And I would be honored if you could stay and have supper with me also. Bobby is working at the Larsons tonight and will be having supper with them, so it would be just us girls."

"Absolutely, lead the way, my dear." With that, Ms. Plummer put her arm in the crook of Mrs. Finney's arm and smiled. "By the way, my Christian name is Alice."

Mrs. Finney returned the smile. "And I am Maureen."

The following day, the morning was taken up with school studies. After the lunch break, it was time to practice dancing. The students were assigned to partners, and a record was put on the Victrola. The strains of a waltz issued forth, and the students dutifully began dancing to the music. Suddenly, Mr. Huffmeister entered the room. The students stopped dancing in confusion.

"Please don't mind me. I am here at Ms. Plummer's request to observe and perhaps to offer some instructions or advice. Everyone, please continue dancing. You were doing very well." He then stepped off to the side of the room, and he began conversing with Ms. Plummer. When he reached out his hand to her and gave her a slight bow, she nodded in compliance, and they walked out into the middle of the floor. He put his hand delicately on her waist, and she put hers on his shoulder. They clasped their free hands together, and they began moving their feet in time to the music, stepping and twirling gracefully.

"See how we are doing this? All of you watch and try to copy us. Step lightly and chant softly one, two, three, one, two, three, counting it over and over."

The music stopped, so Mr. Huffmeister walked up to the Victrola and reset the same record to play once again. Then he walked up to Sarah and asked her to dance. She blushed and was flustered, but she stepped up into position. Mr. Huffmeister smiled at her, and they began to waltz. Sarah kept repeating the mantra of one, two, three over and over in her mind. Suddenly, she no longer had to repeat it as her feet just followed the rhythm on their own. She and Mr. Huffmeister seemed to be gliding effortlessly over the floor.

When the music stopped, Mr. Huffmeister smiled at her and gave her a slight bow. "Thank you, my dear. That was beautiful. Now that you have danced that way once, you will be able to do it again. Now choose another partner, and teach them the steps."

Mr. Huffmeister danced with each girl in the room, and they in turn chose another partner, having varying measures of success. But the tone of the room had changed. The boys no longer seemed as defeated as they had been. It seemed to make a difference that the girls got the hang of the dance and were more willing to work with them so they could be successful at the dance too.

Mr. Huffmeister called a break, and the group scattered. When they reconvened, he paired Rolf with Sarah for the waltz. They started out with Sarah being hesitant. She finally relaxed when she realized that Rolf knew how to waltz. They caught the beat of the music as they gracefully spun about the room. When the music stopped like his father, Rolf smiled at her and gave her a bow. The rest of the practices, both Rolf and Sarah did their best to impart the knowledge of the waltz to their school chums. Each gained a measure of success with their partners who at least enjoyed the large twirling steps as they recited the one-two-three mantra.

The night of the prom, the girls and boys were nervous as they showed up dressed in their finery. The gymnasium had been decorated with banners congratulating the seniors, and colored bunting was draped from the ceiling and strung along the walls. A refreshment area had been set up, and there was a delicious assortment of homemade delicacies displayed.

Mrs. Huffmeister had a photographer on hand, and the girls had stood together as a group dressed in their finery for their picture. The photographer took the names of each participant and promised them that he would supply each of them a copy of the photo. He lined up the boys and made the same promise. Ms. Plummer told both groups that Mrs. Huffmeister was also sending copies of the photographs to her friends back east, along with the thank-you notes. It was a fitting end to the generosity shown by the folks. To see the happy faces of the recipients would be worth a thousand words.

It was time for the festivities to begin. Mr. Hooper gave a short speech focused on the vision of hope for the future for graduating seniors. Then Rolf, who had been selected as the valedictorian, gave a speech. Finally, the announcer called out that the first dance was to be a waltz, and the group began to choose up partners. Rolf walked up to Sarah. "May I have this dance?"

Sarah's cheeks flushed a delicate pink, but she nodded her head in acquiesce. As in practice, they went to the center of the floor and positioned themselves to dance. Then they stepped out in unison in time to the music. Sarah's dress gave off a soft swooshing sound as it swirled around her. Her feet moved in soft graceful steps, matching those of Rolf. They dipped and twirled in matched grace and beauty. Their movements were synchronized, smooth, perfectly timed, and utterly beautiful. The other couples stopped dancing and made a circle around them. So caught up in the dance, Sarah and Rolf were unaware that the others had stopped to watch them. When the music ended and the couple came to a stop, their faces reflected surprised shock that they were surrounded by the crowd who engulfed them in applause.

Mr. Huffmeister stepped forward and smiled at the couple, putting his hand on his son's shoulder. "I have rarely seen the waltz done so well. I knew that Rolf here had some experience with ballroom dancing, but tonight he certainly had the perfect partner. Well done, both of you."

The crowd again showed their appreciation and gave the couple another round of applause. The crowd was regaled with more music, and everyone was encouraged to participate by dancing. There were more waltzes, polkas, and even the Charleston. The night was a huge success as the entire community celebrated the young graduates and welcomed them into the world of adulthood.

5

Church

Miriam's grandmother had been ill for a long time. She had slowly declined, losing her strength and regretfully even her eyesight. The family had done all that they could to try to build her back up by feeding her the juiciest meats, vegetables, and fruits, and administering sundry herbal remedies; but it was to no avail. Grandmother claimed that old age had finally caught up with her and that she could hear the Lord softly calling her home. One day in late May, she lay down for a nap, and she did not wake up again.

Miriam was heartbroken. She had adored her grandmother Hannah. It had fallen to her to assist Grandmother with whatever fetching and carrying that she desired. Before the blindness, Miriam would fetch Grandmother's sewing basket for her, threading the needles and helping to measure and cut the material for the quilts that Grandmother had loved to make. Under Grandmother's tutelage, she had patiently learned to quilt, knit, tat, and crochet. She could now follow the most complex patterns that Grandmother had collected over the years and could make beautiful quilts, dollies, afghans, and delicate edgings for pillowcases and handkerchiefs. While they had shared time together, Grandmother had told her stories about her life in Germany and about her parents dream to immigrate to America. Then while she was still a young girl, that dream had come true. It had been a difficult passage fraught with hardships as they crossed the Atlantic Ocean on a storm-tossed ship. But all those hardships were forgotten when they sailed into New York harbor, and they were greeted by magnificent sight of the Statue of Liberty. Even now, Miriam would be doing a chore somewhere in the house, and she would think that she would hear her Grandmother call out for her. She would rush into the parlor to Grandmother's favorite chair sitting in front of the window before she would remember that the dear, sweet lady was no longer there. Then the grief would hit her afresh with a poignant sense of loss.

It was Sunday morning, and as was their custom, the group of youngsters met in the lane to walk to church together. They had all scrubbed their faces and donned their best clothes for the occasion. They took this particular route because it followed a lazy little creek that meandered through an apple orchard. The blooms had almost totally faded, but the air was still laden with the soft scent of the blossoms, and the petals littered the ground with their snowy whiteness. Honeybees were still busily gathering the last of the nectar and pollen to take back to their hives and conger that golden elixir called honey.

As they reached the town's limits, the lane merged with the main road. The group chatted merrily as they ambled onward toward the church, enjoying the beauty and freshness of the day.

"I got a letter from one of our cousins, and he told us about a missionary in St. Paul, who had been all the way to Africa. At a tent meeting, he told stories about the natives there and the animals like lions and elephants. I wish that I could see an elephant," Jeremiah said.

"That would be something, all right! I myself think that it would be nice to hear another preacher talk about stuff like that instead of things like our sinful natures. I sometimes think that Reverend Arden watches me just so he can get a good sermon on sinfulness and misbehaving. I don't think that I am being so very bad, but sometimes I sure feel bad when he gets done with his preaching," Bobby declared with a sigh. The others refrained from commenting, but that didn't stop them from thinking that very same thought.

Abigail noticed that Miriam was quiet and subdued as she had been since her grandmother's passing. "Hey, Miriam, are things busy at your house with all of your aunts there?"

"Oh yes, it is busy and loud too." Miriam gave a heavy sigh and continued, "They all seem to be arguing all of the time about how to divide up Grandmother's things. They especially can't seem to agree on how to divide the china and the silver. My mother insisted that I was to have the china figures of the little boys and girls that Great-grandmother had brought with her from Germany when she came to America. Grandmother would sit in her chair by the window and watch me when I fed the geese. She said that I looked just like the little girl with the goose, and she even made me a kerchief just like the one that the little girl wears. Mother didn't ask for much of anything else of Grandmother's, so she stood her ground about the little china figures. Well, the aunts finally relented and went back to bickering about the other stuff. Mother just hugged me and told me that we had gotten the best of things anyway, that we had had the privilege of having Grandmother in our lives and sharing the joy of caring for one another. The aunts had never made much effort to come here to see Grandmother, and she had been too frail to make the trip to visit them." Miriam sighed again. She did not understand all that was going on, but she had resolved to be as good and as obedient as she could be so as to not add any more strain to parents, especially her mother.

The group turned a corner, and the white clapboard church came into view. One car had pulled up as close to the church as possible, and two burly men were assisting a small frail woman out of it. After they had gently righted her on her feet, one of the men held her arm as she ascended the stairs and sat down in a rocking chair that was on the porch. "I'll be right back, Mother," he said. He left to move the car to a shady spot under a tree, and while there, he was hailed by a friend. As was their custom, they passed some time talking about crops and livestock in general.

"Oh no, there's crazy old Mrs. Rogers sitting on the porch. I don't like getting too close to her, because I don't want her to get riled and go off on me. Remember on Easter Sunday how upset she got with Jimmy Ware's father. Jimmy fessed up that his father had been drinking pretty heavy that morning and that he had a big fight with Mrs. Ware about going to church. Mrs. Ware called him a heathen, so he decided to go to church just to embarrass her. Well, old Mrs. Rogers sure turned the tables on him when she went off on him. She just kept asking him if he knew Jesus and how that he just has to know Jesus before he dies. She just kept on until Mr. Ware just turned tail and ran out of the church. No one has seen Mr. Ware at church again," said Bobby.

As the parishioners entered the church, some of them greeted Mrs. Rogers while others just passed her by. The story about Mr. Ware was not the only time Mrs. Rogers had spoken out the way she had done so with him.

Ever since the accident, she'd had years before she had become introverted. Most of the time when she was in a social situation, she would just sit quietly staring at nothing in particular or would close her eyes as if she was asleep. When she did engage in conversation, the subjects of heaven, angels, and Jesus were always the focus. Miriam's grandmother had been and continued to be one of the few people who maintained a friendship with her saying that true friendships, especially ones that spanned a lifetime, overcame all obstacles. So once a week, Miriam's father would take his mother to visit her friend, dropping her off on his way to the feed store, and then he would pick her up again on his way home.

"Let's wait until some other folks go up into the church. Then we'll just pass on up with them on the other side of the porch. That way, we won't get near Mrs. Rogers," said Samuel.

Miriam and the others reached the stairs to the church just as the Gutenberg family came noisily up the path. The father and mother always tried their best to keep their nine offspring mannerly and orderly, but they were a somewhat rowdy bunch. The older boys rushed and pushed one another up the stairs, jostling each other, trying to be the first one to go into the church. As planned, Miriam and her friends slipped in amongst them. Then the two older boys engaged in a scuffle, and their bodies temporarily blocked the doorway, keeping the group behind them from entering. Mr. Gutenberg took the situation in hand, and he grabbed each boy by an ear, pushing them ahead of him into the building. The rest of the family followed with Miriam's friends in tow. But in the fray, Miriam was separated from the group and pushed to one side. To her chagrin, she found herself face-to-face with Mrs. Rogers.

Mrs. Rogers seemed oblivious to the altercation and was gently rocking in the chair. Suddenly, she focused on Miriam's face, and a soft smile crept into her countenance. She reached up a hand and gently grazed Miriam's cheek. "Why, you must be Miriam," she said. "You are the image of your grandmother Hannah when she was your age. I should know about that because she and I were best of friends our entire lives. Even at the end, here she took time to come and visit me. But you knew that, didn't you?"

"Yes," said Miriam. "I knew that she, Mrs. Bernhardt, and Mrs. Eckhardt often went together to visit you."

Beckoning to a chair next to her, she said, "Come and sit here by me, child."

Miriam suddenly realized that she was no longer afraid of the old woman; in fact, she wondered why she had been afraid in the first place. Smiling, she pulled the chair even closer to Mrs. Rogers's rocker and sat down.

Mrs. Rogers looked again into Miriam's face and concentrated on her eyes. "My dear, I see such a deep sadness in you. You have no need to carry such a heavy burden of sorrow." She paused for a moment and continued, "I am sure that you have heard stories about me, about how I am not in my right mind since my carriage accident years ago. May I tell you a little bit about what happened to me then? It might help you to understand things that are happening to you now. Your grandmother and I spoke of these things many times, and I believe that it brought her much peace and understanding."

Miriam considered this and answered, "All right, if you think that it will help me and I will try hard to understand."

Mrs. Rogers took a deep breath, then began her story. "Well, when I had that accident, I passed from this world, and I went to heaven. I experienced many wonderful things. Some of which were so wonderful that I can't even put them into words. I can say, though, that I truly experienced the magnificence of heaven. It is so beautiful that anything this world can offer pales in comparison. I was met and welcomed by many friends and relatives that had passed before me, and the overall feeling was of total peace and joy. I was dead to this world, and I was alive in Christ in his heavenly kingdom. I looked into his face, into his amazing eyes, and my joy was boundless. But then I was told that I had to come back, that the Lord still had work for me to do back here on earth but that soon I would come back again, and then I would stay forever. I sometimes so long to be there again that I lose my grip on where I am. But then the Lord will put someone in my path that is so lost, so far from the knowledge of him that I have to speak out and try to reach them. Why, then I am doing the work that I was sent back to do."

Mrs. Rogers's voice softened even more as she said, "Child, your grandmother was a fine Christian woman, and her faith grew even stronger toward the end. So, child, you need to put off your sorrow and instead be happy for your grandmother as she no longer suffers from pain or earthly travails. You will always miss your grandmother for as long as you live, but the day that you also pass from here to that marvelous place, you will be with her again."

Miriam was amazed at the measure of understanding that she experienced at the words spoken by Mrs. Rogers. She had never heard anyone explain heaven in this manner before. She now understood why Mrs. Rogers acted the way that she did and especially why she so wanted to return to heaven. She could now envision her beloved grandmother in heaven waiting for her, and she could especially believe that she would join her there one day. The burden of heavy grief that she had carried had slipped miraculously away and was replaced with the lightheartedness of childhood once again.

Young Mr. Rogers appeared on the porch, and he took his mother's arm, helping her to rise from the rocker. Miriam also arose and took Mrs. Rogers by her other arm. She looked up into the old woman's face and said, "Thank you, Mrs. Rogers, for all of your kind words today. I still miss my grandmother, but somehow it doesn't hurt so much anymore."

"That's good, child." She softly patted Miriam's hand.

The three turned and started to enter the church when Mrs. Rogers paused. She looked down at Miriam and said, "Do you think that you could come by and visit an old lady once in a while? I would like to share some stories of the escapades and scrapes that your grandmother and I got into as children. It think that it would help me so I would not miss my old friend so much. And then we could speak some more about those other things too if you wish."

Miriam smiled. "I would like that very much, Mrs. Rogers."

"Very good. Now go and join your friends. I'm sure that they are very curious, and they will have many questions for you."

Miriam slipped away as the Rogers continued up the isle to their pew. Abigail scooted over and made room for her to sit next to her. As she looked into Miriam's face, she saw that her friend no longer looked so pale and pinched, that a glint of happiness again shone in her eyes.

"What did Mrs. Rogers have to say to you for so long?" asked Abigail. "Weren't you afraid?"

"Oh no! Well, maybe at the very first I was. But after a while, I wasn't afraid anymore, and I don't know why I ever was. She wants me to come and visit with her sometimes, and I really want to do that. She and Grandmother were such good friends, and she misses her as much as I do. I asked her if you and Sarah could come too. I suggested that we could go with your grandmother when she goes to visit again. Mrs. Rogers thought it was a grand idea. Would you like to do that?"

"Yes, I think that I would like that very much."

Right then the service started, so they couldn't talk anymore. Miriam lifted her voice in a song of worship, and she truly felt the love of the Lord again, and the praise welled up from her happy and grateful heart.

A couple of weeks later, Miriam, Sarah, and Abigail took the local ferry downriver to a cherry orchard. They had planned ahead and had brought a picnic basket so they could spend the entire day on their outing. The orchard supplied small baskets to carry and fill with the fruit as they picked it, and they had brought along gunny sacks to bring the fruit back home in.

"What a pretty day this is! And just listen to that loon. I love how its call just echoes off the water like that, don't you?" Sarah remarked with a happy sigh. "And I just love to pick cherries too."

The girls laughed with the simple joy of just being together and sharing a beautiful day.

The ferry pulled up to the wharf, and the girls walked the plank, stepping off onto the dock. It was about a half-mile walk through the small town to get to the orchard. As they passed a small bakery, the smell of freshly baked bread wafted through the air.

"Let's go in and get us a snack for later." Abigail's stomach had lightly rumbled at the yeasty smell. "I know that Mother packed a good lunch, but a sweet will taste good in a bit."

"Um, I agree. Come on," Miriam said as she followed her nose.

The shop was small, but there was a good assortment of bakery items displayed in a glass case. "I'll be with you in just a minute." A voice sang out at the jingle of the bell on the door. A young woman soon appeared from a back room in a flour-dusted apron. She gave the girls a wide friendly smile. "Sorry, I had to get the loaves out of the oven. My boat captain will be in here soon to pick up his order. How can I help you today?"

"We need to get a pastry for each of us. I'll take the blueberry-filled one, please," Sarah said as she made her selection. Both Abigail and Miriam chose a blueberry-filled one also.

As they were paying for their pastries, the bell on the door jingled again, and a man entered the shop. He greeted the woman with a warm hello and a big smile. Seeing that the woman was busy with the girls, he stood back and let them conclude their business.

Abigail had finished stowing the goodies in her basket when she took a closer look at the man. It was then that she recognized Captain Jolly, having met him one time when she was with her father.

"Hello, Captain Jolly, I don't know if you remember me, but I'm Abigail Eckhardt. I was with my father one day when you were picking up a load of lumber at the mill."

"Why, hello there, young lady. Of course I remember you. As I recall, you had on a very fetching bonnet that day. It sported a lovely assortment of spring flowers. I remember that solely because my mother had one that was very similar to it. So what are you and these other fine young ladies up to today?"

"We are going cherry-picking at the orchard, sir."

"In that case, could I impose on you to do a favor for me? You see, I have a great fondness for cherries, but I do not have the time to pick them for myself. I have to take a load to St. Paul and get back again by morning. I had planned to stop and visit with Mr. Heimlich at the mercantile at that time. I will gladly pay you to pick the cherries and deliver them there. Would you be interested in doing this for me? You are under no obligation, of course, if you do not have the time or the inclination to do so."

"Why, Captain Jolly, of course I would be glad to get some cherries for you. We are to meet my father at the mercantile to get a ride home later today, so that is perfect." Abigail did not want to accept payment for her labors, but the captain insisted. They finally settled on the wages for the task, and the girls left the bakery and continued on their way to the orchard.

The fruit was almost to the point of being perfectly ripe and was so prolific that they were able to fill their baskets fairly quickly. "Mother suggested that I pick extra cherries for Mrs. Rogers. We're sure that she would appreciate the fruit, and besides that, it gives me a reason to go and visit her again," Miriam said as she resumed picking the beautiful red fruit.

"That's a wonderful idea. I have wanted to visit with Mrs. Himmel again too. I believe that she also would love to have some cherries. The last time that I saw her at church, she promised to share some of her crochet patterns with me. She has one that you sort of make up the pattern, and it will create your family name. She showed me the one that she made for herself, and she has it framed on her wall. I'm eager to get the pattern and make it up as a gift for Mother as a Christmas present," Abigail said.

"Will you share that pattern with me? I think that my mother would like it too," Miriam stated.

"Me too!" Sarah chimed in. "That is a wonderful idea for a Christmas gift. My mother just loves it when I make things like that. In fact, I think that I will also make one for my hope chest. Then when I marry, it will help me to remember my roots especially when I take my new name. Then I can display them side by side."

"Mother asked me to get about five pounds of cherries for the cherry cordial that she makes. Oops! I wasn't supposed to mention it to anyone. Please forget that I said anything." Miriam begged her friends.

"Why?" Abigail asked her quizzically.

"Well, some of the ladies in the Women's Circle at church are temperance and the cordial is alcoholic, and it can be potent. That is why she only makes a few bottles of it each year." Then she let out a little giggle. "Oh, I shouldn't tell you, but since you're my best friends and I know that you both can keep a secret, I just have to share it. It's nothing really bad anyways, but please, please, please do not breathe a word of this to anyone ever again. Do I have your promise?"

Of course both of the girls did cross their hearts or hope to die as was required of this kind of important disclosure.

"Well, at Christmastime last year, Mother made the mistake of mentioning the cordial at a Women's Circle gathering, and the group as a whole became very critical of her. Some of the women become derogatory to the point that they even questioned her Christianity. In despair, she was compelled to talk to Reverend Arden as to what she should do to rectify the situation. The reverend assured her that he would take the situation in hand, that she was to trust him. When the group next convened, he gently chastised the ladies as to their treatment of this fine woman who had always been an exemplary specimen of Christianity. Furthermore, he stated that his dear departed mother had also made cherry cordial, and it had been a family tradition to serve it with their meal on Christmas Eve. He then turned to Mrs. Holden and gave her a sly wink that only she could see. Readdressing the group, he stated that Mrs. Holden had told him that in light of the temperance movement and now being properly instructed, she had assured him that she would no longer be making the elixir. The ladies, in turn, were properly chastised and were satisfied with the arrangement. In time, the whole subject was forgotten as if it had never happened.

Miriam giggled again as her face lit up with a smile. "Well, starting at that Christmas and every year since, my mother gets a special visitor. The Reverend Arden pays a call, and when my mother sees him off, he has a bottle wrapped in brown paper tucked tightly under his arm. He is so grateful to Mother as this allows him to remember his mother and honor her by keeping a great family tradition." The girls all shared a merry laugh at the story, and of course, they all swore never to reveal it to anyone else.

The three girls had a great day together picking the red fruit for their families and their friends. It was a day of laughter and sharing and just enjoying one another's company. It was as if they knew that they had to make these memories and store them away for the time when life would separate them and would add its own burdens and stresses. When that happened, they could look back to a time when they were young and carefree, full of joy and laughter and most especially of friendship and love

6

Bees

Mrs. Acres is the local beekeeper, and you can often find her bedecked in her veils and gloves with a smoker can tending to her hives. The smoke calms the bees, which make it possible for her to harvest the honey. If you visit her and promise to be very still and quiet, she will allow you to watch while she removes the wooden trays from the hives. She then stacks them in a large washtub and carries it all to the shed to process. This process involves using a heated knife to cut open the wax combs so the honey can drain out; then it is strained and put into jars. She knows just which hives are ready to harvest, and she always leaves enough so the hive will continue to survive. Mr. Heimlich owns the local mercantile, and he gladly takes all the honey that she brings in as he had no lack of buyers for it.

As for the wax that is left behind, she has a use for it also. She melts it down and makes candles from it. Beeswax candles are highly prized as they make the purest white candles that burn clean and bright. She is an expert at dipping the slim tapers. Sometimes, she infuses the wax with color, staining it red, blue, pink, yellow, or green. She sometimes also permeates the wax with different scents. The local children gather the rose hips, juniper berries, and the mulberries that she needs to make the oils for the scents. The pennies that she pays them for these items usually end up at the local mercantile. Mr. Heimlich always has a good supply of penny candy displayed in glass jars on the front counter. Most highly prized of these sugary treats are the licorice whips, peppermint sticks, root beer barrels, and lemon drops.

Carrying a basket, Abigail most often makes the rounds of the neighborhood, asking if she can collect rose hips from the bushes. The folks know that she collects the hips without harming the plants, so they let her take as much as she wants. They discovered that this process also serves as a good, light pruning for the plants. She does sell some of the hips to Mrs. Acres, and she saves the rest to use in her soapmaking. Mother taught her how to make fine glycerin soap, and Mrs. Acres had taught her how to make the oils to scent it. She uses some of the soap as gifts and the rest she takes to the mercantile to sell. Not only does the soap smell wonderful; she had also figured out how to imbed rose petals, small dried flowers, leaves, and other greenery into the soap, making it pretty as well.

"Why, I sure am glad you brought in a supply of your soaps, Miss Abigail. I was about down to the last bar, and some of the ladies get quite put out when I don't have any in stock when they come in to shop," said Mr. Heimlich. "And I really like how you wrap them in that pretty paper and tie it with the bits of ribbon. It makes the ladies feel like they are getting themselves something really special. Pamper themselves like."

Just then Mrs. Acres walked into the store carrying a box of jars filled with honey.

"Why, Mrs. Acres, let me take that box from you." Mr. Heimlich rushed to relieve her of her heavy burden. "This must be my day for deliveries. First, Abigail comes in with her soap, and then here you are with your honey. I was getting short of both items, so I am mighty glad to get my stock refilled. Is this all of it?"

"No, I have another larger box out in my wagon, and then I have yet another box full back at my house. I couldn't fit all three boxes in the wagon at one time as I didn't wish to overload the little wagon and possibly break the jars."

A man stepped forward, tipping his hat as he addressed Mrs. Acres. "Pardon me, madam. I'm Captain Jolly, and I am a patron and friend of Mr. Heimlich here. I would be honored if you would allow me to go out and fetch that other box for you."

"Why, I guess that would be all right." She was looking quizzically at Mr. Heimlich.

Suddenly, Mr. Heimlich stepped forward, clearing his throat and smiling broadly. "Well, Captain, if you will just allow me to do the introductions. Mrs. Acres, this here is Captain Jolly. We have been friends, and avid checkers opponents, for a number of years, and I certainly can vouch for his character. And this here is Mrs. Acres. She is our resident beekeeper and candlestick maker. She started the honey business a number of years ago, when she discovered the throat-soothing properties of the golden elixir." Mr. Heimlich had nodded from one to the other.

"I'm mighty glad to meet you, madam. I too use honey to calm the sore throat that comes with a cold. I always buy my honey here as I found that it seems to work the best for me. I'm pleased and honored to meet the supplier," said Captain Jolly, again tipping his hat to her.

"And I am glad to meet you, sir," she said, giving him a small shy smile.

"Hum, ah, I'll be right back with that box, madam." A blush had infused Captain Jolly's face, and he ducked his head as he hurried out the door. He quickly retrieved the box of honey and carried it into the store, placing it on the counter next to Mr. Heimlich.

Mrs. Acres had drifted across the store and was speaking with Abigail. The captain, not wishing to be overheard, leaned over and whispered to his friend, "Hey, old friend, I have a question for you. Is there a Mr. Acres in the picture?"

Mr. Heimlich's eyebrows raised almost to the ceiling as he whispered back, "No, he passed a number of years ago, had cancer of the throat, thus the need for honey. Why?"

"Oh, no reason really. Just curious is all."

Mrs. Acres and Abigail came walking back up to the counter. "I thank you, Captain. That was very kind of you to fetch that box for me."

Mrs. Acres's voice was softly musical. The captain's face sported a slight pink blush as he mumbled a, "You're welcome, madam."

"Hum." Mr. Heimlich cleared his throat. "Mrs. Acres, you say that you have another box back at the house?"

"Yes, I certainly do. First, Abigail and I have a bit of shopping and visiting that we wish to do, so may I leave the wagon here for about an hour? Then I'll go back home and get the second load."

The captain took the opportunity to butt into the conversation. "Uh, Mrs. Acres, uh, if you would like, uh, I mean that is if you wouldn't mind. Well, I have things to do also for about an hour. Then I could meet you back here and take you back to your house to fetch that honey."

"Why, that is so very kind, but I just couldn't impose on you in that way." Mrs. Acres was somewhat flustered at the impromptu offer.

"Really, madam, it is no imposition at all," Captain Jolly recounted.

"Well, Mrs. Acres, if Captain Jolly gives you a ride, then I could come along and get those patterns from you. Then I would be back here at the store in plenty of time for Father to pick me up. And, Captain, I'm sure that Father would love a chance to visit with you," Abigail said with a smile.

"Well, I guess that would be all right. Abigail and I will meet you back here in about an hour then, Captain. Thank you again for your kindness." Mrs. Acres was relieved that Abigail would be with her in the captain's truck. She didn't know why she felt so uncomfortable being alone with the man except that she found him attractive, and that had not happened in a very long time.

"Good, good, an hour then, madam." And the Captain nodded his head at her.

"Come, Abigail, we need to go and see Mrs. Himmel and deliver this honey to her." She nodded to the two men with a smile and walked out of the door.

"Well, Captain, I usually have a business lull just about now. How about we have a rousing game of checkers?" Mr. Heimlich said as he reached for the game board that kept beneath the counter.

"Nope, I don't have time right now. I got to get to the barber, then go back to the boat. I only have an hour. Maybe we'll have a game later this evening," the captain said as he hurried for the door, leaving Mr. Heimlich holding the checkers game and scratching his head.

Abigail and Mrs. Acres walked slowly toward Mrs. Himmel's house, chatting as they strolled along.

"Abigail, I have to tell you that your soaps are absolutely heavenly. I have so enjoyed my baths of late. And I love how you imbedded the rose petals into the soap too. I have also heard the praise from the other ladies who have purchased your soap at the store. Mr. Heimlich is right. He does get complaints when his stock gets low. You have a good product that is in high demand. I'm so very proud of you, my dear!" Mrs. Acres was gushing with her praise.

Abigail was blushing with gratitude at Mrs. Acres's high remarks. "Thank you so much, Mrs. Acres. Mother had told me how much the soap was liked, but I thought it was just her way of encouraging me to keep me productive. It is so nice to know that you and others really do like the soaps too. I wouldn't have been able to scent them if you had not shared with me how to make the oils. I thank you for that. This does encourage me to make more, so I will have a stock to sell after school starts again in the fall. It will be hard enough to find the time to do my studies, much less make the soaps. Do you know that Mrs. Huffmeister has placed an order for twenty bars of the rose soap? She wants to send it back east to her friends as Christmas presents. I was amazed when she asked me about it at church last Sunday."

"Well, you shouldn't have been surprised, my dear. It makes a lovely gift, and it should travel well when it is shipped. I'm so very glad for you." Mrs. Acres gave Abigail a light squeeze on her arm in pleasure.

"I am most happy because I have a special use for the money that I will earn. It is a surprise for Mother and Father for Christmas, so I can't divulge what it is, but it makes me giddy with happiness to think about it." Abigail gave a little giggle.

"What a sweet girl you are. You are always thinking about others ahead of yourself. But, of course, I saw that characteristic in you from the very beginning. Well, now, what do you have in that bag for Mrs. Himmel?" Mrs. Acres was curious.

"I'm returning some books to her that she had loaned to Mother. They belonged to the late Mr. Himmel, some of his Audubon collection." Abigail was reluctant to say why her mother had needed the books until there was suddenly a merry glint in Mrs. Acres's eyes.

"So she did take my suggestion and borrowed the books to copy a liking of the blue jay to add to her quilt. Did she find a good pictures of all of the animals that inhabit her garden? How I would love to see what she is doing, but I will be patient until fair time. And I will keep all of this secret too, as she has requested," Mrs. Acres said conspiratorially.

"Oh, I am so glad that Mother confided in you and Mrs. Himmel. She has been so secretive and has worked so diligently on the quilt. I have only seen bits and pieces of it as she has worked on smaller parts of it in the evenings, and even then we do not discuss just exactly what she is working on. Mother has stated that the less said, the easier it is to keep it under wraps, don't you think so too?" Abigail asked.

"Yes, my dear, I am waiting with bated breath to see the quilt too. Your mother is such a dear lady and an even dearer friend. I am sure that this quilt is sure to be one of the finest examples of needlework that I will ever see," Mrs. Acres said confidently. Then Mrs. Acres changed the subject. "Um, my dear, this is the first that I have met Captain Jolly. If you don't mind my asking, just how did you come to know him?"

"Oh, the first time that I met him was at the mill with Father and Mother. Mother, and I had packed a special lunch for Father and brought it over to him. The captain was picking up a load of specialty wood, black maple I believe, and was going to be delivering it to a cabinetry shop in Minneapolis. He was kind enough to give Mother and me a ride back across the lake that day. That was when he offered to transport us to the cities for a shopping trip sometime. Mother accepted his offer, and we plan on going a little later this summer. I think it's going to be an exciting adventure. I've been to the cities twice, but I have never traveled by boat before. Captain

Jolly is even going to let us stay at his room at the boarding house so that we can shop for two full days. Father told Mother that this is a great opportunity and that she deserves a little diversion. He has repeatedly assured Mother that he and my brothers will be just fine on their own while we are gone. Grandmother will also be there to ride herd if the need arises. Father is even thinking that they may attempt a little fishing trip in our absence."

"My, that is a wonderful opportunity. I must remember to talk to your mother about it. I know of a couple of little specialty shops in Minneapolis that she may be interested in browsing through. I'm sure that you both will have a marvelous time." Mrs. Acres smiled at her little friend and gave her a light pat on the back.

Mrs. Himmel was so glad to have some company. Abigail was no stranger as she, Miriam, and Sarah had made a point of visiting ever since Abigail had delivered vegetables earlier that summer. The girls were surprised to find that Mrs. Himmel was a well-read and well-traveled person as well. She had some very interesting stories that she shared with the girls about her journeys. It had created a longing in the girls to go themselves and to see some of the places that the older woman had been to. Abigail was content just to go to the cities for now. She was sure that even this little trip was going to broaden her horizons. When Abigail told the old woman about the planned trip, she became very animated.

"Oh, I do need to talk to your mother about this trip. Perhaps I can impose upon her to do a bit of business for me that I have put off for far too long. Yes, I will certainly be calling her this very week about it." She nodded her head as if setting it in her mind. "Now what else have you been up to lately, my dear?" She effectively changed the subject, steering the conversation in a totally different direction. Her mind, though, was still on the original subject as she fleshed out her idea.

Mrs. Acres and Abigail finished with their visit and ambled back toward the mercantile. The day was beautiful filled with sunshine and fresh air. They talked extensively as they walked, enjoying one another's company as well as the exercise. Many of the neighbors were taking a break from their daily chores and were sitting on their porches, taking in the ambiance of the extraordinary summer weather. Words of greeting and small bits of news were exchanged between the walkers and the porch sitters.

Consequently, it took the two a bit more than an hour to get back to the mercantile, and as Mrs. Acres entered the store, she had full intentions of apologizing to the captain for their tardiness. Instead, she was caught speechless when the captain greeted her. His hair had been freshly cut, his beard trimmed, and he sported a suit and tie rather than the bib overalls in which he had previously been attired.

Mrs. Acres finally overcame her surprise and found her voice. "Oh, Captain Jolly, I truly do apologize for being late. We were greeted by our neighbors from their porches, and it took a bit more time than anticipated for them to catch us up on the local news."

"No need to apologize, dear lady. I just got back here myself, so it has turned out to be perfect timing. Are you and the young lady ready to go and retrieve your load of honey?" The captain was extremely solicitous of the two friends.

At just that point, Mr. Eckhardt entered the mercantile. "Father, you are here earlier than I had thought you would be. Captain Jolly has offered to give Mrs. Acres a ride back to her house to pick up some honey. Would it be all right with you for me to go along so I can get some patterns?"

"Why, hello there, Captain. It is so good to see you again." Father shook the Captain's hand in greeting. "And, yes, dear girl, I have no problem with you finishing your errands. Mrs. Acres, my wife has requested your presence at our house for supper this evening. Are you free to come, or had you made other plans?"

"Thank you for the invitation. No, I have no other plans, so of course I would love to come. There is something that I have wanted to talk over with her, and this would be a perfect opportunity." Mrs. Acres beamed as she thought of her friend and the curiosity that she had concerning the quilt.

Suddenly, Mr. Eckhardt turned to the captain. "And you, sir, are also invited, and this time I will take no excuses from you."

"Well, I have no excuses to offer, and I thank you for the invitation. I am taking these two beautiful ladies to procure the honey, and I was also hoping for a tour of the honey farm. I would be happy to deliver them to your residence in time for supper if that is all right with you, of course." Captain Jolly had a decided twinkle in his eye.

"That is totally fine with me, Captain. Mother and I will look forward to seeing all of you at the house in just a bit then." Abigail was looking strangely at her gather as he was wearing a huge grin on his face, looking much like the picture of the Cheshire cat in the *Alice and Wonderland* book.

"Shall we go?" The captain walked to the door and held it open while the group exited the mercantile.

Father waited for the door to close before he turned quizzically to his friend. "Did I just witness what I think I did?"

"Aye, my friend, you certainly did. Could have knocked me over with a feather when he walked in here all dolled up like that. I think our Captain Jolly has been smitten. Not that I blame him, as Mrs. Acres is a fine figure of a woman." The merchant was grinning from ear to ear.

"Well, this promises to be a very interesting evening. I can't wait to get home and share this with the missus. Let me get the few things on my list here so I can get going. Looks like you do not have any one to play checkers with tonight. In fact, you may have lost your partner for good if the lady returns the captain's interest." Both of the men shared a smile at the thought.

A little more than an hour later, the trio arrived at the Eckhardt residence. Abigail hurried to help Mother with the last-minute preparations for dinner while Father entertained his two friends with glasses of lemonade on the front porch. Mr. Eckhardt realized that Mrs. Acres and the captain seemed to be comfortable in each other's presence. He chuckled to himself as he observed each of them gaze serendipitously at each other when they thought that the other was not looking.

Mrs. Eckhardt called everyone into to the dinner table, making sure that the two guests were seated next to each other. After consuming a fine meal, the men and boys helped to clear the table before they retired to the porch. It didn't take long for the ladies to clean up the dishes, and they joined the group.

"Captain, could you tell us some stories about your trips down the river? Have you been all the way down to the end of the Mississippi? How long did it take you? Did you get to see the ocean?" Jeremiah was doing his mile-a-minute talking and asking tons of questions. The captain smiled as he tried his best to field the multiple inquires, realizing that both Father and Samuel were also interested in the answers.

The ladies had left the group and entered the house on a secret mission, and when they rejoined the men on the porch, they all had very satisfied smiles on their faces.

"Jeremiah, why don't you and Samuel play some checkers now and let us grown-ups talk a bit. I am sure that the captain would be glad to share more of his stories at a later time." Father gently steered Jeremiah in another direction.

The adults talked and shared until the sun finally began to set. Mrs. Acres then smiled at her friend and patted her arm. "It is getting late, and although I thoroughly enjoyed the meal and the ensuing companionship, I'm afraid that I must call an end to the night. Thank you so much for such a wonderful dinner."

At that, Mr. Eckhardt arose from his chair. "I will bring the car up and drive you home."

The captain stood up and cleared his throat. "No need for you to make a special trip my good friend. If it pleases the lady, I would be honored to escort her to her home."

Mrs. Acres blushed prettily. "Thank you, Captain, I think that is a capital idea."

The group all said their good-byes, and the Eckhardts waved to their friends as they drove out of sight.

"Well, my dear, I do believe that there is a spark there on the captain's part. What kind of a feeling did you get from Mrs. Acres?" Father had his arm around his wife's waist as they enjoyed the twilight and the earthy odors the land gave off as it cooled.

Mrs. Eckhardt smiled as she looked up into her husband's face. "I think that my dear friend is open to possibilities that she previously had not believed could exist anymore. They are both wonderful people, and I wish them well. Romance, who would have thought?"

7

First Day of Work

The temperature had dropped overnight, causing dew to form. Because of that, everything had a light coating of the moisture, including the intricately spun spider's webs. These droplets were strung on each delicate strand of the web, so later when they were lit by the sun's rays, they would sparkle, much resembling gems that had been cut and highly faceted.

It was their first official day at their job for Mr. Larson, and Samuel and Abigail walked down the road to the farm.

"I like to be out early in the day like this. Listen, the Larsons' rooster is already crowing up a storm. It sounds as if he is yelling for us to hurry up. Bobby is staying at the farm, and he is sure to be feeding some of the other animals already. There he is. Hi, Bobby!" Samuel waved at his friend.

"Hey, it's about time that you got here. I fed the chickens already and put feed down for the cows. Guess we had better go and find those old bovines. Are you ready?" Bobby had a running dialogue going as he hurried toward the pasture gate.

The three gamely set out to scour the woods for the cows. After a time, they heard the soft tinkling of the bell that the lead cow was wearing. As they drew closer to the sound, they spotted her lying down in a small meadow, contentedly chewing her cud. The rest of the herd was there also, lying close by, surrounding her. Abigail laughed because the group looked like a women's social gathering she had attended just last week. Was this group also discussing recipes or exchanging quilt patterns? As Bobby called out, "Come, boss," the cows inelegantly rose to their feet and started ambling down the path that would end at the dairy barn.

Nameplates for each cow had been fashioned by Mr. Larson and had been hung above the stanchions. As each cow entered the barn, she went to the stanchion that had her nameplate over it.

"Hey, Bobby, do the cows know how to read, or do they just go to the same spot every time?" Samuel asked with a laugh.

"Right, Samuel, the cows can read." Bobby began laughing at the joke. "Naw, it's just that they get milked twice a day, so the cows have been trained to go to the same stanchion every time." Each cow stood munching their pile of grain contentedly while the children got the three-legged stools and pails and proceeded with the milking. The barn was soon filled with the distinct sound that the milk makes when it hits the side of the metal pail. The barn cats lined up behind the cows and began meowing, begging for their treat. With a little maneuvering and careful aim, a stream of milk could be shot into a waiting cat's mouth. If the aim was off, the cats didn't mind much, as they would get each drop later when they later gave themselves a thorough tongue bath. Bobby poured some of the milk into a pie plate so that even the littlest kitten could share in the bounty.

After the morning milking was finished, the cows were released so they could return to the meadow to graze until the process would be repeated in the evening. The large milk cans were put to cool in the spring well that was unique to Mr. Larson's farm. Mr. Larson had discovered that this little spring emitted a steady stream of water that ran constantly cool and clear. He had dug a large hole below the spring and lined the area with rocks, creating a pool. He then covered that with a wooden frame house effectively, making a cooling house. It was large enough to hold four large milk cans and still left room for other food items like butter and vegetables. In the summer, he would chill a whole watermelon by immersing it in the cool water. Chilling it enhanced its juicy goodness, and it was a welcome treat on a hot summer's day.

Mucking the barn was the next necessary chore to be done. With three people tackling it, the odiferous task was done in short order. As Bobby and Samuel fed the rest of the livestock, Abigail went to weed the garden. They joined her at the last to help harvest the vegetables that were ripe and ready to be picked. Mrs. Larson had instructed that the vegetables were to be equally split and put into two burlap sacks. One sack was to be delivered to Mr. Marples and the other to Mrs. Himmel. Both of these elderly folks could no longer care for a garden on their own, so Mrs. Larson shared her surplus with them.

They got the morning chores done a little before eleven o'clock. The reward for these labors was that a few afternoon hours could be spent relaxing by swimming at the lake. Mother had packed a picnic lunch, and they headed to the favorite swimming spot on the lakeshore. It had a little sandy beach area, and it boasted a small dock as well. Even though it was the first week in June, the water was still a little chilly. Small minnows played in the shallows, and from out on the lake, they could hear the plaintive call of a loon.

"I'm going to eat first. I'm starving!" said Samuel.

"Let's sink the bags of vegetables in the water so they will keep cool until we deliver them," said Bobby. "Put a rock in each bag so they won't float away."

After they had secured the vegetables, they spread out the blanket they had brought with them. When the lunch pail was unpacked, they found that there were sandwiches, apple fritters, lemonade, and sliced fresh tomatoes from the garden. Samuel stripped off his clothing, revealing his swim trunks that he had on underneath, and the others followed suit. They plopped down on the blanket, and Abigail distributed the food evenly between them.

"What a feast! I could do this every day all summer long and never get tired of it!" Samuel said with a sigh of satisfaction as he munched heartily.

"Just eat up so we can get to the swimming!" Abigail said laughingly.

They consumed all of the goodies and sat contentedly, sipping the lemonade. With a last big gulp followed with a satisfied sigh,

Bobby brushed the crumbs from his hands and stood up. A large grin split his face. "Last one in is a rotten egg!" With this last, he sprinted toward the dock as fast as he could run.

Samuel jumped up and sprinted after him, uttering a loud whoop. They pounded down the dock and launched themselves off the end of it. Both curled into a ball, and their bodies hit the water with full force, causing tremendous splashes. When they surfaced from the dunking, they both had huge smiles on their faces.

"Make way because here I come!" Abigail yelled as she jumped from the dock and hit the water. Her body caused a huge splash as well that washed over the boys, making them sputter as it hit them in their faces. All of them shook the water off and laughed loudly. The coolness of the water was a shock to their hot bodies but was thoroughly enjoyed as they splashed and floated.

When they had their fill of the water antics, they padded out of the water and piled back onto the blanket to dry out. Within an hour of lying under the sun, their swim attire had reduced to just a slight dampness.

"Guess it's time to go and deliver the vegetables. After that, we need to get back for the evening milking," Bobby said.

They gathered the picnic supplies, retrieved the bags of vegetables, and proceeded down the road toward town. As they passed Mrs. Acres's place, they spotted her out tending to her hives. She spied them as they waved and called out a cheery hello. "Where are you youngsters off to?" she queried.

"We're taking these vegetables from Mrs. Larson to Mr. Marples and Mrs. Himmel," said Abigail.

"Why, that is wonderful. Would you be willing to take them some honey from me? I am behind in my chores, and it would be a great help to me if you could deliver it. Mrs. Himmel swears that the honey mixed with vinegar makes her arthritis better, and she has almost run out. If it helps to relieve her pain even a little bit, it is a blessing. Would you mind?"

"Why, we would be glad to," said Abigail.

"Good. Wait here, and I'll be right back." Mrs. Acres hurried away. When she came back, she had two jars of honey, and they added one to each of the bags. "Tell them both that I will be stopping in to visit with them later this week. They are such dear old souls, and they just love company, and we neighbors have to watch out for one another. I'm sure that they will appreciate your coming to visit with them," said Mrs. Acres. "Thanks again for your help, and do enjoy yourselves." She smiled and turned back to her hives.

The children made their deliveries to their elderly neighbors. Both of them were so appreciative and grateful for the thoughtfulness and generosity that their neighbors extended to them. The deliveries took longer than the youngsters had anticipated because the recipients made a fuss over them and wanted them to sit a spell and visit.

They finally took their leave by saying that they had to get back to the dairy to prepare for the evening milking. So with fond good-byes coupled with promises to come to visit again, the children headed back.

"I didn't know that Mr. Marples had worked at the lumber mill all of his life. He worked for Mrs. Himmel's brother after he had bought the mill. That's how he learned so much about wood. Those animals that he carves look so real that I expected the squirrel to jump right out of the window and climb a tree and chatter," said Bobby.

"I know! He says that he sells his carvings at the mercantile over in Brainerd and even all the way down in the cities. He has an order now from a customer that wants a life-sized beaver carved," Samuel said in wonder.

"When I told him that I wished that I could carve like that, he upped and offered to teach me how. I told him that I wouldn't have time for any lessons until the Larsons get back because of the milking, and he said that would be fine to wait. He said he was proud of us, that running that dairy was a big undertaking, and he was sure that we would do the job right. That was a mighty fine thing for him to say," Bobby said.

Mother had a light supper ready for them when they got to the house. After they had eaten, Samuel and Abigail quickly doffed their still somewhat damp swim wear for drier clothing. They all took their time as they walked up the road to the dairy farm. When they got to the barn at the Larsons, the cows had come in on their own and were waiting in the corral. After doing the milking along with the accompanying chores, there was still a good measure of daylight left. The boys sat in the rockers, and Abigail curled up in the porch swing, and each enjoyed a cookie and a glass of cold milk.

"Well, we made it through the first day, and Father says that he is proud of us. He was the second person today to say that. I guess this really is a big responsibility. I hadn't thought of it that way before. I was just proud to be able to earn some money on my own. It makes me feel pretty grown up," said Samuel.

"I knew that it was going to be a lot of work but that we would be up to it. Mr. Larson was pretty sick for a couple of weeks last year, and I pretty much carried the load for a while. He had Lars Anderson come and help out a time or two, but then he saw that I knew what needed to be done and that I could do it too. He's told me since then that he didn't know what he would do without me. I just know that the Larsons are mighty fine folk and they care a lot about me. I don't know what my mother and I would have done if I couldn't have worked here. Mother depended on the money that I earned to help out with the bills. It had been mighty hard for her when Pa left. Now I get to use my earnings any way that I want to. I have spent some of it, but I want to put the rest of it into a savings account. I don't know what I want yet, though, but it will be nice to have it when I need it," Bobby declared.

Samuel and Abigail stood up to leave for home as the light waned, and the fireflies began their lighting ritual.

"We'll be back bright and early in the morning."

"See you then." The earth began cooling as the night air descended, and it gave up a rich, loamy odor. The darkening sky filled with bright twinkling stars.

"I guess that we have life pretty good. I was just working to earn extra spending money, but Bobby gave his to his mother to help out. I need to remember to be thankful for the blessings that the Lord gives to me," said Samuel.

The next day was Tuesday, and it was quilting day. All of the ladies showed up for the event. The town knew that the Larsons were out of town and that Bobby and the Eckhardt youngsters were running the farm in their absence, and that was why Abigail was not at the bee.

Mrs. Huffmeister and Mrs. Finney were both in attendance along with Ms. Plummer, the school teacher. As always, the younger girls were included in this ladies' endeavor.

All of the attendees had brought along scraps of material to be cut into the pieces that would be sewn together to fashion the quilt tops. Sarah, Miriam, and Brianna made themselves useful, sorting the material by color, and some of the other ladies had chosen patterns and assembled the templates so the material could be cut into pieces. Still others took the cut pieces and sewed them together, making squares. Mrs. Finney was in charge of taking the finished squares and ironing the seams flat so that they all fit together nicely. Soon a beautiful quilt top emerged. The next step was to take the finished quilt top and sandwich it with a batting and the backing. As they were only tying the quilt, they put it on a frame, lightly basted it, and began tying it off.

They had one quilt well on its way to being finished and had started a second one when the group broke for the noon meal. The entire bee was a time of fellowship, and the ladies took the opportunity to share news of the community. There was news of births, deaths, and all other events in between.

After the meal had been consumed and all of the dishes cleaned up, Ms. Plummer stood up at the front of the room and asked the ladies for their attention.

"Ladies, I have an announcement to make that is such wonderful news that I am literally giddy with happiness. As you all know at the end of our school year, Mrs. Huffmeister had collaborated with her friends back east, and our local children had wonderful clothing to wear to the graduation festivities. The entire event was aptly deemed a huge success. Following a suggestion made by Brianna, Mrs. Huffmeister provided for a photographer to take pictures of the attendees dressed in their donated finery, and then she had copies of the photos sent back east so the benefactors could see the results of their generous contributions. I am pleased to announce that those pictures so touched the marvelous people back east, that they plan to repeat the donations again in the spring." This information caused the room to erupt in thunderous applause. "Thank you, ladies, but there is more. There is yet another outstanding result from this incident. When the benefactress, Mrs. Smythe, saw the picture of our own Brianna in the green dress that she had donated, it touched her very deeply. Her daughter who had passed away a year ago loved to design clothing. She would visualize a dress by looking at material. She would then create a pattern and have the garment made up. When the girl saw her finished creation, she told her mother that she could envision the person who would wear it. In her mind's eye, she saw a beautiful, willowy red-haired girl, and that she was dancing. As we all know, it was Brianna who chose that specific dress, and she did indeed wear it to a dance. Brianna, will you please come up here?" Ms. Plummer gestured to an extremely surprised Brianna, who blushingly joined her teacher at the front of the room. "Now if you would please give Mrs. Huffmeister your attention, as she wishes to share some information with you."

The ladies clapped as Ms. Plummer stepped back and guided Brianna to stand next to the frail lady.

Mrs. Huffmeister smiled at the assembled group and began speaking. "Thank you, ladies, for your patience and undivided attention. The news I have concerns this very fine young lady standing before you. I waited to share this information with her until all of the particulars were totally set, as I did not wish to get hopes up just to have them dashed. Thankfully, all of the plans have come to fruition and have turned out even better than I could have hoped for. Brianna, dear, Ms. Plummer told me about the efforts that have been made on your behalf for you to attend college and obtain a teaching degree. When my friend, Mrs. Smythe, saw the picture of you in the dress and heard about your aspirations to attend college, she made some inquires. She had Ms. Plummer send transcripts of your grades and obtain letters of recommendation from people in the community confirming your stellar character. Mrs. Smythe then submitted this information to a friend of hers who is the dean of a college located very close to her home in New York. After reviewing all of the information, the dean is now delighted to extend an offer for you to attend his college. This offer includes a full scholarship that covers all of your tuition, books plus room and board."

The room exploded in applause while Brianna stood completely stunned by the offer. Ms. Plummer and some of the other ladies hurried to give her hugs of delight and congratulations, and she was finally able to mumble. "Thank you." Sarah and Miriam hurried up to give her hugs, and she finally was able to shake off the shock and gave out small squeals of delight. Her eyes were shining with unshed tears, and her face almost split with the luminous smile that was plastered there.

"Oh, Abigail is going to be in a tizzy because she missed this. And I also know that she is going to be as thrilled for you as we are. What say you that we all go over to her house tonight when she gets back from the Larsons? That way, you can share the news with her in person. Let me check with Mrs. Eckhardt to make sure that it will be all right with her." Sarah knew that her friend would want to hear all of the details from Brianna herself and that she would want to hug her friend in congratulation.

"There is a bit more, my dear." Ms. Plummer also had a few tears in her eyes as she got the room to quiet down so she could speak again. "Mrs. Smythe realized that Brianna would require some clothing while she attends classes, and to that end, she has sent some of her daughter's patterns, along with appropriate materials to make the garments." With that, she lifted a sheet and revealed some material that had been piled up on the table. "So, ladies, this is no longer a quilting bee. Instead with your assistance, we will use these materials and dressmaker form to make a wardrobe for Brianna, that is, if you all agree."

The room again exploded with applause and noisy affirmation that the group was more than willing to take on the new task. The ladies swarmed up to the table to view the patterns and the material that had been supplied. There were ohs and ahs as they fingered the fine quality of the fabric. They were also surprised when they saw that matching threads and embellishments had also been included.

"It is going to be a treat to work with this fabric. Mrs. Bernhardt, will you begin laying out the pattern as I get the dress form adjusted?

Stand right here, Brianna, so that I can take your measurements." Mrs. Finney was smiling with her measuring tape in hand, and she had a filled pin cushion fastened to her wrist in anticipation.

"When I looked through the fabrics, I found silk to make undergarments too. There is enough for two camisoles and a slip, and there are lace inserts to make them really fine. I haven't seen this quality of material since I left New York City. I worked as a seamstress in a fine dress shop there until we came west and settled here in Minnesota." Mrs. Finney had a soft smile on her face. "We certainly are going to get you fitted out fine."

"I am so overwhelmed that I don't even know what to say except thank you. Yes, thank all of you. You are all so wonderful to do this for me." Brianna had tears in her eyes once again as her gaze swept over the room, and she looked into each and every face there. She stopped when she got to Mrs. Huffmeister. "Thank you especially, Mrs. Huffmeister. Could I get Mrs. Smythe's address from you? I need to write her a special thank-you note."

"Of course I will get it for you. But I do have a bit more good news for you too." Brianna gave her a puzzled look. "Mrs. Smythe knows that New York is a very long way from Minnesota and, though your studies will take up much of your time, that you will have weekends and holidays off. If you would care to, she would like you to spend any or all of that time at her house as a guest. She has also approached her lady friends about your finances, and a number of the ladies have committed to giving you a monthly stipend to cover any other expenses you may have. They are putting aside five dollars a month for you."

"What? Oh my, I just don't know what to say." She looked around at her friends, and this time, she could no longer contain her tears.

Mrs. Huffmeister patted her on her shoulder to comfort her. "From what I have been told by others and what I have seen for myself, you are an exceptional young lady. You just need to go and do your very best, and I am sure that you will succeed. We are all so very happy for you."

Ms. Plummer had tears in her eyes as she hugged Brianna. "She is right, my dear girl. You are to go and realize your future. I am certain that you will excel in your scholastic studies and that you will obtain the education that you have always dreamed of. Then you will be the educator and in turn will lead our young folks so that they too can attain their dreams. I am so happy for you, and I will also miss you terribly."

"And so will we!" With that, Sarah and Miriam both hugged their friend.

A War Story

It had been hot and sultry all morning. The air was heavy with the heat, and the heavily overcast sky threatened rain. It was now just past noon, and the clouds had turned black. Rain was welcomed as there had been a dry spell, and the crops needed the moisture.

The morning milking was finished, and the group had completed the accompanying tasks. They had devoured a light lunch that included the strawberries gleaned from the garden. This was a singular treat especially as they had been topped with some of the heavy cream skimmed from one of the milk buckets.

The youngsters climbed up into the hay loft, and from there, they could see a good portion of the farm. The animals sensed the coming storm and began to take shelter. The hens gathered their chicks and urged them into the coop. The cats lurked within the barn doorway, ready to scoot farther inside at the first hint of raindrops. The cows had wandered out to find pasture with sweet grass to munch on. The horses remained in the coral area, waiting for the rain to come and cool them off. The pigs too were waiting expectantly for the rain to create a puddle in their sty so they could enjoy a lovely mud bath.

"Umm," said Samuel as he rubbed his stomach appreciatively. "I'm going to be a little sorry when the Larsons come back on Saturday. We have to talk to Mother about putting in some strawberry plants so we have them all of the time."

"Well, Mr. Marples and Mrs. Himmel sure enjoyed them too," said Abigail. "Of course they also really liked the vegetables we brought to them. They always make such a fuss over us when we bring the vegetables like we are company or something. I think they just get lonely, so I've asked Mrs. Himmel if she would like me to just stop by sometimes just to talk awhile. She liked that idea just fine. This last time when I stayed a little longer, she told me a story about her family when she was a little girl in Germany. Would you like to hear it? It's rather a long story, but I'm sure that you will like it."

"Sure!" the two boys said in unison. So they all snuggled down into the sweet-smelling hay.

Well, it seems that the German Kaiser and the leader of Poland were always fighting over their boundaries. In fact, when her grandfather was born, the nearby town was considered to be Germany, but when her grandmother was born there three years later, it was considered to be part of Poland. Consequently, they considered themselves of a mixed heritage.

When Mrs. Himmel's parents married, the young couple moved onto the farm with his parents, the Muellers. It was a small farm that had been in the Mueller family for three generations. It was self-sufficient in that it had an apple orchard and some cleared fields, and it also boasted a creek, which trickled merrily between several small hillocks. The house itself was built adjacent to one of the hills, and a family of foxes took to using a small cave in the hillside as a den. But the foxes were destructive in that if they could find no other prey, they would kill Mr. Mueller's chickens. As this could not be tolerated, the elder Mr. Mueller hunted the foxes out until none were left. Then, as to not waste a good thing, he enlarged the little cave, fashioned a door for it, and used it as a root cellar. Because of the war and the pilfering that went on, they disguised the entrance by encouraging vines and other foliage to grow over the door. This concealed it from any casual observer and many times proved its worth as their provisions were spared for the family rather than ending up in a marauding soldier's belly.

Mrs. Himmel's father was an only child, so he inherited the homestead when his father passed. It made a fine home for his wife and four children. Mrs. Himmel was the youngest child and the only girl. She and her brothers all had chores assigned to them, which included working in the garden and the apple orchard and feeding and caring for the chickens and goats. When they had finished their chores for the day, they spent many carefree hours fishing in the creek. Fresh caught fish were a welcome staple of their daily diet.

But their happiness ended when Mr. Mueller was called to go to war. The Kaiser had once again become disenchanted with Germany's boundaries and was attacking Poland to expand them. The family said their good-byes amidst many tears and hugs as they knew that this could well be the last time the family would be whole. Many of the neighboring women had been widowed more than once when their husbands did not return from the fighting. The couple had been talking for many years about moving to America, but they could not devise a plan to actually make it happen. They received letters from relatives who had gone to America and settled there in a place called Minnesota. In those letters, they encouraged the Muellers to come and live with them. Now the war was here again, so they would have to put their dreams on hold once more.

In the following months, the war raged on, but so far, it had not come too close to the little farm. The family prayed every day for the fighting to end and for all of them to be together again. Then one day, they were awakened by cannon fire. At first, it had sounded rather like distant thunder, but as the day lengthened, it grew steadily closer. Mrs. Mueller decided that it was time to leave the farm for a while and to take her children to a safer place. They would prepare to leave in the morning at first light. She and the children spent the last few hours of daylight packing their few belongings, wondering what would be left when they could finally return. At dusk, she went out to catch the goats and milk them. She would then make sure that they were penned for the night as she would not have time to chase them down in the morning. She hated to think of it, but she might have to sell them to obtain food or lodging for herself and the children.

She caught and tethered the goats, milked them, and then led them to the shed to lock them in for the night. When she opened the shed door, she was startled by a dark shape lying against the back wall. The form moved, and as she turned to run, a voice weakly called out to her in German to please help him. Even though she was frightened, she stopped and turned back to the form. It was then that she saw that it was a man and that he wore the uniform of a Polish officer. It was also apparent that he was wounded, as his head and his right leg were wrapped in crude bloody bandages.

Mrs. Mueller had a strong Christian faith and was brought to remembrance of the scriptures that said to be kind to your enemies. She was also mindful that her beloved mother-in-law had been of Polish heritage and that the older couple had not only shared their home but had also lived their faith daily. She knew that she could not turn her back on this man, so in Polish, she told him that she would help him. The children were shocked when she entered the house with the soldier but listened to her as she cautioned them to silence. She instructed the oldest boy to go back out to the shed to erase any evidence that the soldier may have left there and then to stay outside and keep watch in case anyone should come. She had the other children unpack all of the belongings as they would no longer be leaving.

As she set to tending his wounds, she discovered that his head gash was not too deep, but it still required a couple of stitches. This she did, trying to be careful not to cause him any unjust agony. The leg wound was much more serious as the bayonet that had been used had bit deeply, causing a deep puncture. She nervously advised him that, to treat this wound, she would have to cauterize it, not only to stop the bleeding but that to also seal the wound and kill any infection in it. To do so, she would have to heat the metal fireplace iron and apply it to the gash. It would be painful, but it would cause the cut to heal quickly and cleanly. He agreed to the treatment, only stating that he wished that he had a bottle of brandy to drink first. Instead, he took a large piece of cloth and crammed it into his mouth, biting down on it and then nodded to her to begin. As she applied the hot metal to the wound, he mercifully passed out. She quickly applied healing ointment to the injury and bandaged it. When he awakened an hour later, she shared some of the soup from their supper with him. He thanked her and stated that he wanted to leave as soon as possible as it would be dangerous for her and the children if he was discovered there. She argued with him that his wounds were too serious for him to travel, that he needed to rest and regain his strength. That was when she told him about the root cellar and that she was sure that he would not be discovered there. He agreed that it was a good solution but advised that he would leave as soon as he was able. She and the oldest boy helped the injured man hobble to the cellar. Even in the gathering dark, he discerned that it was indeed a good hiding place and that he would be safe there. She had brought bedding along to make a pallet and got him settled, telling him that she would be back in the morning to check on him. Weakened by the pain and the loss of blood, he gratefully laid his head down and drifted into a deep sleep. As she left, she carefully concealed the door with the foliage.

Back at the house, she again cautioned the children to silence and cleaned up all evidence of his presence. Just as she got everything straightened and put away, the oldest boy came running into the house excitedly, telling her that someone was coming up the road. As she looked around quickly to make sure that all was in order, there was a loud knocking at the door. When she opened the door, a German lieutenant pushed past her into the house. His eyes scanned the room, taking in the children sitting quietly in the corner, their eyes huge with fear as they focused on him. He asked where her husband was. She told him that he was on the war front, fighting for the Kaiser. He nodded his head as if in agreement; then he advised her that some of the fighting was now very close and that Polish soldiers could come upon them. He asked her if she had already seen any of the enemy in the area as they had been tracking a wounded Polish officer but had lost his trail nearby. She assured him that they had not seen anyone, but they would certainly be on guard for any strangers. He advised her to contact him if she did see anything out of the ordinary. At that point, a soldier came up to the door and said that he had scouted the area and that it was clear. He also gave an accounting of the livestock saying that there were six chickens in the coup and a shed containing one ram goat and two nanny goats. Then he smiled and lifted his hand where he had three good-sized fish on a string, saying that he had retrieved them from traps that were set in the creek. The lieutenant told the young man to take two of the chickens and the ram. He stated that he was leaving the other livestock only because her husband was the serving the Kaiser and that he too was gleaning food wherever he was serving. The army must be fed so they could stay strong for the fighting.

After the German soldiers had left, the oldest son told his mother that the soldiers had almost stepped on the door of the root cellar but hadn't discover it. He told how he had lured the soldiers away to the creek to the fish that were in the traps. Mrs. Mueller praised him for his quick thinking and said that from now on they would have to keep watch in case the soldiers returned. They would be staying now and helping the injured man until he was well enough to leave. She gathered her children to her and praised them for their courage and their silence. If the Polish soldier was discovered, it would be a death sentence for all of them, but she also knew that it was God's will to help this man and, in turn, God would protect them.

As Mrs. Mueller nursed and cared for the young man, they had opportunities to talk. He told her that his name was Jablonski and of his father's unhappiness that he preferred to serve in the army rather than to work in the family business. She shared with him her husband's dream of moving to America. The young man told her often how much he appreciated her nursing him and her courage to assist and hide him. He had heard her son lure the soldiers from his hiding place, and his gratitude was boundless. All she could say to him was that she and her children were all Christians and it was their duty to God to help him.

The young man stayed hidden in the root cellar until his head no longer throbbed, and the cut on his leg had a thick healthy scab. He had slowly regained his strength to the point that he would exercise under the cover of night by walking in the apple orchard. At first, he used a stick as a crutch just to maintain his balance, but he grew steadily stronger each day. One day, he finally told Mrs. Mueller that he would be leaving as soon as it was dark, that he was well enough to travel and he needed to return to his regiment. He thanked her again for all of her help but that he could no longer expect them to jeopardize their safety for him. She told him again that they had only done their Christian duty and that they would pray for him to get through the war safely. The next morning, when she went to the root cellar, it was empty and showed no sign of his ever having been there except for the bedding that he had used for his pallet. She sent up a prayer for him and wondered if she would ever see him again.

The war raged on for another six months before peace was declared and new boundary lines were drawn. Sadly, Mrs. Mueller received official word that her husband had died on the battlefield. She was left to deal with her grief and also the death of the dream of going to America.

About two months later, she was thoroughly surprised as a fine carriage came down the road and turned into the lane leading up to her house. As she approached the carriage, the young man, Lieutenant Jablonski, emerged. As she lifted her hand to offer a handshake, he laughed and embraced her with a hug. Instead of a uniform, he now wore fine clothes and appeared to be well and fit. He claimed that his healing was solely due to her excellent nursing skills, that he barely even limped from the wounds. He then inquired about her husband and was saddened to hear of his demise. When she invited him into the house, she was prepared to offer him some cookies that she had made that morning using the last of her sugar. He surprised her by asking if she would accept some small gifts that he had brought for her and the children. When she accepted, he had the driver begin to carry boxes into the house. The children excitedly began pulling items out, squealing with delight over the staples of flour, sugar, coffee, and even a loaf of bread. The largest box produced the biggest smiles as it contained an entire leg of ham. When he produced a smaller bag from his jacket pocket, the children looked at him curiously. Then when he held the bag up and shook it saying the word *candy*, their eyes began to sparkle. Smiling, the woman took the bag from him and told the children that they could have it after they had eaten. She put together a wonderful lunch of sandwiches and fresh vegetables. After the meal had been consumed, she opened the bag of candy. It was an assortment that included licorice whips, peppermint sticks, and lemon drops. Each child took one piece, saying that they would savor it and make it last.

The woman put coffee on to brew while she cleaned up and stored the food. Then the two friends settled down with cups of coffee and cookies and began to share what had happened in their lives since they had last been together. The young man told her about the perils he had faced to get through enemy lines and make it back to his regiment. He still suffered some dizzy spells caused by the head wound and had a slight limp from the leg injury. His superiors decided that because of these injuries he would be exempt from rejoining the fighting until he had fully recovered. Fate stepped in, and peace was declared, which ended the fighting. His father was grateful that he had not been more severely injured and declared that once he was healed he could finally join him in running the business.

She shared her grief over her husband's death and the worry she had of trying to run the farm by herself. Her oldest son had already taken on the majority of the chores, but there were some things that even together it was difficult for them to handle. She also shared her sadness that the dream of going to America was no longer feasible.

They talked for a while more until the young man stated that he had to return home to Poland. He asked if he could come again, and she assured him that he would always be welcome. He leaned out the window of the carriage, smiling and waving at her and the children as he disappeared down the road.

A few months went by, and the woman was amazed at how she was able to make the food gifts last. The ham had been stored in the root cellar, where the coolness had kept the meat from spoiling. They had fashioned many fine meals from it, and she had even shared some of it with her elderly neighbor. The woman was grateful as she had not had any meat for a long time, much less ham. The German army had taken all of her pigs when they had been in the area, and she didn't want to slaughter her chickens as she needed the eggs that they produced. She had been subsiding on the vegetables she got from her garden, so the ham was a special treat.

One morning as Mrs. Mueller and her son were finishing some repairs to the goat shed, they heard a wheeled vehicle coming down the road. Soon a fine carriage came into view, and she recognized it as belonging to the young man. As it pulled up to the house, the young man leaned out of the window and waved to her. He alighted from the vehicle and pulled down the step for the other occupants, and he assisted two older men to step out. As Mrs. Mueller approached the group, the young man hugged her once again and then introduced the others to her. One of the men was his father, and the other, a Mr. Lewinsky, was a bookkeeper at this father's business. Both men greeted her warmly.

Young Mr. Jablonski informed her that he had again brought gifts and instructed the driver to take the boxes into the house. The elder Jablonski asked if she could give them a tour of the farm that they especially wanted to see the root cellar where she had hidden his son while he was healing from his injuries. She happily obliged, taking them to the creek first, which was running briskly. If you looked carefully, you could see the fish as they maneuvered among the rocks that made up the bed of the creek. They then went through the apple orchard, where the trees were laden with still ripening fruit. They finally came back to the cellar. Mr. Jablonski was amazed that it was so carefully hidden. He had known approximately where it was but could not find it until it had been shown to him. They all went inside, and the men were surprised at how large and cool that it was. The two older men smiled and nodded as if in agreement with one another about something.

Whey they all returned to the house, the children were excitedly chattering about a cake the gentlemen had brought, and the men laughingly prevailed on Mrs. Mueller to brew some coffee to serve with it. The young Jablonski again produced a candy-filled paper sack from his pocket and gave it to Mrs. Mueller. She decided to save its contents until after the children had eaten their meal, especially as they would each be allowed a slice of the cake and one sweet at a time would suffice.

Mrs. Mueller prepared sandwiches fashioned from the ham that the young man had brought. Later, as the group relaxed and enjoyed the cake and coffee, the older Mr. Jablonski revealed that their visit had an ulterior motive. It seemed that Mr. Lewinsky had two sons, and the elder son desired to have the family homestead to raise his family on. Rather than split the homestead up, the younger son decided to procure a farm of his own. Mr. Lewinsky had come along today not only to meet the wonderful woman who had risked so much to save his employer's son but also to look for a farm. He was very impressed with this little farm with its orchard and creek. He was wondering if she would be interested in selling the farm, and perhaps she could then use the money to fulfill her dream of immigrating to America.

Mrs. Mueller was flabbergasted as she had continued to pray for this very thing even after it seemed that it was impossible for it to happen. She still feared that if the family stayed in Germany, her sons would meet the same fate as their father. The Kaiser was relentless in his quest for more land no matter the cost of the lives of his soldiers. Now here was the answer to her prayers. She was so overwhelmed that she could not speak for a while. At last, she was able to gasp out a resounding yes. A very happy Mr. Jablonski also revealed that he would be adding a stipend in appreciation for all she had risked for his son. He was convinced that his son would have been lost to him if she had not helped him.

"And that was how Mrs. Himmel ended up here in Minnesota. Her oldest brother began working at the lumber mill as soon as they got here. In time, he ended up saving his money, using it to eventually buy the mill with a partner, Mr. Himmel, who married his sister. Mrs. Himmel inherited the mill when both men passed and has owned the mill ever since," said Abigail.

They all sat quietly for a few moments, reflecting on Mrs. Himmel's mother's courage not only to risk all by helping an enemy but also to move her family here, leaving all she knew behind in Germany.

"What is so wonderful is that Mrs. Himmel gives all the glory to the Lord. He answered their prayers and gave them all the strength and courage every day to do all that needed to be done," said Abigail.

Just then a bolt of lightning sliced through the sky. It was quickly followed by a tremendous boom of thunder that made the air vibrate with its force.

"Wow! I wonder if that is what a cannon being fired sounds like?" asked Samuel. He had actually ducked down in reflex from the sound. "That certainly would scare me if I had to live where that was happening. Mrs. Mueller must have been one brave lady and have a strong faith to stay and help that man rather than take her children and leave. The Lord surely must have given her the courage she needed to do that."

"I'm glad that she moved here and didn't stay in Germany. I don't know if I could live where there was war all of the time," said Bobby. "I guess that I have a lot to be grateful for."

Abigail looked out the loft door. The wind had picked up and it had a chill to it cooling the sultry air. Suddenly, the clouds split open, and the rain began pelting down on the roof of the barn. The horses stood in a group stoically, accepting the rain as it ran off them in sheets. The children laughed as they watched the antics of the pigs. They were squealing excitedly, running in circles and plopping down in the huge mud puddle that was forming. Their long anticipated mud bath had begun.

It was a wonderful day to be up in the hayloft. The sweet smell of the hay had mixed with the clean fresh scent of the rain. Here in the loft, they were protected from the fury of the storm. Its energy was soon spent, and it left a world that had been washed clean. The sun came out and turned the clinging raindrops into sparkling diamonds.

Missionary

Everyone was so excited! There was going to be a special church tent meeting in Brainerd, and we were going to make the trip along with the Larsons. The main speaker at the event was a missionary who had been to Africa. He was going to share some amazing stories about the strange animals and the even stranger people whom he had found there. He also had crates filled with artifacts that included an elephant's foot and a full lion's head with its pelt. It was a six-hour trip, so we had to leave very early in the morning. Mr. Larson had a brother who lived just outside of Brainerd, and he had arranged for a number of families to camp out on his property. After breakfast, we had to load the camping gear and bedding onto a trailer and then stop and pick up the Larsons. Bobby's mother was letting him come too, so he came to spend the night with us. We were all so excited that we could barely sleep. This trip was a rare adventure in our lives.

When the group stopped at the Larsons, the children all piled onto the trailer, while the adults enjoyed the comforts of traveling inside the car. A nest of mattresses covered with blankets had been laid down in the center of the trailer. The bedding would make for comfortable sleeping while camping, and for now, the youngsters settled down in the middle of the pile to enjoy the ride. Traveling this way was an extra bonus of fun as far as the youngsters were concerned.

"I'm so glad that you are coming with us, Bobby. It is going to be ever so much more fun with all of us together," said Samuel.

"Me too! Mr. Larson got Lars Anderson to take care of the milking so we could all go. It is just for two days, and Mr. Larson thought that it was important for me to hear this missionary. The Larsons are really fine folk, and they care a lot about me," said Bobby.

"Father and Mr. Larson are fashioning a tent cover for the trailer, and Mother and Mrs. Larson are going to be sleeping inside on these mattresses. But the rest of us are going to be making pallets and sleeping right out under the stars. Father says that it is going to be fine weather for this," said Samuel.

"I heard Mother and Mrs. Larson talking about the food that they plan to make. They are bringing a large pan called a Dutch oven to make a big apple cobbler in! I'm excited because they are going to teach me how to cook over an open campfire. It's very different than cooking inside on the stove," said Abigail.

"Ummm! Apple cobbler is my favorite!" Samuel began rubbing his stomach in gastronomic anticipation.

"Oh, Samuel, every kind of dessert is your favorite!" Then she laughed aloud because Samuel just grinned and rubbed his belly even more.

The roads were dry, and a soft breeze kept everyone cool and comfortable. The sun rose, and it slowly warmed the earth. At noontime, after crossing a small creek, Father pulled up under a large tree. The menfolk including the boys pulled out fishing poles just to see if they could catch a fish or two from the little creek while the women set out the food. The girls had taken out the blankets and spread them on the ground for everyone to sit on. The group gathered and gave thanks before they devoured the picnic of sandwiches, hard-boiled eggs, and large juicy pickles. Samuel and Jeremiah had fetched the pails of still-cool water that they had brought from the spring at Mr. Larson's farm. All dipped their cups and slaked their thirst.

As they were eating, they enjoyed the cool breezes, and they began watching the animals that came to the creek to drink. The birds were singing their songs when suddenly there was a tussle between a blue jay and a red-winged blackbird. The blue jay had a large dragonfly in its beak, and the red-winged blackbird had hold of one of its feet, and they were having a tug of war. Well, the blackbird let go trying to get a better hold, and the blue jay got so surprised that he let go too. The dragonfly took advantage of its freedom and quickly flew away. In the end, both birds had lost an opportunity for a juicy meal. It was just too funny, and everyone enjoyed a good laugh.

"Everyone needs to finish up," said Mother. "When we get to the camping area, we are hoping to get the camp set up quickly so we can go shopping at the large mercantile in Brainerd. They have so much more at that store than we have in town. I am hoping to find some pretty material to make some dresses. Abigail, this last year, you have outgrown just about all of your clothing."

"Yes, Abigail, you are growing into such a fine young lady," said Mrs. Larson with a soft sweet smile. The Larsons had no children, so Mrs. Larson looked on all children as being her own. She was ever ready with a word of encouragement and extended small acts of kindness toward them.

They finished their meal, and as the women repacked the food items, the men shook out the bedding and secured it on the trailer. Looking at his watch, Mr. Eckhardt estimated that they still had about two hours left to travel to reach the campsite. As they traveled, the children kept occupied by playing word games; the men talked about crops and livestock; while the women shared recipes, sewing ideas, and patterns. When they reached the farm, Mr. Larson guided them to the camp area. Some years before, a house had stood in the little clearing, but it had burned down and had not been rebuilt. There were still a functional well and an outhouse, so it made an ideal campsite. As the grown-ups unpacked the trailer and set up the camp, the children gathered firewood. Mr. Larson's brother had kindly supplied some larger logs, so all that was needed was some kindling and smaller pieces of wood to feed the cook fires. He had even supplied some planks of wood and larger cuts of logs, using them to fashion crude benches for seating.

As the group worked, two other cars drew up, and the other families spilled noisily out of them. It was their neighbors, the Bernhardts and the Holdens. Sarah, Anne, Randy, Miriam, and Jerald joined the other children in the collecting firewood. All of the parents greeted one another and began making plans for the trip into town for shopping and for the missionary's program later in the evening.

As the wood began piling up, the men in the group started fires so the women could begin cooking the meal. It had been decided to pool all of their bounty so that all could enjoy the wonderful food. The girls settled with their mothers and began helping with the cooking preparations by peeling and cleaning the vegetables to be used in the stew. The heavy cast-iron pots had been put on the hot coals and were already filled with simmering chunks of meat. Abigail's mother had the Dutch oven filled with apple cobbler and was setting it on the coals. The camp smelled heavenly, and everyone's mouths watered in anticipation.

Mr. Larson's brother, along with his wife and children, arrived at the gathering. They were warmly welcomed, and the group was quick to thank them for their generosity in allowing them to camp the property. The Larsons claimed that they were glad for the company and that they had brought along some contributions to add to the festivities. Mr. Larson had brought a specialty of his, a sugar-cured smoked ham, and Mrs. Larson had a large chocolate cake covered with a fudge frosting. Everyone was looking forward to the potluck meal, and the children decided that instead of picking just one dessert, they were going to ask for just a few bites of everything so that they could taste of them all.

After the delicious meal had been devoured and the dishes were cleaned up, everyone climbed into vehicles for the trip to town. Mrs. Larson said that the mercantile was going to stay open right up to the last minute in order to accommodate all of the travelers who had come to see the missionary. Randy had brought along some jars of honey to sell, and the others had lists of things that they wanted to purchase. As they got closer to town, they were amazed at the large crowds of people that were already there. They found an empty lot to park in and began walking toward the mercantile. The town had a center square, and the group could see that a large tent had been erected in the middle of it.

The mercantile was filled with shoppers, and even though the owner was busy, he took the time to buy Randy's jars of honey. He barely had the jars displayed on the counter when folks began adding them to their baskets.

"I'm glad that you brought so much honey, Randy, because at this rate, I might sell out of it very soon! Plus I have already sold all of the jars that Mrs. Acres had brought in today too. She was accompanied by a Mrs. Rogers and her son. A number of folks from your town have come to see the missionary." The owner of the mercantile was smiling widely as he waited on all of the shoppers.

Randy was just happy to be able to buy the supplies he needed to process more honey. He had never had so much money in his entire life before. He had plans to build more hives, and now he was getting some of the other specialty items he needed to process the honey and the wax. The other members of their group had made their purchases too and were taking the items back to the cars. After locking the items in the trunks, they started back to the square. Vendors had put up makeshift booths and were selling their wares to the milling crowds of people. Some vendors had things like leather goods, handmade toys, and clothing items; and others were selling food items such as pastries and sausages. Their group had feasted so well that they were not tempted to buy any of the food items even though the pastries looked absolutely mouthwatering.

Excitement was high among the gathered throng, as there were rumors that tonight's program was going to be filled with revelations and surprises. At the ringing of a bell, folks began filing into the tent to procure seating on the rough benches that had been provided. The walls of the tent had been pulled up on three of its sides, leaving just the flap at the head of the tent down. There was a stage erected in front of the flap where a podium was set up, and it was surrounded by wooden boxes. A cooling breeze wafted through the tent, keeping the milling crowd comfortable.

"I heard some folks talking about the missionary and the things that he had brought back with him from Africa. I've never seen anything from Africa before. I wonder if they are in those crates up front," said Bobby.

"I guess that we are about to find out. Here comes Reverend Arnold and that other man must be the missionary. Why, he looks perfectly ordinary to me. I thought that he would look different having spent so much time in Africa," Samuel stated.

"Oh, Samuel, you are so silly. Why would he look different? He's from Wisconsin you know," said Abigail. "I'm curious about those crates too."

Just then Reverend Arnold stepped up to the podium. The crowd quieted, and he opened the meeting with prayer. After speaking for a few minutes and thanking the folks for coming he called the missionary, a Mr. Griswold, forward and introduced him to the crowd. Mr. Griswold again called the group to pray, then began to tell about his life, his calling to the mission field and how that had led him to Africa.

"I have some articles in these crates that I brought back with me from Africa so you can see for yourself how different it is to live there. I will open the crates at the end of the program, and all who wish to may come forward and see them. But, first, tonight, I have a special surprise to share with all of you. Our purpose as missionaries is to offer the heathens solid Bible teaching about the love of the Lord and convert them to Christianity. They then witness by sharing their faith with others, and they in turn are converted. One young man desired more, and he asked if there was any way that he could study to become an ordained minister. He was convinced that by doing so, he would be so much better prepared to reach his people with the need to turn from their heathen traditions and accept Christ as their Savior. After much consideration, he traveled to America with us and has just finished two years of intensive studies at a Bible college, receiving his doctorate in divinity. Though he is anticipating returning to Africa and serving his people, he has consented to delay his return and travel with us for a while. It is now my great pleasure to introduce him to you. Ladies and gentlemen, I present Reverend Jawwana Uhmah."

As he said this, he stepped to the back of the podium and pulled the tent flap aside. There stood a black man dressed in strange colorful garb complete with a tall headdress that had a long tail fashioned from long reeds hanging from the top of it. His face, arms, and hands were covered with patterns of white dots. The crowd gasped, and a loud babble arose. Some children were so startled that they began crying. The black man stepped up to the podium and raised his hand for silence. When the crowd quieted, he began to speak in English with a strange soft, almost musical, accent.

"Greetings, my friends in the Lord. I am Reverend Jawwana Uhmah, and I am so very happy to be here." He smiled; then he reached up and removed the headdress and placed it by his feet. "I need to remove this as it makes too much noise when I try to speak, and tonight I have some very important things that I wish to share with you. First, I wish to talk to you about the courageous missionaries who traveled all the way from America to my home in Africa to tell me—yes, me—about Jesus and his love for me. Many of my people were suspicious of these strangers, and some even wanted to kill them." He then turned and pointed at the missionary. "But these good people refused to be afraid and continued to speak about this Jesus, his love for us and our need to have him in our lives. I knew from the start that my life had changed forever. Then these good people found a way for me to come to America, and I have been greatly blessed to be able to study the Bible in such depth. I am now preparing to return to Africa and share my faith with my fellow countrymen. They desperately need to hear the message about Christ and his great love for all mankind. I am eager to share his message and am grateful to have the opportunity to serve my Lord. I am especially excited as I have also been approached to work on translating the Bible into my native language."

He continued speaking for another hour with the crowd so fascinated that they hung on his every word. He ended by telling them that he was living proof of how important it was to support the missionary efforts, and he thanked them for coming to the meeting this night. He was humbled that they would make the effort to travel such distances to see this strange African man, a simple man, who was delighted to share his faith in Christ.

When he finished speaking, the crowd rose to their feet and gave Reverend Uhmah a standing ovation that went on and on until he quieted them. He then invited them all to come forward to see the articles displayed in the crates and to answer any questions that they might have. The people surged to the front, anxious to see just what strange things were contained in those mysterious crates. They were the most fascinated by the preserved elephant's foot and the lion's head and pelt. Of course, there were also many questions about the tribal clothing, including the necklace of lion's claws and the body painting. The meeting continued long after it was originally planned because the people did not want to leave. Finally, Reverend Arnold had to call a halt to the proceedings as they had to pack everything up to go to the Twin Cities for engagements they had scheduled there.

The four families finally loaded up into their vehicles to head back to their camp. They were all still so wound up that they couldn't stop talking. Even after they had bedded down, the children continued to whisper. The wonder of the things that they had seen and heard had expanded the boundaries of their world and stretched their faith. Randy was the one who seemed the most touched by the happenings of the night. He had sold all of his honey at the mercantile, and when the missionaries had passed the plate for donations, he had secretly put half of his earnings in the plate. After they got back to the camp, he talked quietly to his father and mother, telling them what he had done.

"From now on, I'm going to give half of my honey money to the missionary fund. We have churches everywhere here, and the Africans don't have any. I need to help."

"Son, that is the most wonderful thing that I have ever heard. This is a very grown-up thing for you to do, and I believe that it was the Lord who brought you to this decision. You are growing into a very fine young man, and I'm so proud of you," Mr. Bernhardt declared. He put his arm around his son and hugged him snuggly while his mother held tightly to his hand.

The trip back home the next day was filled with conversation about the missionary and all of the strange and wonderful things that they had seen. The church had always been faithful to do special collections to support the missionaries, and the children decided that from now on, they would work even harder to raise even more money. They now had a new understanding of missions and a knowing that this was the Lord's work for them.

Randy was at the local mercantile once more to pick up more jars for his honey. Mr. Heimlich had placed an order for them, and he was happy to sell all the honey that Randy brought in.

"You are doing really well with your honey business, aren't you, son? Your daddy comes and brags about you on a regular basis. He is so proud of you, and so am I. Well, are you too busy to help me straighten up the back storeroom and get it organized? I have gotten a few shipments in and just haven't had the time to properly restock." Mr. Heimlich put the question out, then got sidetracked taking care of a rush of customers. When he finally had time to catch his breath, he had lost track of Randy, so he assumed that the boy had taken his jars and left. About thirty minutes later, he had to retrieve some items from the storeroom; and to his surprise, he found Randy busily cleaning, organizing, and stocking goods.

"Why, I thought that you had picked up your jars and left. Have you been back here the entire time? Sure enough, you have been, because it is looking mighty fine. You always do such a good job that I can always find just what I need because you always put everything away in its proper place. You have no idea just how much that helps me out, and once again, I say thank you, Randy. Make sure you get your wages before you leave today. There goes the bell, so I guess that I had better get up front and wait on the customer." He tousled Randy's hair and went to the front of the store.

Randy spent another thirty minutes, and he got the restocking done before he needed to go back home to do his chores. He took off the apron that he wore while working and hung it up on the nail. When he walked out front, he was surprised to see his father talking with Mr. Heimlich and Zachariah Rogers.

"Father, I'll go home right now and get the chores done. Mr. Heimlich wanted me to work in the storeroom for a while, and it just took me longer." Randy was apologizing for being a bit late at starting his regular chores at home.

"Don't worry, Randy. Mr. Heimlich told me that you were helping him with the restocking. He always tells me what a fine job that you do too. I got off a little early today so we can ride home together. We'll start the chores a little late tonight, but we'll still have plenty of time to get them done before dark. As long as we are not late for dinner, I certainly don't want to upset your mother by being late for that." Mr. Bernhardt would not disrespect his wife by being late for supper.

"So how is your mother doing today, Zachariah? I heard Mr. Eckhardt say that he is planning on bringing his mother and Mrs. Himmel to visit with her tomorrow."

"I am thankful for that. She does so enjoy visiting with her friends. It lifts her spirits and helps her to have a good day. Unfortunately, today has been one of her bad days." Mr. Rogers complained lightly.

"I'm sorry to hear that. She is a fine woman who has been through a lot." Mr. Bernhardt commiserated with the young man.

"I just wish that I understood what she was talking about sometimes. This thing with the man from Africa has really got her stirred up. She started muttering again, and it usually involves something about my grandfather and how I am his namesake. Then sometimes she mentions something about the treasure that is a legacy. I just don't know what she means by that, so it is very confusing. Now my grandfather was a very fine man, and he not only had convictions. He actually lived them as well. He was horrified by slavery, and when he had a chance to personally rectify that issue one time, he did it without reservation."

"If you have a little time, I would like to share with you just what kind of a man that he was." When the two men nodded, he cleared his throat and swallowed, and then he started his story.

"He had a reputation for goodwill and fairness. I believe that you've all heard about the old colored man that lived on the farm for a number of years, and Grandfather wouldn't put up with anyone showing that man anything but respect. He said that the man's great grandfather had been in line to become chief of his tribe somewhere in southern Africa, that is, until slavers captured him and changed his destiny. He was brought to America by those slavers as a teenager and expected to live as a slave until the day he died. He always talked about escaping and trying to make it to Canada. His son was freed by the Civil War, but he did not have the will to leave the South. Now this old man was the only surviving child, as the rest of his siblings had all died at an early age of some kind of disease. Well, when his father passed, he decided to follow his grandfather's dream and go to Canada, where there was less prejudice to deal with. It was the middle of winter, and he only got as far north as Minnesota, ending up half frozen in the barn on my grandfather's farm. Instead of turning him away as many would have done, my grandfather offered him friendship and gave him sanctuary. Together, they built him a small but well-appointed log house to live in, and Grandfather paid him fair wages in exchange for his care of the farm animals and the garden. The old man found a peace that he had never known before. Because of his advanced age and failing health, he knew that he would never get to Canada. He was grateful to my grandfather for the care and friendship that he had given him in the last years of his life. Now comes the really strange part of the story."

When Mr. Rogers asked for a root beer, Mr. Heimlich brought enough for everyone. When they tried to pay for it, he refused to take their money. "This is the most entertainment that I have had in a while, so I am glad to extend a small treat just so I can hear the rest of the story. Go ahead, son, and finish it up."

"Thank you, my friend. I have not shared this story in a very long time, and I don't think my mother has either. But it is not something that you forget." He took a long swig on his drink before he continued. "One night the old colored man was very sick. He knew that he was dying and that he didn't have much time left. My grandfather was at his bedside ministering to him, trying to keep him as comfortable as possible. A fever was ravaging the man, sapping his strength. He was mumbling about something to himself in a strange language that Grandfather could not understand. Then in a moment of clarity, the man spoke to my grandfather, thanking him for making his last years so wonderful. It was only in these last years on the farm that he finally felt safe and had finally felt free. He had a gift that he wanted to give to Grandfather, the only thing of value that had been passed down from his great-grandfather. He told my grandfather to save it and give it to his grandson, who would be his namesake. It would be his legacy. Of course, I am that grandson."

Mr. Rogers stopped for a moment and rubbed his hands through his hair. "I never have known just what it was that the old man gave to my grandfather. He and mother just referred to it as the treasure, and they said that it was a legacy. Supposedly, it is hidden somewhere on the farm, but I was not told where. Since Mother became ill, her memory has clouded. Sometimes, she will just sit in her chair, saying, 'I just can't remember.' She will just repeat the statement over and over again. Quite frankly, I think that it is just a family legend that doesn't have a bit of truth to it." He gave himself a little shrug and let out a small laugh. "It doesn't really matter anyways. The farm has always been self-sufficient, so though Mother and I have not been rich, we have been comfortable. I just wish that Mother could let this story go and find some peace."

"That's a great story, son. Thanks for sharing it. A little mystery in life gives everything a little spice. I'm sure that it will all come out sometime." Mr. Heimlich gave the young man a manly pat on the back.

"Well, Randy and I do have to get to the house." He turned toward Zachariah. "I will keep you and your mother is prayer just like I always have. You are a fine young man, and your care of your mother is exemplary. Just keep your chin up and keep doing the good that you have been doing. See you all later." Randy and his father waved as they headed out the door to go home.

10

Summer Camp

When the group arrived at the campgrounds, the girls and boys were directed to their respective bunkhouses. They were instructed to get unpacked, make up their bunks, and then to report to the cookhouse at eleven o'clock for lunch and orientation.

Abigail, Sarah, and Miriam were the first arrivals in the girls bunkhouse. "I'm glad that we got here early so that we could get bunks close together. I was afraid that we would be scattered around the room," Abigail said happily.

"Oh, me too!" Sarah replied. "I wonder if all of the bunks are going to fill up. Well, we have some time before we need to meet in the cookhouse. Do you want to go out and look around?"

Just then the door opened, and two girls walked in. They looked at the three girls in the corner, and they seemed to hesitate as they looked around the room deciding which bunks that they wanted to use. Abigail, Sarah, and Miriam did not mean to stare; but one of the girls was black. Abigail was the first to shake herself out of her shock. She got up from her bunk and walked up to the girls with a warm smile on her face. She stuck out her hand to the black girl.

"Hi! I'm Abigail, and those are my friends, Sarah and Miriam."

The black girl smiled and took the proffered hand, shaking it gently. "And I am Benah Uhmah, and this is my friend, Charlotte Miller."

Sarah and Miriam had finally also recovered, and they came and shook hands with the two girls. Finally, Abigail broke the tension when she laughed. "Oh, look at us, like we need to be so formal. It's our first time at camp, so we are new at everything."

"It is our first time too." Benah spoke in a soft singsong accented voice.

"Hey, why don't you bunk over by us? That is, only if you want to. We were the first ones here, so we had first choice, so we took the bunks in the farthest corner." Sarah invited them, but she didn't want to seem pushy.

It was Charlotte's and Benah's turn to be surprised. Most times, their arrival anywhere was met with opposition, and even cold rebuttal. Benah searched Sarah's face, looking to see if the offer was genuine.

"Oh yes, please, come on over by us," "Yes, please do," both Abigail and Miriam chimed in.

Charlotte and Benah exchanged a look, and then their faces lit up with huge smiles.

"Yes, thank you. It will be good to bunk by all of you." Benah visually relaxed and picked up her suitcase, crossing the room toward the bunks. Two of the bunks were set into a corner somewhat off by themselves. "Yes, I think that this will work well. What do you think? Do you want the top bunk or the bottom one?"

"You are the one who always wants to be up in the trees, so I will take the bottom bunk." Charlotte smiled as she teased her friend.

Soon other girls entered the building. There were looks of surprise from them when they spied Benah, but Abigail and the others were quick to greet the new arrivals and do the introductions. After the initial surprise of having a black girl in their midst, Abigail's stream of friendly chatter set the tone, and all of the girls began to relax. Sarah and Miriam also kept the conversation going by asking the newest arrivals questions about where they were from and whether or not this was their first time at camp. The room was filled with friendly chatter.

Then two more girls entered the room, chatting noisily until one of them spotted Benah. Her conversation stopped in midsentence, and it was as if a cold winter wind had poured through the room, chilling the very air. The new girls put their things on the bunks that were closest to the door and opened their suitcases. They were whispering very loudly, with one girl obviously trying to calm the other, but she was having no part of it. Finally, the girl who was being the most vocal put her arm on her friend's arm. "Oh no, this won't do at all. We will just have to see about this!" Then she turned in a huff, glaring at Benah as she trounced out of the door.

"Well, Charlotte, here we go again," Benah said with resignation.

"Yes, my friend, but I have a feeling that it's going to turn out better this time. I believe that the Lord has a work to do here, and we are in the middle of it." Charlotte smiled at her dark friend and held out her hand to her. Benah smiled back and took her hand, squeezing it lightly.

Abigail crossed the room and approached the new girl, gracing her with a warm smile. "Hi! I'm Abigail."

"Hi! I'm Barbara Smith. I'm from Minneapolis." She let out a heavy sigh and gave Abigail a crooked smile. "The girl who huffed out of the room is my cousin from Atlanta, Annabel Rawlings. She came to visit me for the summer, and my parents thought that it would be a fun thing for us to come to camp. But I'm afraid that she is upset about that other girl being here." She gestured toward Benah. "There is not a problem as far as I'm concerned, but being raised in the South, Annabel has specific ideas about what is proper between her and people of color. Oh, I do hope that Annabel will work this out so it does not ruin our time here."

Before Barbara could say anything more, Annabel returned. Abigail quickly introduced herself, and though Annabel returned her greeting, she was cold and withdrawn. Then Annabel turned toward Barbara, effectively snubbing Abigail. "Let's get our things put away so that we can go down by the lakeshore. I want to see these blue lakes up close that you have been talking incessantly about." She quickly stowed her suitcase and then grabbed Barbara's arm as they exited out of the door.

Abigail had crossed the room back toward her friends. Benah reached out and laid her hand lightly on Abigail's arm. "Do not stress, my friend. This is a common reaction that I get to my presence, especially from people that are from the southern part of America." She looked around into the faces of the other girls, and a soft smile played over her lips. "Your offers of friendship and acceptance are a wonderful gift, and I thank you for it. Now let's put this from our minds and go to the cookshack. I don't know about the rest of you, but I am very hungry."

The lighthearted group of girls headed for the cookshack, their soft merry chatter filling the air. As was her way, Benah ignored the stares and whispers and just kept asking questions about the camp and the activities that they would be participating in. Many of the campers' faces displayed looks of curiosity or confusion. The only glaring looks that had been aimed at her had come from Annabel. In the cookshack, the girls picked up trays and began walking down the line, filling the trays with plates of delicious-looking food. There was an empty table off to one side, and the group sat down, filling half of it. Some of the other campers approached the group and tentatively asked if they could join them. "Of course, you can! Please sit down." Abigail warmly welcomed them. Soon the table was full with everyone introducing themselves and stating where they were from. Of course, everyone was the most interested in Benah, and they were surprised when she told them that her father was ordained as a minister. It was then that Abigail realized that her father was the African minister they had met at the tent meeting in Brainerd.

Reverend Arden, along with the adult counselors, entered the cookshack. They picked up trays and filled them as they went down the chow line. A small table was reserved for them, and as they sat down to eat, the reverend's eyes surveyed the room. His gaze settled on the table with Benah and the other girls, and a smile lit up his face as he saw that the group was interacting with smiles and laughter. He then stood for a moment to address the room. "After you have finished eating and cleared your dishes, you may go to the activity board and sign up for whatever activity that you would like to participate in for the afternoon. Then proceed to the fire pit so we can begin orientation. We will join you all shortly."

Everyone excitedly gathered outside to study the postings on the activity board and to sign up as instructed. When the adults exited the cookshack, all of the campers had gyrated to the pit area and had found seating on the benches surrounding the pit.

"My, it is so good to see the familiar faces of the return campers and to be able to welcome so many new ones. Let's open this year's activities with prayers for safety and good health and to thank God for this time we that we have together to share and to grow in his word." As the reverend dropped his head in prayer, Annabel was whispering furiously in Barbara's ear.

"I can't believe that they expect me to do menial labor. On top of that, I am assigned to the cookshack at the same time as that darky and on our last morning too! Humph, I guess that they expect me to work right alongside her. Well, I plan on keeping as much distance from her as I can and do as little work as possible." Annabel's tone was fraught with frustrated drama.

The reverend finished the prayer and had continued speaking. "Well, we certainly have a diverse group this year. Not only do we have campers from other states such as Wisconsin, Iowa, and Georgia. We also have one person from Africa. In reality, we have always been diverse as you represent so many different nationalities. Some of you are first-generation American, and many of you speak at least two languages. Along with English, you speak the language of your parents and grandparents' home countries of Germany, Poland, Italy, Ireland, Sweden, and now Africa." He paused to look around at the circle of faces. "With that said, I am going to release you to enjoy the activities that you have chosen to participate in. There are a certain number of openings for each activity, so make sure that you fill in the allotted spaces on the sign-up board. Also make sure that you chose some activities that are new to you so you have the opportunity to be challenged. Now for the schedule. The hours of 8:00 to 9:00 a.m. and 6:00 to 7:00 p.m. are reserved for Bible study meeting here at the fire pit. The time from after lunch, which is at 11:00 a.m. until 1:00 p.m., is free time. You can do what you wish as long as you do not leave the immediate campground. We have Mr. and Mrs. Dale as our counselors, who will not only lead you in your activities, but if you have any problems or concerns, they are more than willing to spend time talking with you about them. Added to that, we are blessed with a wonderful cookshack crew led by Mrs. Bates. It takes a lot of work to feed such a large group of people, so it is imperative that you do not miss your work time when you are assigned to the cookshack. The crew greatly appreciates all of the helpful and willing hands. Now you are released to use your free time as you wish until the first activity at one o'clock."

Abigail and the other four girls hurried back to the bunkhouse to change into their swimwear, anxious to take a dip in the beautiful little lake.

"I have been so hot today that the lake is going to feel absolutely delicious." Sarah crooned. "Benah, I know that you have been pestered with so many questions about your country, but it is just so different there than it is here, and it is so interesting that we just can't help ourselves. We are so curious that we just have to ask questions."

"Oh, Sarah"—Benah's eyes were shining with merriment—"you are so dramatic that you could be an actress on stage. I do not mind the questions at all. In fact, I am glad that everyone shows so much interest in my country." The group had been walking toward the lake as they talked. Benah looked up and saw the beautiful blue water, and her face split into a grin. "Now how do you say it? The last one in is a bad egg?" With that, Benah raced toward the dock ahead of the rest of them.

The girls broke out with peals of laughter as they sprinted after her. "It's a rotten egg," Abigail shouted out with a laugh.

Benah got to the end of the dock first and plunged into the water. The others were right behind her, and they caused a tremendous wave as they all jumped in. The girls were all laughing as they came up from their dunking, and they began splashing one another, playing a game of water tag.

"Oh, it is so nice to be able to just jump in the water and not have to check for crocodiles and hippos first. And the water is so clean and cool too." Benah's observations stopped the girls in midstokes.

"Crocodiles and hippos?" Miriam spurted out in surprise. "Why, I would never have thought of that." The others chimed in with her. It was a totally new concept to all of them.

Suddenly, Samuel and some of the other boys came running toward the lake, yelling and whooping at the top of their lungs. They too all jumped off the dock, thoroughly drenching the girls with the large waves that they made as they hit the water. The girls took the drenching in good humor, and everyone began laughing and splashing one another.

"Guess what Benah just told us? That in her country before they can swim, they have to check and make sure that there are not any crocodiles or hippos. Isn't that wild?" Miriam saw that the information was as much of a shock to the boys as it had been to them.

Samuel recovered first, and he said that he had an idea. "Let's all swim out to the dock. I have thought up a game that I think that everyone will like." When they were all sitting on the dock, he presented the game to them. "We will take turns being a crocodile or a hippo. A crocodile will grab a leg or an arm and pull on it, while a hippo will just rub a leg or an arm. When you have been 'crocked,' then it is your turn at being the crocodile. Anyone can be a hippo at any time. We can make up other rules as we go along just as long as we all agree on it."

"Hey, it sounds like a great game! You go first because it was your idea," Bobby piped up.

Soon the group was having a wonderful time trying to avoid the crocodile and getting grazed by the hippos. It turned out that Benah was the best crocodile. She amazed everyone at how long she could hold her breath underwater. It gave her an advantage as she could sneak up on the others and "crock" them before they even knew that she was close to them.

Mr. and Mrs. Dale haled the group from a spot on the shore. "You look like you are having a good time, but you need to come on in now!" Mrs. Dale merrily called out. As they all gathered on blankets under a tree, Mrs. Dale was pulling articles out of some boxes. There were strips of cloth, a belt, and some sticks of varying lengths. Mr. Dale was holding a set of crude crutches.

"This is not only a swim time, but it is also a first aid class. We are going to cover some common injuries and rudimentary first aid that you can apply until you can get somewhere to get proper medical attention."

They spent the next two hours being lectured on first aid. As many of the boys did spend time out in the woods hunting and could get hurt by accident, it was very informative. They then spent time applying bandages for wounds and splints used for broken bones. The crutches were the biggest hit with the boys. They took turns limping around, trying to work both crutches in unison. It made for some comic relief as most ended up in a heap on the ground.

"You have been a very attentive group, and we appreciate your cooperation. Now we are going to swim out to the dock, and we will practice how to save someone who is drowning." Mr. Dale had changed into his swim trunks in preparation of this part of the training. "You sure were having a good time when we arrived. Were you playing a game when we came up?" They explained about Benah's crocodiles and hippos and the game that they had made out of it.

"Oh my!" exclaimed Mrs. Dale. "I don't know if I could deal with large animals like that in the water. I have a hard enough time with the small fish that want to nibble on my toes when I dangle my feet in the water." She gave an obvious shiver.

Mr. Dale, on the other hand, was fascinated with the concept. When they got out to the dock, he demonstrated the proper way to help someone who was drowning. He then worked with the young campers as they practiced drowning and being saved. When he felt that they had mastered the skill, he announced that the teaching was ended. He then surprised them by joining them in their game, proving that he was also adept at being the "crock."

The next day, Benah again surprised the group during the rope bridge and tree-climbing activities when she appeared in leggings made from tanned deer hide. A few months earlier, she had accompanied her father when he had been invited by the Chippewa Indians to visit their village. She had not only been impressed with their tanning skills, but she was also intrigued with the clothing that the women had fashioned from the tanned hides. She in turn amazed them with her skill at hunting using a simple sling and rocks to bring down squirrels and rabbits. The women had then gifted her with the leggings that she found were comfortable as well as functional, even if they were not considered proper female attire in the general American public. She was anxious to introduce the concept to the women of her country using hides from their native animals to construct them. Being unhampered by skirts, she was able to keep up with the boys on the rope bridge, and she excelled at the tree climbing.

"How did you learn to climb trees so well?" Samuel asked as he sat down on a hefty tree limb next to Benah.

"In my country, we often have to climb trees to escape from danger. Thankfully, the warthogs, rhinos, and the water buffalo cannot climb trees!" she said with a merry laugh.

Samuel laughed along with her. "You have so many more dangerous animals to deal with than we do. First, it was crocodiles and hippos. And now it is warthogs, rhinos, and water buffalos. Your people must be very brave to live among so many vicious animals. Not to mention the lions. Our domestic cats are really good at climbing trees. How about the lions? Can they climb as well?"

"Oh yes. But they pretty much stay out on the savannah. Though they sometimes do come and attack our cattle. Then the herders have to scare them off or kill them. My people have gotten very good with using hunting rifles, so the attacks are not very frequent.

"We only have to contend with the occasional bear and sometimes wolves but not so very often. And we usually have to be out in the woods to encounter either of them."

He was shaking his head softly from side to side. Then he looked at her with a smile. "I want you to know that I am right proud to have met you and had a chance to hear about your country. It has shown me that it is a big world out there, and I hope to see more of it someday. Perhaps I could even travel to your Africa."

"You would be welcome in my country anytime. I wish that all of my new friends here could come and experience my country as I have had the privilege to experience America." Just then Bobby was calling out searching for his friends. They all tramped back to the camp together, sharing an easy camaraderie. The boys had gotten over their shock of Benah's physical prowess and had come to respect this girl from Africa. She was as skilled at hunting as they were and had proven it when she had rid Mrs. Bate's garden of the pesky rabbits using nothing more than a sling and rocks. Then she had happily schooled them in the making and use of the sling. Many of the boys and even some of the girls were beginning to become proficient using the simple weapon. Mrs. Bates had cooked Benah a rabbit stew in appreciation of her ridding her garden of the furry pests. Mr. Bates, in appreciation of being relieved of the nagging the pesky critters, had tanned the rabbit skins and presented them to Benah.

Benah was so physically adept that she could keep up, or even surpass, the boys at climbing the trees and maneuvering the rope bridges and ladders. The other girls watched her fearlessness at performing these activities, and it had inspired them to participate. They had surprised themselves at how much fun they had doing these tasks, and they had enjoyed a good laugh when their efforts turned up short. Benah was quick to encourage them and gave them pointers on how to succeed and even sometimes excel at the tasks.

It had been a week of surprises for the entire group as a whole. Not only had they been challenged to grow spiritually with the Bible teachings, but those teachings had practical application through having Benah attending the camp. The adults had spent the week showing how when people are different that it leads to learning about other cultures and accepting that the differences were a good thing.

Prejudice

Evening arrived with a blazing sunset, which settled into twilight. Then the sky totally blackened, and the dark canopy was filled with millions of stars. The earth gave off a poignant mix of woodsy odors that intermingled with the smoke of the burning wood in the fire pit. The fire gave off a flickering glow, lighting the faces that encircled the pit.

It was the last night at camp, and it was to be a time of sharing. Each camper was advised to be prepared to talk about something that they had learned during the last week, be it a new skill or a Bible verse, or they could even just share a funny anecdote. As each youngster took their turn, the faces of the listeners reflected the peace and happiness that they had enjoyed during the past week.

The last person left to speak was Benah. As she stood up, she was joined by Reverend Arden. The reverend shared a soft word with Benah, and then with a smile, he gave her an encouraging pat on her arm. A scowl crossed Annabel's face as she turned toward Barbara. "Just look at the darky. What could she possibly have to talk about? I don't understand why Reverend Arden even allowed her to come to this camp. I guess he just felt sorry for her and with her being a minister's daughter and all. Well, the only place her father will ever have any kind of a church will be in Africa." The comment was dripping with acid. The reverend overheard Annabel's remark, and he turned and gave her a long look. The girl had the grace to look ashamed and dropped her head, finding something very interesting on her shoe.

Reverend Arden then turned and smiled as he addressed the group. "Well, from all of the stories that everyone has shared tonight, it seems to have been a good week for all. I have heard of challenges met with courage and growth derived from those experiences. This year, we had campers not only from other parts of the United States but it also became international with Benah's arrival. The friendships that were formed this week are truly a gift from God, and those relationships will last not only a lifetime but will be eternal as well. Now Benah wishes to share her story with you. Some things that she is going to tell you may shock and dismay you, but there is a powerful lesson in it. What she is going to share proves the power and grace of our God and his love for all. Go ahead, Benah." His gave her an encouraging smile and then sat down.

"You know that I have come from Africa with my father, who has studied to become an ordained minister. We will be returning to our country in about a month, and my father will begin sharing his faith with our people. Traditionally, we are a very fierce people, so the gospel message of love, peace, and joy has met with resistance. But my father and I also know that the truth will prevail over the traditions and superstitions." Benah stopped, and a small soft smile graced her countenance as she looked around at her newfound friends. It seemed that everyone was hanging on her every word, and she nervously took a deep breath and continued.

"I will now tell you the story that my father and grandfather have told me since I was a small child. My great-great-grandfather was a fierce warrior, a great hunter, and was also a natural leader. When there was war between the tribes, he proved to be strong and fearless in battle. In time, the other tribes feared and respected him to the point that they avoided any altercations with him and with our tribe as a whole. Then one day, the unthinkable happened. An entire group of people from our tribe disappeared. Some women had gone to the river to wash clothes and fill their water jugs, but they did not return. When someone went to check on them, all that was found were odd pieces of clothing and a broken water jug. My great-great-grandfather and the men of our tribe gathered their weapons and headed toward the camp of an adjoining tribe, certain that they had abducted the women. On the trail, they met the men from that other tribe, and the two began fighting with each other. It didn't take long for my great-great-grandfather to understand that both tribes had people who had turned up missing and that they were each blaming the other. He called a truce, and as they shared information, they quickly decided that it would be best to work together to find out what had really happened to them. Both tribes desperately wanted to get their people back. Trackers from each group began searching, and they found a faint trail. Swift runners were sent ahead, and they were told that once they found the missing tribe members to wait for the rest of the group to catch up. Then they would work together to rescue them from whoever had abducted them and to bring them back home."

Benah paused to catch her breath. This was a powerful story, and she wasn't sure how the people would receive what she was about to share. Charlotte had been her friend for the last two years, and she already knew the story. Both Benah and Charlotte had been happily surprised at the acceptance they had received from most of the girls here at camp. In fact, Abigail, Sarah, and Miriam had warmly embraced them with open friendship. Benah treasured the friendships that she had formed with them this past week, and she hoped that this information would not change how these girls felt about her. Charlotte had assured her that these girls would not withdraw their support and friendship. She looked toward Charlotte and Reverend Arden, and they both gave her an encouraging smile.

"It didn't take long for my great-great-grandfather and the others to realize that the trail was heading for the coast. Suddenly, the group heard a very loud noise, somewhat like a lightning strike yet different. This was the first time that they were to hear a rifle shot, but it would not be the last. A few minutes later, they stumbled across one of the runners. He was lying on the ground, bleeding profusely from a wound in his side. He advised them that the others had been taken to the seashore, where they were being loaded into a boat. One of their party stayed behind with the injured man, while the others hurried ahead to the shore. When they got there, they saw a small boat rowing toward the largest ship that they had ever seen. In the rowboat, they saw some white men holding big sticks while some natives were working the oars. Huddled together in the center of the small craft were some of the people from the villages, along with the captured second runner. The large ship was anchored too far from shore to swim to, so all they could do was stand on the beach and watch, screaming and shaking their spears in frustration. The captors were relentless as they forced the group up onto the ship, whipping and beating those who tried to resist. Once they were all on board, the ship unfurled its sails and sailed out of sight. In dejection, the group turned and headed back the way they had come, puzzling over what had happened and wondering what, if anything, they could do to get their people back and most importantly to keep it from happening again. The wounded runner was still alive when they got back to him. In gasping breaths, he told them how the white men had tied everyone together and then had taken them by groups to the ship. As the two runners had watched from the edge of the jungle, the white men were loading the last group into the rowboat. Finally, when the last white man was going to get into the boat, the young men realized that the others were not going to get there in time to stop what was happening. So both young men raced at the boat, yelling as fiercely as they could with their spears upraised. As they neared the boat, one of the white men picked up a large stick. He pointed it at the first runner, and the stick belched fire with a tremendous roar, and the young man felt something punch him in his side. He fell to the ground and then got up and started running, staggering and falling, but he managed to reach the edge of the jungle. When he looked back, he saw that the other runner had been captured and that all were headed out to the ship. One of the women in the boat was crying and staring at where he had disappeared into the jungle. It was the last time she and her bother would ever see each other. He died before they could get him back to the village, and no natives ever saw or heard of her or any of the other villagers again."

Benah paused to again look around the campfire at the faces of her listeners. All were quiet, and the expressions on their faces varied. Some appeared stunned while others reflected various stages of shock, devastation, and distress.

Benah began again in her soft voice with its distinct accent. "My great-great-grandfather refused to give up. He was determined to find the members of his tribe, and he wanted to know who had taken them and why. He intended to have his people returned to the village, and he proposed to keep this horrific event from being repeated. He bravely traveled to the other tribes, risking being killed by his enemies just so he could find out if they too had experienced this kind of trouble. What he discovered affected him deeply. Many of the tribes that he approached had also had members that had been taken by the white men. To his horror, he learned that once they were taken, they were then sold into slavery throughout the world. It was a bitter realization that not only would he not be able to rescue his people but also that it would be difficult if not impossible to stop the slavers from coming back again and again.

"Then he did something that was totally unheard of in their history. He invited the leaders of all of the tribes to come to our village to talk about the slavers and what they could do to stop them from raiding their villages. The tribes had to put their differences aside and to agree that this would be a meeting of peace and cooper-ation. All who attended the meeting agreed that the slavers were now the enemy and not each other. The only way that they would be able to defeat the slavers would be to cooperate and show a united front against them.

"The meeting was successful, but the only way the tribes would totally cooperate was if my great-great-grandfather agreed to be the head leader. Over the years, as they came to respect his foresight and leadership and they honored him with the title of king, more and more tribes were added to the original group. Unfortunately, they couldn't stop the slavers completely, but they were able to occasion-ally fight them off and sometimes even to rescue the ones who had been abducted. They made a point of torturing and killing every white man that they captured, and then they displayed the mutilated bodies on the seashore as a warning. The slavers eventually stopped their raiding, but by then hatred of the white man was so ingrained that they continued to torture and kill all white men for two generations until one fateful night my grandfather had a dream."

The Reverend Arden called for a short break. Some people headed for the bathrooms, and others grouped around the snack table, where there were cookies and lemonade laid out. Abigail, Sarah, and Miriam gathered around Benah, bringing her some of the sweets. They talked about how wonderful this week had been and how they were going to miss their friends Benah and Charlotte. Benah basked in their outpouring of support.

The reverend called the group back to the fire pit. Some of the boys had brought some more wood, and they threw it all into the flames. The comforting fire gave off soft popping sounds as the wood was consumed. Benah stood up to tell the rest of her story.

"The throne was passed down through the generations, and after my great-grandfather died, my grandfather became king. The slavers were still raiding periodically, but there were much fewer attacks. Still, it meant instant death to any white men who wandered into the tribe's territory no matter who they were or why they had come. Then one night, my grandfather had a dream. In this dream, he saw large cities with many buildings and roads. What really amazed him was that the cities were populated with people of many colors all living together in them. When he awakened, he realized that the dream had been revealed to him so he could lead his people into the future. He especially understood that his people would have a hard time changing centuries of their beliefs and superstitions, and he also realized that he did not know how to teach them how to accept those changes.

"Then one day the answer was revealed to him. He heard of some white men who were traveling up the river with a guide. In the past, he would have immediately sent out hunters to kill them, but this time he gave orders that the hunters were to meet the men and bring them to him unharmed. The hunters did as they were told certain that the white men were to be tortured and killed in the village. To their surprise, when the men were put before the king, they were invited to sit and talk as if they were guests. The villagers were set to spill blood, but after about an hour of talking with the men through an interpreter, the king stood up and addressed his people. He told them that these men, though they were white, they were not slavers and they were to be treated as honored guests. He stated that he would continue to question them carefully for a time and if they showed any signs of meaning to harm the people that he would deal with them at that time. Of course the villagers were confused and upset, but the king stood firm to the point that he said if anyone caused harm to these men, they were the ones who would be tortured and put to death.

"As time passed, these white men who were actually missionaries won the trust of the king, my grandfather. Some of the people remained suspicious and antagonistic, but they obeyed the king's commands that the men were not to be harmed. The missionaries stayed in the village, and they were allowed to build structures to live and work in, and as they learned the local language, they began sharing the gospel. My father watched the white men and how they met the hostility of the people with the love of the Lord. It impressed him so much that he questioned them even deeper about their faith.

"Then one day the most extraordinary event happened. More white men came to the village and asked the king if they could take some samples of earth to have it tested. They believed that it contained copper and if it did that it could be mined. The king did not know how this copper could be so important, but he agreed to the testing. After a little time, the men returned and told the king that though there was copper it was of a low grade. They still wanted to mine it, but it was not worth as much as they first thought. One of the missionaries who had become suspicious of these men had a brother who was a geologist back in America. He secretly sent some samples of the ore to him to have it tested. His brother reported back that the ore was of excellent quality and when mined it would be worth a lot of money. He even supplied the names of reputable men who already owned a mining company in Africa who might be interested in doing the actual mining.

"When the king found out about the deception, he was furious, but the gentle teachings of the missionaries had begun a work in him. Even though he had not as yet become a Christian, he had respect for these men who had come into his village and had been bringing him and his people into an understanding of the larger world outside of his land. So he asked his missionary friend for advice as to what he should do. They both knew that in former days the dishonest men would have forfeited their lives for their deception. The young missionary pointed out that they should be grateful that these schemers had been exposed before any real harm had been done, and he suggested that they be exiled instead. My grandfather agreed that by handling the situation this way, he would be showing the world that he and his tribe were now civilized and were no longer the ferocious heathens as depicted from their earlier history. It also demonstrated that they were now forward-thinking men, and that they are ready to be a productive part of this ever-growing and evolving world.

"My country is now one of the major suppliers of copper for the entire world. My grandfather's understanding of business and financing has grown to the point that he can stand alongside businessmen from all over the world. and they show him deference and respect. From the proceeds of the sale of the copper, our people now enjoy many modern amenities, such as schools and hospitals. Medical care is administered by people who we have sent to foreign countries to receive their training as nurses and doctors and others who have been educated as teachers. All who attended school have returned to teach and minister to their own people.

"Those of our people who wish to work at the mines and to change to more modern ways of living can do so. They move to our cities and build new houses with modern amenities. But those who do not wish to change the way that they have lived for centuries are also allowed to do so without prejudice. They live in the same type of housing as our ancestors did, and they hunt and forage the same way as before.

"As my father was growing up, he learned the copper business right alongside my grandfather. When we return to our country, he will assume the throne as my grandfather wishes to step down. As king, he had made a point of seeing as much of Africa as he could, enjoying the diversity and richness of his native country, and now he wants to travel and see the rest of the world. Over the years, he invited the leaders of his fellow African countries to come and see what he was doing in his own country, and he shared concepts with them that they could apply to their own land and people. Now he wants to continue to be an ambassador to all of Africa and whenever possible to assist them in their economic and social growth.

"I am standing here before you today only because my grandfather was willing to put aside his superstitions and prejudices. If he had not done so, my country could have shared the fate of some of the other countries in Africa have. Some tribes have been hunted down and annihilated, not only by white men but by other Africans who desired the riches and resources of their land. Through the dream that he had, my grandfather understood that wickedness and greed do not know color boundaries, but neither do friendship and prosperity." Benah's face glowed with happiness as she smiled at the people surrounding the fire. "I have been so blessed to have had the opportunity to come to America and especially to spend this last week here among other Christians.

"When I return to Africa, as is our custom, I am to be married. My father and his best friend arranged this union when my fiancé and I were just babies. My fiancé's name is Kinto Menoweua. We have grown up together, so even though it is an arranged marriage, we also know and love one another. He is a faster runner than I am, but I am the better hunter. He will be graduating from Yale in two weeks with a degree in business, and he will be taking his father's place at the mining company. But, most important, because of the missionaries' influence in our lives, we are both blessed to have learned about and to accept Jesus as our Lord and Savior. Thank you for allowing me to share my story with you." With that, she gave the group a warm smile and sat down next to her friends.

"Thank you, Benah, for sharing with us, and thank all of you for your attention this evening. Now, as it is past lights out, I will ask all of you to go directly to the bunkhouses. We will share our last meal together at noon tomorrow, and then everyone will head back home. I believe that this has been the best year at camp we have ever had. Remember to thank the Lord in your prayers tonight for all of the blessings that he has poured out on us this past week."

The next day, the camp was preparing to shut down right after the lunch meal, and everyone had been assigned a cleanup task. It was especially a busy time in the cookshack. Benah had made a habit of spending her free time there, and she had again come in early to work. Over the past weeks, Mrs. Bates had taken odd moments to share her recipes with Benah and teaching her how to cook American food. "For a long time, I have wanted to learn how to make these foods that I have come to enjoy so much. How happy my husband will be with me when I can serve him some of the foods that he has eaten for the past four years. Thank you for your teaching and your patience." This morning, Benah had learned how to make cornmeal mush, corn bread, and hush puppies. "This has all turned out so well. I just hope that I will be able to do this again on my own."

"Oh, I am certain that you will do just fine. In fact, in time, I believe that you will even come up with some variations of your own made from traditional ingredients that you have in your own country. You have been an excellent student and a tremendous help." Then Mrs. Bates gave her a big hug. "I am going to miss you, my dear, and I wish you the very best. Now I think it is time to get back to preparing the lunch meal." Mrs. Bates tried to hide that she was dabbing at her eyes.

The door opened, and Annabel and Barbara walked into the kitchen as this was their assigned work time. Annabel was looking around skeptically with a pouty look on her face. Spying them, Mrs. Bates directed the girls to grab an apron and to start peeling the potatoes that were going to be served at the lunch meal. Both girls took the proffered paring knifes and headed for the bags of potatoes situated in a corner of the kitchen. "Look at how many potatoes there are," Annabel exclaimed as she rolled her eyes dramatically. She continued to complain as she and Barbara spent the next hour peeling the potatoes and putting them into large roasting pans.

"We're finished with the potatoes. Where do you want them?" Barbara asked Mrs. Bates.

"Please just set them on the table next to the stove for now. I will finish preparing them and get them into the oven. You have both done a fine job on them. Can I get you to snap the green beans now?"

"Sure, but may I go to the bathroom first?" Barbara queried.

"That will be fine, Barbara." Mrs. Bates nodded her head. With that, Barbara rushed out of the room.

"Well, I guess that means that I have to carry these over to the table by myself," Annabel complained to herself under her breath. With a dramatic sigh, she lifted the heavy pan and maneuvered her way through the kitchen and set it on the table.

"Annabel, you need to slowly back away from the table. You must move slowly and quietly. Do not jump or turn fast." Benah's voice was very soft and very close.

"What are you talking about? Just who do you think you are talking to me in this manner?" Annabel's voice was loud and indignant.

Suddenly, she heard a strange sound emanating from under the stove close to her feet. When she looked down, it was if the blood froze in her veins. A timber rattler was curled up just under the edge of the stove. The snake's tail was vibrating, letting out its distinctive rattling sound. It slowly uncurled and began slithering toward her. She took one small step backward and then another, but the snake kept coming in her direction. Then things occurred so fast that she couldn't keep track of exactly what happened. In a blur, she saw a black hand grab the snake, and then its head went flying. When she saw the blood, she fainted.

Reverend Arden was waiting with Benah in the doctor's waiting room. Mrs. Dale had gone with Annabel into the examination room, and the door had been shut for at least a half an hour. Finally, the door opened, and the doctor walked out and approached the reverend.

"Annabel is going to be just fine. She has a bump on her head from when she fainted but otherwise has no other injuries. If what Mrs. Dale tells me is true, then I believe that she owes a bit of thanks to this young woman who dispatched the snake before it had a chance to strike her."

"Well, that is wonderful news. Yes, Benah killed the snake before it got to Annabel, though I am still uncertain how it was managed. Just how were you able to do that?" the reverend asked curiously.

"There are very many snakes in my country, and they especially like to get into the beds of the children and babies. For that reason, all women carry a knife, and we are very skilled at dispatching them. This way, many children have been saved from harm." Benah sounded nonchalant as she spoke.

Just then Annabel and Mrs. Dale came out of the examination room. Mrs. Dale, who had also been in the kitchen at the time, was looking a Benah and shaking her head in wonderment. "I have never seen anything like it. Benah just reached out and grabbed that snake right behind its head, and the next thing I know that snake's head is flying across the room! Benah acted so fast that I don't think that snake even saw her coming!"

"I know," Annabel said with wonder. "I saw a flash of movement and then the headless snake and the blood." She closed her eyes and shuddered. Then she opened her eyes and gazed into Benah's face with a puzzled expression. "Benah, I have been so mean to you this past week, and yet you risked getting hurt for me. Why?"

Benah took Annabel's hand, and with a beautiful smile, she simply said, "Because you are my sister in Christ. I believe that there is no room for prejudice in the Lord's kingdom, and above all, I am to be at peace with everyone."

The Secret

It was not quite light out yet, but Jeremiah was up and ready to go. The older children had gone to church camp, and Jeremiah was feeling left out. Father had arranged this fishing trip for him with Mr. Boggs so he would have a summer adventure also. Father and Mr. Boggs had become friends years ago when they had worked together at the lumber mill. Mr. Boggs had injured his leg when a chain holding some large logs broke. His leg had been trapped between the logs, which had broken the bones in a number of places. Even after the leg had healed, he needed to use a cane to walk, making it impossible for him to climb up onto the loads the way he used to. Seeing that he was good with numbers and measuring, Mrs. Himmel, the mill owner, gave him a job that was less taxing on him physically. She put him in charge of the tally sheets, and soon he had a new system in place that cut down on waste and increased the profits from each log that was processed. Before Mr. Boggs retired, Mrs. Himmel asked him if he could recommend someone to fill his position. Mr. Boggs advised her that not only was Father a top-notch employee, but as he had already been assisting him at times, he was already familiar with the tally sheets and his system of measuring and accounting. She agreed wholeheartedly with his recommendation, and Father was promoted to the position.

Headlights turning into the driveway signaled that Mr. Boggs had arrived. Father helped Jeremiah stow his fishing pole and camping gear; plus he had placed a large picnic basket in the back of the truck under a tarp. Then he shook hands with Mr. Boggs, greeting his old friend warmly. As they conversed in quiet tones, Jeremiah climbed into the cab and patiently waited. Presently, when Mr. Boggs joined him, Jeremiah smiled hugely and gave him a cheery hello.

"You two have a good time today, and I hope that the fish are biting. Jeremiah, I need for you to try and not talk an arm off Mr. Boggs. Fish for supper would be a welcome treat, but they won't bite if you talk them to death." Father gave out a jolly laugh at his joke. "The missus packed a goodly picnic spread for your enjoyment. Jeremiah is a growing boy, and he can sometimes pack away enough food for two." He smiled brightly at the youngster and leaned over, tussling Jeremiah's hair.

"You be sure to thank your missus for the victuals for me. I know that they will surpass my poor attempts at cooking, so they are mighty welcome." With that, Mr. Boggs tipped his hat and started the engine, putting it in gear. Jeremiah's father stood and watched as the truck turned onto the road and drove out of sight.

The morning was cool, and there was a light breeze, along with some clouds that could harbor rain sometime in the day. But the schedule had been set, so the two were prepared for the wet if it happened. Each had brought a full change of clothing and towels for when they took a swim.

As usual, Jeremiah was curious about the tarp covering the bed of the truck. When Mr. Boggs had lifted a corner of it for his father to stow the hamper of food, all that Jeremiah had seen was a pile of burlap bags, a wagon, and some fishing gear. He had been warned by his father not to ask any questions about it, but it didn't stop the questions in his mind. He figured that sometime later in the trip, Mr. Boggs would tell him what everything was going to be used for.

Jeremiah's eyes shone with excitement, and he could no longer hold himself in. He began peppering Mr. Boggs with questions. "Do you think that we will catch a lot of fish? How long will it take to get there? I'm not very hungry yet, but I will be pretty soon. I know that Mother put some cookies in the basket because I saw her do it." Jeremiah babbled on with Mr. Boggs, giving and occasional, "Uh, hum." Jeremiah talked for about a half hour until he finally ran out of steam.

Mr. Boggs just smiled to himself. This boy so reminded him of his little brother. David had been as full of questions and life as Jeremiah was. The two brothers had been very close with little David, following him around wherever he went as if he was a second shadow. Then one day when the lad was eleven years old, he awoke one morning with a raging fever. He was so hot that you were almost burned when you touched his skin. Nothing they did brought the fever down, and within a few short hours, it had consumed him. At the last, the little lad had a final lucid moment, and he looked his big brother in the eyes and smiled. With dried cracked lips and a croaking voice, he told him, "You are the best brother anyone could ever ask for." Then a surprising thing happened. His face settled into a picture of peace, and it seemed to glow from within. "The angels are coming for me now." Then he closed his eyes, not to open them again. Mr. Boggs did not set a lot of store in religion. His father had been the gardener for a large estate, and though the owner was fair in his dealings with his help, it was still a hard life. His mother was the only one in the family who cared to pray, and as far as he could see, it sure didn't seem to help much. They still struggled financially, and they were still sick just as often as their neighbors. Despite his lack of faith, a part of him hoped that there was a heaven and that his little brother had gone there. Not wanting to be a gardener like his father, he had left England, hoping to find another way of life. Not liking the hustle and bustle of the east coast, he had traveled as far west as Minnesota and had found a job at the mill. He seemed to have an aptitude for the lumber business, and he had made some good friends. He was content.

Mr. Boggs shook off his reverie as if shedding a heavy coat. He had not thought of his little brother in this depth in a long time. He figured that it was being with Jeremiah that had brought it on. When he looked over at the boy, he found him lying down on the seat, staring up at the sky, looking thorough a square he had fashioned with his hands.

"Mr. Boggs, these are great clouds! I've found a bunch of animals. There was a dog, a gaggle of geese, a rabbit, a frog, a turtle, and a bird. No, the bird was a real bird. I think it was an eagle, the kind with the white head. He was far away, but he must be really big, because I could see him real good. Do you think that he might have a nest close by?" Jeremiah asked.

"We are at the fishing spot, and, yes, there are bald eagles that nest by the lake. They like the fishing as much as we do. You see the waterfall at that escarpment over there? It keeps the lake filled up, and it spills over a little dam out into the river. The dam is made up of big rocks that were put there by nature a long time ago. We will walk down to it later, and I will show it to you. Sometimes, when the river is flooding, it will spill back into the lake. When big fish come in with the flood, they get trapped when the river goes down. I have seen some very large walleyes that have lived here for a long time. I almost caught one before that I estimate was almost thirty inches long. He put up a good fight, and just as I was going to get him, my fishing line broke. There is a big fish out there that has my hook in it, and I want it back," Mr. Boggs said with a jolly laugh.

The two set up their little camp and pulled their fishing gear out. Jeremiah had gone to the lake's edge and captured minnows and bloodsuckers to use as bait. The wind had picked up, making little white caps on the water. The clouds had been gathering together and threatened to pour out some rain on them. This was the perfect weather for walleye fishing, and within a couple of hours, they had one of the stringers filled with fish.

"Look at all of the fish we have caught. And we would have more except we let the smaller ones go. I've never had so much fun fishing before. How many more are we going to get? Gosh, I'm really getting hungry. Can we have our picnic now?" Jeremiah's stomach gave out a very loud rumble.

"No need to growl at me, young man!" Mr. Boggs said with a chuckle. "We can stop to eat now. I am anxious to see what your mother has sent for us. I usually just roast some fish to eat, so this will be a treat."

Jeremiah's mother had indeed packed them a feast. As they finished up with the cookies, Mr. Boggs gave Jeremiah a peculiar look and became very serious.

"Jeremiah, I am about to share certain information with you. Your father assures me that you are indeed a trustworthy young man and that you will keep it secret. It means that you cannot reveal this information to anyone."

Jeremiah's eyes grew large, and he gave a nervous swallow. "My father said that about me? Does he know the secret too?"

"Yes, he has known about it for many years. If I share it with you, do you think that you could keep this secret too? I need your assurances before I reveal it to you." Mr. Boggs seemed so very solemn, but Jeremiah was quick to answer.

"I promise that I can keep your secret just like my father said."

"Good boy, I had a feeling that I could trust you. That is why you were chosen to come on this trip with me." Mr. Boggs gave Jeremiah a big grin. "Now we need to get the gear that I have under the tarp and go on a hike."

Mr. Boggs lifted the tarp that covered the bed of the truck and removed burlap sacks, a small wagon, and a shovel. He then took some wooden panels and positioned them in brackets on all four sides of the wagon and put the sacks and shovel inside. "Now we are going on a little hike. It's not far, and we will have a great view of the lake from a ledge. If the eagles are using the same nest that they used before, we will be able to see it clearly."

As they started walking toward the escarpment, the land was sloping steadily upward. At first, they followed the lakeshore, and then a faint trail bisected some large boulders. "This is a game trail. It goes all the way to the top of the escarpment." Mr. Boggs led the way, and he stopped a few minutes later. "Follow me. The ledge is just on the other side of these boulders." He scrambled up over the rocks with Jeremiah right behind him. They arrived on a large flat rock that jutted out over the lake. "Step carefully. There are loose rocks here, and if you slip, you will have a long fall into the lake."

The view from the rock ledge was as spectacular as Mr. Boggs had promised. They could see their little camp area, the river, and the lake where it spilled over the dam into it. "Look," said Jeremiah. "There's an eagle now! Wow, it just dove into the lake, and it caught a fish! I've never seen anything like that before. Hey, it's coming this way. Oh boy, that bird is really big!"

The eagle flew toward them, and then it veered to a nest that had been built in the top of a dead tree. The tree was fairly close to the ledge and was almost parallel with it. Two little eaglets popped up from inside the nest and were greedily grabbing for the fish in the adult bird's talons.

Jeremiah started laughing at their antics. "They sure are hungry. It's a good thing that she's such a good fisherman."

"That's the male eagle," Mr. Boggs corrected him. "He takes an active part in supplying his offspring with food. The female must still be off hunting somewhere. It seems that he got the goods first today," Mr. Boggs said with a laugh.

They stood and watched a few minutes more. Then they went back to the trail to finish their hike. An outcropping of rocks appeared up ahead, and a cleft in the rocks revealed the entrance to a cave.

"We're here," said Mr. Boggs.

"Do any wild animals live in there? Is there a bear or a mountain lion?" Jeremiah started his excited babbling.

"Slow down, son. The only animals that live in this cave are bats. And now it is time for you to learn the big secret. We are going into the cave, and I need for you to talk softly, or we will startle the residents. Are you ready?"

"Yes, sir." Jeremiah was a little scared, but he was more excited than anything else. He had never been in a cave before, nor had he ever seen a large group of bats. Oh, sometimes there were bats in a barn, and you could see them flying at dusk, but he was sure that this was going to be different.

They picked up the bags and shovel and stepped into the cave. They had to wait just a bit while their eyes adjusted to the dark interior; then they walked a little father into the cave. "Here, you hold the bag open while I shovel." Mr. Boggs scooped some of the material that covered the floor of the cave into the bag.

"What is that?" asked Jeremiah when he heard some rustling.

"Look at the ceiling. What do you see?" quizzed Mr. Boggs.

Jeremiah peered intently at the ceiling. At first, he didn't see anything. Then, all of a sudden, it seemed almost as if the ceiling was moving. He looked harder, and then he finally made out that what he was looking at. "Bats, lots and lots of bats!" he loudly exclaimed.

"Shhh! We need to talk softly so we don't startle them. They won't harm you, but it is rather unsettling to have them swarming around you. I counted some of the bats one time, and believe it or not, there were about fifty of them in just one square foot of space. Now you just hold that bag steady while I do the shoveling. This is the answer to your question about my garden. Bat guano is some of the best fertilizer in the whole world," Mr. Boggs said softly.

They worked quietly, and soon they had filled all of the bags. Mr. Boggs had fashioned handles from the rope he had used to secure each bag, so it made it easier for them to carry the bags out of the cave going back until they had them all.

Mr. Boggs set the last bag down in the wagon and then mopped his brow with a large handkerchief. "Now you know the secret of my garden. I mix the contents of these bags in with my garden soil, and it makes my vegetables grow. I come here and get a supply, and every spring when I work up my garden, I just plow it on in. Then I plant the seeds and watch the plants grow and grow and grow."

"How did you think to do it?" Jeremiah was puzzled.

"Let's get this load back to camp first. Then I will tell you the story."

The little wagon was stacked high with the bags of guano, but, thankfully, it was a downhill trek to get back to the camp. They loaded the bags, wagon, and shovel into the bed of the truck and fastened the tarp down. It was just midafternoon, and the threatened rain had blown off.

"Let's dip our lines in the lake for another hour or so. Then we can head back home. I can tell you the story as we fish." They walked back to the lakeshore, baited their lines, and threw them into the water.

Mr. Boggs settled down on the log at the water's edge that he used for a chair. He adjusted his fishing pole, took a deep breath, and began. "I learned the secret of bat guano from my father. He was the head gardener on a large estate in England. One day, he took notice that the foliage grew exceptionally well around a certain tree that bats congregated in, so he took soil from around the tree and, first, put it around the earl's prized roses. Soon, he was using it in all of the gardens, and the Earl became known for his exceptionally healthy roses and the large size and amount of produce that came from his gardens. Of course, my father had told the earl about the bat guano, and the earl swore him to secrecy. He was allowed to share the information only with me as I was his main helper. Eventually, he built bat houses to draw even more bats so they would nest in them, and he could reap the guano."

"Do other people know about bat guano?" Jeremiah was curious.

"Oh yes, others eventually figured it out. That doesn't seem to be the case with folks around here, though." The old man chuckled with mirth. "I take some joy in my secret, especially when some folks try to trick the information out of me. I know that it could be construed as being selfish for not sharing the information, and someday I may let the cat out of the bag. But not yet, as I am still having too much fun. I am counting on you keeping all of this under your hat. Is that too much to ask?"

"No, I will keep your secret just as I promised I would." Jeremiah smiled. "It is a great joke on the town. Everyone has wondered how you get your vegetables to grow so big. Say, how did you find this bat cave anyway?"

"Ah, now that is a story too. I have a friend who is a tugboat captain on the river, and he told me about this little lake with its wonderful fishing. After coming and having had great success here a time or two, I decided that it was time to go exploring. As I hiked up to the escarpment and stepped out on the rock ledge, the threatening rain became even more ominous. The wind had picked up, and there were black clouds rolling in. Being the stubborn man that I am, I decided that I just wasn't done exploring yet. So I clambered back down onto the trail and continued the climb. That was when I discovered the cave. Just as I got to the entrance of it, the clouds opened up, and the rain came down in buckets. Well, I ducked into the cave, hoping that it was not occupied by any fierce critters. I soon realized that even though the cave seemed to have inhabitants, I was safe from becoming an afternoon snack. I had not brought a light with me, so I hunkered down close to the opening and waited for the rain to abate. The storm spent itself rather quickly, so I went back to my camp to get a lantern and returned to the cave to see what I could find. Imagine my surprise when I discovered that the inhabitants were none other than a colony of bats. They had been housing here for some time because the guano had built up and it is quite deep. Well, it took me no time at all to start making trips back here on a regular basis not only to fish but to also harvest the guano and use it in my garden. I have been doing this for many a year, and no one has found me out yet."

With that, the fishing pole in his hand gave a decided jerk. He quickly pulled on the line, setting the hook, and in a short while, he reeled in a good-sized walleye. "Well, son, that about fills our stringer here. There are plenty for each of us and some to share with our neighbors too. Are you ready to call it a day?"

"Oh yes, sir," Jeremiah said.

"All right, let's get our gear loaded up and head back home then. I want to clean a few of these fish first. It is still early enough that I will have time to deliver them to our friends."

As Mr. Boggs set to scaling and cleaning the fish, Jeremiah set to work, putting out the campfire that they had made. He made absolutely sure that there were no live embers left. Then he patrolled the area, making sure that no trash was left behind. He carefully stacked the excess firewood neatly against a tree. It would be saved there for the next fishing trip. The camp spot was neat and clean, and all the equipment had been loaded and stowed.

"I think that we need a quick swim to clean the guano and the fish scales off. Are you game?" Mr. Boggs asked with a grin.

"Hey, last one in is a rotten egg!" Jeremiah said as he began swiftly stripping his clothes off. He shimmied into his trunks and went flying toward the lake.

"You win, you little scamp!" Mr. Boggs yelled after him. "Should have known that he would be as slippery as an eel and as fast as an antelope," he said under his breath with a smile.

The two swam and splashed about for about a half hour, enjoying the warm, clear water. Then they dried themselves off and got into the truck to make the trip home.

"Well, Jeremiah, did you enjoy yourself today? I must say that for me it has been one of the best days of fishing that I have had in a while. I have certainly appreciated your assistance with the guano, and you did your fair share at catching this fine mess of fish too."

"Oh yes, sir! It was the best time I have ever had fishing. And the cave is really great! Thank you so much for letting me come along with you."

"I'm the one who needs to thank you." Mr. Boggs paused for a moment. "So would you like to come along with me again sometime?"

"Oh yes, sir!" Jeremiah exclaimed exuberantly. His smile almost split his face in half. With that, Mr. Boggs grinned and started the truck, happy that he and the boy had become fast friends.

13

Blueberry Picking

It was a beautiful Minnesota summer morning. The sun was shining, but the air still had a slight chill to it, and there was a light breeze playing with the leaves on the trees. Small puffs of white clouds dotted the clear blue sky. It was the first of summer break, and the events that were planned had not begun yet. Miriam and Jerald had come early to visit their friends. Miriam had brought some crochet patterns she had found in a chest in her grandmother's room that she was eager to share with Abigail. The two girls had positioned themselves on some soft pillows in the porch swing, and they were studying the patterns intently. Samuel, Jeremiah, and Jerald were busily sorting through a box of rocks on the porch steps. Samuel was an avid collector, and he had a fairly wide assortment that he had gathered over the years. The distinct sound of a horse trotting caused Abigail to look up from her task. She was surprised to see her friends Sarah, Anne, Randy, and their baby sister Ellie coming up the road in a pony cart. Randy's dog, Jack, was with them, but he was prone to following rabbit trails, so he would take off on a run at a moment's notice. Later, he would show up again out of breath with his tongue lolling wetly out the side of his mouth and looking very pleased with himself. Each time he returned, he would always go directly to Randy and snuffle his hand as if he had to check and make sure that Randy was all right. There was no doubt who his owner was.

"Hey! We're going blueberry picking. Want to come along?" Sarah called out to them. "Father was out chasing a stray cow and found a big patch a little ways from here, so we're going to try and find it."

"Sure. Let me ask Mother and get some pails. We will have to pick lots and lots of berries, though," Samuel said.

"You're right. We need to be positive about this. All of those berries will make fillings for many a pie and some wonderful jelly too," Sarah chimed in.

Mother happily supplied each of them with a sturdy pail, and then she even put together a lunch with an added treat for all of them. She gave Abigail a basket that she had filled with sandwiches and pickles, plus the apple pasties she had made just that morning.

"It looks like the weather is going to be good today, so have fun and get lots of berries. And watch out for little Ellie. Make sure that she doesn't wander off." Mother admonished them as she waved to them from the porch. The children waved back until the little cart was lost to sight around a curve in the road. She rest assured that the little one was in good hands as they were all good children and they were also highly responsible. She smiled as she turned back toward the house, a scheme suddenly developing in her mind. With the children occupied and out from underfoot, she would be able to work on her quilt without curious prying eyes around.

She was thinking about how very early this morning she had gone out to her flower garden to see if it needed watering. It was barely past sunrise, and there had been a cool snap overnight, and to her surprise, she had found a large bumblebee hanging upside down from a lady's slipper leaf. It must have gotten dark, and the night air had cooled so quickly that the chilled bee perched on the leaf of the flower rather than to risk getting lost in the dark trying to get back to its hive. The sight had so tickled her that she giggled. "Why, Mr. Bumble, is there a Mrs. Bumble that is going to be concerned that you did not come home last night? Will she be suspicious and search you to see if she can find strange pollen on you?" The silly thought quickly turned into the idea of the bee becoming embroidered onto the quilt. She could hardly wait to start, but she was not sure if she had the correct shade of yellow thread to use for the bee, and after all, Mr. Bumble deserved only the very best. Her heart was light as she went to check her sewing box. To her consternation, she found that she indeed did not have any yellow thread at all.

"Well, I guess that I am going to have to make a trip to the mercantile. Perhaps I need to stop and see Mrs. Acres first. She may have a picture of a bee that I can use as a pattern. I know that she has already seen the garden part of my quilt, but now I have to share my ideas of the animals and insects with her. I'm sure that she would keep this part secret too, and frankly I am dying to talk about it. My, I am a silly woman to be so secretive about something like a quilt." She laughed aloud at her having such a nonsensical conversation with herself.

With that, she placed her hat on her head, and she hummed merrily as she thought about the blueberry pie that she hoped she was going to make for supper. The pie all depended on the children and what kind of success they had in finding the berry patch and how many berries that they could pick. She was smiling to herself as she firmly closed the front door and started down the road in the direction of town.

Mrs. Acres's house was on the route that she was taking to the mercantile, and she was glad to see that she was out tending her garden.

"Good morning!" Mrs. Eckhardt's voice was cheerful as she hailed her friend.

"Well, good morning to you too!" Mrs. Acres called back. "Where are you off to today?"

"Well, actually, I was hoping to get your help with something. Do you have a few minutes? There is something that I'd like to ask you about," Mrs. Eckhardt quizzed her friend.

Mrs. Acres had removed her gardening gloves as she exited her garden and closed the gate. "Why, of course. Let's go on up to the house, and I will brew us some tea."

The ladies made small talk as they heated water for a large pot of tea. Taking the tea and a plate of cookies, they settled themselves in the rockers on the large porch.

"Now what is on your mind?" Mrs. Acres's curiosity was piqued.

Mrs. Eckhardt set her teacup down, and she took a deep breath. "You know that I am doing the quilt of my flower garden and that I have not only the flowers, but I also am including some of the animals and insects that inhabit it. Well, I had a new inspiration this morning when I met Mr. Bumble." Both ladies shared a good laugh as Mrs. Eckhardt described the plight of the frigid Mr. Bumble hanging precariously from the leaf. "I was hoping that you would have a picture of a bee that I could use as a pattern so I could embroider it onto the quilt also."

"Why, I think that the whole idea is absolutely charming! Of course, I have a number of books on beekeeping, and I am sure that you can find a suitable picture in one of them. When we last spoke of your quilt, you were still trying to decide just what other animals that you were going to include from your garden. Have you made your choices?" Mrs. Acres was curious.

"Yes, I did, but only after much deliberation. I am going to have a shy rabbit peeking out from under some foliage, a caterpillar on the gate, a butterfly perched on a hollyhock, and then perhaps a blue jay staring at a ladybug climbing on the trellis." She had almost become dreamy as she described her ideas in detail. "Oh my, I am carrying on, aren't I?"

"No, no, I am totally fascinated. Then you did you find some suitable pictures in Mrs. Himmel's books?"

"Oh yes, her set of Audubon books that had belonged to her late husband was a treasure trove for me. In them, I found the perfect pictures of all of the animals that I have found visiting at different times in my garden. But I do so want to get a picture of a bee from you. After all, it is only fitting as you are the resident beekeeper. Then I have need to go to the mercantile as I do not have any yellow embroidery thread." Mrs. Eckhardt's eyes sparkled with excitement. "Would you care to come with me?"

"I would love to, my dear. Just let me get my hat, and we can go. If you don't mind, I would also like to stop at Mrs. Himmel's as I have a jar of honey that I need to deliver to her."

"Absolutely! I have wanted to visit her to update her on the quilt's progress so this a perfect opportunity."

As Mrs. Acres went to retrieve her hat, Mrs. Eckhardt quickly gathered the tea dishes, her face aglow with a large smile. "I was so glad that you shared the information with me about those books. I had hoped to keep the information about the quilt a secret from everyone until I entered it in the County Fair in August, but I am glad that circumstances made it necessary to reveal it to you, dear ladies."

"Oh, my dear, both Mrs. Himmel and I are the souls of discretion. Your secret will be safe with us. Not much exciting happens in this town, so this little intrigue is tickling both of us. I, for one, will be waiting with bated breath for the unveiling of it at fair time." Mrs. Acres gave her friend a conspiratorial smile.

The sturdy little pony had no problem hauling the group in the cart as he plodded merrily along. There was still a slight chill in the air leftover from the night's cool spell, and the leaves on the trees were gently tossing in the breeze, which caused the sun's rays to make a moving dapple pattern over everything.

The older children began talking about how much fun camp had been for them. Jeremiah listened to them knowing that he wasn't going to be able to go to camp until the summer after next. But he'd had such a wonderful time fishing with Mr. Boggs that he was no longer envious of the others. In fact, he actually felt superior in the way that he had been honored to become a part of a very adult secret. Plus the fishing itself had really been great. He had caught more fish that one time than he had ever caught before. But he was especially glad that he and Mr. Boggs had become friends.

"Oh, I'll be glad when I am old enough to go to camp. It has been boring with nothing to do this summer." Jerald sounded just a bit pouty about things.

"Yeah, camp will be fun for sure, but I did have a good time fishing with Mr. Boggs. It was really great seeing that bald eagles nest and the male feeding the little ones the fish he had caught. Mr. Boggs said that the fish must have been at least twenty inches. It would have been a keeper for sure. And those little ones were really tearing it up." Jeremiah laughed at the remembrance. "Hey, Jerald, there is supposed to be a nest out by the dam. Would you like to go with me and see if we can find it?"

"That does sound like fun. Can we go tomorrow?"

"Sure. I will have to get my chores done first, but then we can pack a picnic and take our fishing poles along. There are supposed to be some big walleyes waiting to be caught. Who knows, maybe we will get lucky." Jeremiah had learned a number of fishing tricks from Mr. Boggs, and he was eager to see if he could get them to work on his own.

"Look. There's the pile of rocks that Father said to watch for. The blueberry patch should be just a little ways into the woods," said Sarah.

They urged the little pony off the road onto a small trail, and soon they came to a clearing. It was filled with blueberry bushes with the fruit in various sizes and stages of ripeness. The boys quickly unhitched the pony and hobbled him so that he could graze. Then each child grabbed a pail and started picking the round blue fruit, filling the pails and then dumping them into the large washtub they had brought along just for that purpose. Before long, they all sported blue rings around their mouths as the berries were just too delicious to not eat some of them as they picked. After they had picked for about two hours, they stopped to rest. Abigail got the basket from the cart, and everyone took one of the apple pasties. They had also brought a water pail and a dipper. The water was still cool from the well and tasted good as they washed down the sweet savory treats.

"It was so nice of Mother to give us these apple pasties. I think that she had planned on having them for our dessert for supper tonight, but now we will be bringing the blueberries back, so I guess that she will make us a pie." Abigail took a bite of her pasty, thoroughly enjoying it.

"Um, um, as much as I like eating the berries right off the bushes, I like the pie even better. Don't you, Abigail?" Samuel had been a true boy and finished his pasty in just three huge bites.

"Oh, Samuel"—Abigail was laughing—"you had better be as fast at filling your bucket with berries as you are at filling your stomach with food!"

"Look, we have the washtub about half full already, and if we keep picking another couple of hours, it will be really full," said Samuel, "so I suggest that we get back to it. I have to prove that I am the best berry picker here, and my prize will be getting the biggest piece of the pie tonight." With a conqueror's smirk, he walked up to a larger bush and began busily gathering the little blue fruit.

Little Ellie had lost interest in the actual picking but had found other amusements. As Sarah went back to filling her bucket with fruit, Ellie spent her time putting ants in her bucket and then letting them back out again.

It hadn't been two hours yet, but Jeremiah announced that he was hungry again. As the sun had reached its midday cycle, the group gathered at the cart and unpacked the heavily laden picnic basket. They ate slowly, savoring the generously filled ham-and-cheese sandwiches, and their mouths puckered as the sour pickles dribbled their juices down chins.

"Mother sure made some good sandwiches for us, and she whipped them up fast too. It was almost as if she couldn't wait for us to go. I wonder what she is going to do today."

"Well, Jeremiah, she did say something about going to visit Mrs. Acres." Abigail knew it involved something about the quilt. but she was determined to honor Mother's wishes and not to reveal anything about it to anyone. She found that this was especially hard, as she usually didn't keep anything secret from her dearest friends. But she took heart in the fact that all would be revealed in time, and her friends would understand why she did not share this with them. She was beginning to realize that keeping a confidence was an important part of growing up.

"Let's pick just a little while longer. Then we can head back home. I didn't think that there would be so many berries, and I just want to keep filling up the bucket. But Little Ellie is getting tired and will need to nap soon," said Sarah.

Randy had stayed close to Sarah and Ellie until he spotted a squirrel. The little critter seemed intent on chattering at Randy as if he were scolding him for taking the berries. Randy was fascinated, and he followed the noisy little beast as it jumped from tree to tree, leading Randy in a circle. The three had drifted away from the rest and were now at the far side of the clearing. Sarah took Ellie and moved to where the bushes were a little taller, so it was easier for her to get to the berries. The bending and stooping had made her back tired. Now she had to reach up a bit to pick the fruit, but it was a welcome change. Little Ellie was happily engrossed with the ants again.

Jack had gone off on a number of expeditions and had galloped off on yet another one. Suddenly, he was back at Randy's side, a low growl emitting from his throat as he looked past Sarah and Ellie.

"What's wrong, Jack?" Randy asked as he put his hand on Jack's ruff. His breath caught in his throat when he scanned the woods, and he spotted a large black bear just at the edge of the berry patch. "Easy, boy." Randy walked quietly toward Sarah, waving one arm, trying to get her attention. When he reached Ellie, he stooped down and picked her up. He did not want to yell and startle Sarah or to frighten the bear, but he knew that they had to leave quickly. For the moment, the bear was intent on eating berries as if it wasn't aware that the group was there.

Sarah finally looked up, and her face sported a quizzical expression when she finally saw Randy gesturing to her. Then she caught another movement out of the corner of her eye. Her eyes grew huge when she turned toward the movement and saw that a bear was only about two hundred yards away from her. Grasping her pail, she slowly and quietly walked toward Randy and Ellie and away from the bear. Samuel had also already seen the bear and was making a shushing gesture while he pointed the others toward the ponycart. Not fully understanding what was going on but seeing the tension in Samuel's face, they followed his instructions and began to walk toward the cart. Samuel had reached the cart and was hurriedly hitching the pony to it. Curiosity made Jeremiah look back behind him, and then he too saw the bear. The others were getting close to the cart, and he not only made the shushing gesture but was also signaling them to hurry. That was when a cub came out of the woods from behind the bear. Looking first at the cub and then toward the group of youngsters, the mother bear began woofing and shaking her head from side to side.

Jack had been staying close to Randy, but when the bear began woofing, he sprang into action. He left Randy's side and ran toward the she bear, circling her and barking furiously. Samuel had finished hitching the nervous little pony into the traces and was assisting the others up into the cart. He got into the driver's seat and told them to hold on tight, and they started down the trail out to the road. Samuel didn't have to urge the little pony to go; the little guy's feet barely touched the ground as they flew out of the woods. They could hear Jack barking back in the distance, but the sound was fading farther and farther back on the other side of the clearing. When they got to the road, they turned and headed for home as fast as the little horse could go. It made for a rough ride, but they all just clung to the cart and didn't complain.

"Where's Jack? Do you see him? I can't hear him anymore," fretted Randy. "I hope he's all right. Here, Jack! Here, Jack!" he called out to the retreating woods.

After a time, Samuel surmised that the bear was no longer a threat, so he slowed the pony down, and they traveled at a more leisurely pace, but the fear and excitement still had their hearts beating fast and hard.

Randy was still fretting about Jack, but the others advised him that Jack was a smart dog, and they were sure that he was all right. Jeremiah was quick to comfort his friend and point out Jack's prowess. "Yeah, Randy, and Jack knows his way home. He runs so fast that he might even be back home before you get there. Did you see how he kept jumping round and round in front of that bear? But he was so fast that the bear didn't get anywhere near him." Randy was somewhat mollified, but he just wanted his dog back at his side.

They had not traveled too far down the road when suddenly Jack came running out of the woods. Samuel stopped the cart, and Jack jumped up into the midst of the children. The grateful group showered him with hugs and vigorous pats. The dog had been running hard, so he was panting and out of breath, but to Randy's joy, he did not appear to be hurt. "Look, he's all right! Not a scratch on him!" Jeremiah gave the panting dog a vigorous neck rub and ear scratch. They all hailed him as a hero for saving them from the bear, and he was promised many treats when they got back home.

"I was so scared! That bush I was by was so tall that I never even saw that old bear until she was right there. You did such a good job, Randy. You already had little Ellie and were heading for safety before I even knew what was going on." Sarah lavished praise on her brother.

"It was Jack that really saved the day, though. He was so brave. He got the bear's attention and kept her busy so we could all get away in the cart. It might have turned very differently had he not been there and been so brave." Samuel's praise for his dog made Randy almost burst with pride.

"It was the baby bear being there that caused the she bear to get so upset. I know that I wanted little Ellie to be safe, so I guess I know why the bear acted the way that she did." Sarah grew thoughtful.

"Look! We all still have our buckets with the berries, and the washtub is full too," said Miriam. "I'm glad that we have all of the pails because I certainly would not have gone back after them."

The rest of the group laughingly agreed with her. What a story they would have to tell at the supper table tonight. The rest of the trip home was uneventful, but each one had time to ponder on how close they had come to possible disaster.

When the group returned to their respective houses, they regaled the adults with the story about the bear and Jack's courageous actions. Mr. Bernhardt now had another good reason he had allowed Jack to become part of the family. Berry picking was always a good pastime, and all who ventured out to do it knew that they had to keep an eye out for the bears. The large animals were known to usually be pretty tame, and they did not display any aggression as long as the humans exited the area. He was sure that this she bear only acted the way that she did was because of the presence of the cub.

"When you go back picking again, I want you to be especially diligent in watching for bears now that we know that one has a cub.

Of course, Jack will be going on each expedition, and he will be put on guard. He has proven to be a brave and conscientious watchdog. We will make sure that he receives an ample reward for his courageous deeds today." Father was making light of the situation, but in truth, he said this in all seriousness. The group would have probably been fine as long as they had left the area quickly, but Jack did jump in and take charge, which gave the group more time to escape safely.

With great pomp and ceremony, Jack was presented with a large meaty bone as an award for his bravery. Jack promptly took his prize and disappeared under the porch with it.

When Mrs. Bernhardt put a blueberry pie on the table for dessert, Ellie made them all laugh when she stated, "That's not a blueberry pie. That's a bearberry pie!" And that is what the family calls the pie to this day.

14

Up a Tree

Rolf had visitors from back east. His cousin Donald, along with their friend Eric, had come so they could see this Minnesota that Rolf had moved to. They wanted to experience for themselves the tens of thousands of lakes with the awesome fishing and hunting that Rolf so frequently bragged to them about. He claimed that it made up for the lack of social engagements and fine entertainment offered by life in the east. They saw that, indeed, the pace was much slower, and they too were enjoying the quietness. Oh yes, a day in the lush wilds of Minnesota were a far cry from rush and bustle of carriage packed city streets.

Early Saturday morning, they set out for an adventure with their rifles and fishing poles. The best fishing within hiking distance was where the water spilled over the dam, creating a large pool. Rumor had it that there was a huge walleye in that pond, and everyone wanted to be the one to hook it. Also, while they were hiking, they could hunt squirrels and rabbits. It was setting up to be a very enjoyable day for three friends who were full of life and vigor.

"The dam is just up ahead, and I'm feeling lucky today. That walleye will be the center attraction on the dinner table tonight if I have my way," claimed Rolf.

"Ha, ha! Everyone knows that I am the best fisherman in the family, so that big one belongs to me," Donald said with a confident smirk.

"Wait just a minute! I have plans on landing that fish myself, so you two can just quit fighting over it." Eric laughed.

When they reached the dam, the water was merrily rushing over the top of it, creating a gentle roar. The boys wasted no time threading their hooks with plump minnows and casting their lines into the water. Within a couple of hours, they had a stinger full of fish, though the big one had eluded them all.

The sun had risen halfway, and the day had grown warm. The boys set their fishing rods aside and donned swimming shorts. They were soon swimming, appearing much like the fish that they had caught earlier. Getting hungry, they broke out the picnic lunch they had brought along and devoured it while they dried off.

"Let's get some hunting in on our way back. I think that the squirrels are finally awake, so I will have something to shoot at," said Eric.

"All right, but I want to take a different route back. I haven't explored very much, so let's follow the creek for a while, then cut back toward town," said Rolf.

The boys got a couple of shots off at some squirrels, but they were too fast, and they missed the mark each time. A couple of rabbits were not as fortunate, and Donald was looking forward to having the cook make them into a tasty stew.

It had been a good day, and the three had enjoyed being together again. Rolf had come to the conclusion that he really liked living in Minnesota, but he was also looking forward to going back east to attend college in the fall. He was going to be living with his cousin Donald while he went to school. The three boys were such good friends that they had signed up and been accepted to attend the same university. They felt sure that it would prove to be a grand time for all of them.

They left off following the creek and followed a meandering trail cross-country when they came upon a fenced field.

"I think the road to town is just on the other side of this field. When we get to the tree there in the middle, I can climb up to find out for sure," said Rolf.

They climbed over the fence and were almost to the tree when they heard a bull bellowing.

"What was that? Oh no! There's a bull in here! Run! Get to the tree and climb!" Rolf yelled.

The boys were running as fast as they could when Rolf stepped into a gopher hole and fell. The other two boys had climbed to safety in the tree, and they looked around for Rolf. The bull now had its head down and was charging toward Rolf. He had managed to get up, but it was obvious that he had injured his ankle, so he was painfully and slowly limping toward the tree.

"Hurry, Rolf! Run! The bull is coming!" cried Donald.

Rolf hobbled faster and made it to the tree, but it was apparent that he would not be able to climb.

"Here! Grab our hands, and we will pull you up. Reach!" yelled Eric.

They pulled Rolf to safety just as the bull reached the base of the tree. The enraged animal circled the tree, tossing his huge head with its vicious horns, snorting and pawing the ground in frustration.

"Where did he come from? He's huge! And he's really mean too! He would have gored us if he had gotten to us," exclaimed Donald.

"I don't know who he belongs to. I've never seen this field before, so I didn't know about him." Rolf was in misery. His ankle began swelling and was already turning black and blue. "I'd better take this boot off while I still can. Well, that feels better, but I don't think that I will be able to get the boot on again. I don't think that I will be able to walk on it either," he said worriedly. In the meantime, the bull decided that he was not going anywhere. After circling the tree for some time and looking up and snorting at his quarry in frustration, he finally lay down in the shade right under the tree and closed his eyes for a nap. The boys were not fools. They knew if they tried to get out of the tree, the bull would be right on them again.

"The real question here is, how are we going to get out of this mess? I can see a house and the road over there, but with your hurt ankle, you wouldn't be able to outrun the bull. But don't feel bad, because I'm not sure that I could outrun that beast either," said

Donald. "The only thing we can do is hope that someone will come along on the road and be able to help us."

Hours had passed, and it was now late afternoon. The boys were disheartened as there had been no movement at the house or any traffic on the road either. Just then, a car appeared on the road heading out from town. The boys began yelling as loud as they could, but whoever was in the car did not slow down but just continued on their way.

The yelling had an adverse effect on the bull by waking him from his nap. He immediately began circling the tree once more, huffing and pawing the ground.

"Hey, look, there is someone over by the fence. You there! Help us! The bull has us stuck up in this tree!" yelled Donald excitedly.

Rolf looked toward the fence. "Oh no. It's that dumb kid and his dumb dog. Well, maybe he can go and get us some help anyway. Hey, Randy! Go get us some help!"

Randy started running down the fence line but away from town instead of toward it.

"Hey, Randy! Go the other way! You're going the wrong way! Go to town, and get us some help." Thoroughly frustrated, he commented to the other boys. "See, I told you he was dumb! He's not being any help at all."

Randy just continued running and circled the pasture until he was opposite the road.

"What's he doing?" asked Eric.

Randy climbed over the fence into the pasture with his dog, Jack, at his side. He then began waving his arms and yelling wildly. Jack joined him by running in circles and barking. The bull turned toward the noise. With a wicked gleam in his eyes, he began snorting and pawing the ground; then he dropped his huge head and charged toward the boy and the dog.

"Look! He's got the bull to go after him. Let's make a run for it!" said Eric. The three boys did not waste any time getting out of the tree and heading for the fence. Eric had loaded up with the gear while Donald helped Rolf hobble as fast as he could.

Just as the bull reached Randy, he scooted back over the fence while Jack ran in circles around the bull, barking to keep his attention. Randy was banging on the fence and yelling trying to keep the bull distracted until the boys could make it to safety on the other side of the pasture.

Just then Rolf misstepped again, and both boys tumbled to the ground. The movement caught the bull's eye. He turned from Randy and raced off toward the boys. Eric had made it to the fence and had thrown the gear over it when he turned back toward Rolf and Donald. He saw that the bull was racing back toward them, and the sight made his blood run cold. He bravely turned and ran back to assist Donald in supporting Rolf; then all three of them straggled as fast as they could toward the fence.

"He's almost here! We're not going to make it!" Donald yelled as he looked back to see the bull bearing down on them.

Then out of nowhere, the dog charged the bull, flying at it and smacking it in the side of its neck and shoulder area. The surprised bull veered and then staggered to a stop, trying to locate what had hit him. The dog jumped in front of the beast, barking and lunging at the bull's face just barely keeping out of reach of its horns. The bull's confusion only lasted a few moments. He lunged and swung his head again at the dog just barely missing him, and then he focused on the boys once more. The three had made it to the fence, and Eric and Donald almost threw Rolf over it and began scrambling over it themselves. In his haste, Eric's foot slipped, his boot catching on the rail, which caused him to fall back down inside the fence right in the bull's path. Randy had come running back from around the pasture and saw Eric fall inside the fence. He quickly pulled his shirt off, and moving away from Eric, he began vigorously waving the shirt and yelling at the top of his lungs. The bull saw the shirt and veered turning toward it. He steamed up to the fence and hooked the shirt on his horns, tossing it up into the air. When it hit the ground, he bellowed and tossed it again. Then when it was on the ground once more, he violently pawed the shirt, ripping it to shreds. The boys were mesmerized by the ferocity of the bull's attack on the shirt. Thankfully, Eric had taken the opportunity to scramble over the fence. He lay breathlessly on the ground knowing that he had just missed being stomped to bits by the beast.

Randy was dazed and out of breath from his exertions, but he stirred when he felt a familiar wet nose nudge his hand. "Jack!" he said as he patted the dog on the head. "Are you all right?" He began running his hands over the dog's body, checking him for injuries. The dog was not bleeding, but he seemed to be a little shaky when he put his weight on his front leg.

"I think you got hurt a little bit on your side when you hit the bull," Randy stated. "I don't think that it is too bad though." Randy and Jack walked up to the trio of very grateful boys.

"Randy, what you and Jack did was very brave. We could not have made it to the fence if you hadn't have helped us. Thank you both," Rolf said.

"Yeah, thank you. You did a fine job keeping that bull busy. We were almost to the fence when we fell down. Without your help, we would have been goners for sure. You have one brave dog there to take on a nasty beast like that. We would have ended up like your shirt if not for you. I can still almost feel those hooves pounding me into the ground," said Eric with a shudder.

"Well, now we need to get Rolf to the doctor. Hey, wait, there's a truck coming up the road," Donald stated cheerfully as he began waving the truck down.

The neighbor was happy to give the boys a lift into town. He delivered them to Dr. Holliday's office and then went to the bank to tell Mr. Huffmeister what had happened to his son and his friends. The doctor thoroughly examined Rolf's ankle and pronounced that it was just badly sprained. He wrapped it securely and gave Rolf a pair of crutches. "Now you put some ice on that ankle when you get home, and stay off that leg for a few days. I will be by to check on you and reassess the injury then." He also examined Jack and surmised that the dog was just a bit bruised from his encounter with the bull. He was lavish in his praise to Randy about the courageous heart that the dog possessed. A grateful Mr. Huffmeister loaded the boys and the dog into his car to take them all home. Somehow in the fray, the

COURAGE RISES FROM THE ASHES

boys had managed to hang onto the fish and the rabbits, so despite their misadventures, they were going to have a fine supper after all.

Mr. Huffmeister dropped Rolf and the boys off first. "You boys get those fish cleaned, and the cook will fry them up for dinner, but I don't think that she is going to take kindly to skinning those rabbits."

"I'll skin them for you, Mr. Huffmeister. My father taught me how to do it, and I know how to tan the pelts too." Randy was quick to offer his assistance.

"Very good, and in that case, you are invited to have rabbit stew at my house for dinner tomorrow night. And you are also welcome to have the pelts too if you want them." He turned to the three young men and gave them a hard look. "You all can thank this young man again for saving you from that bull and for helping to prepare the rabbits. You three will go to Randy's house in the morning to retrieve the rabbits and then will go back and bring him to dinner tomorrow night. I, for one, am looking forward to having that rabbit stew. Is this plan all right with you, Randy?"

"Yes, sir, I really like rabbit stew, and I'll have the rabbits ready in the morning." Randy was stunned at the invitation for supper. He knew that usually only important folks like the mayor and the sheriff were invited to eat at the banker's house.

"It is settled then. Come on, Randy and I will give you and this brave dog a ride home. I will discuss all of this with your father and gain his permission, which I am sure that he will grant without reservation." Mr. Huffmeister held the car door open so Randy and Jack could get in. They left the three boys to take the mess of fish and clean them.

The next day, a car pulled up in the yard, and Randy went out to meet it. Donald was driving, and when he got parked, both he and Eric helped Rolf to get out of it. Rolf had his ankle firmly wrapped with a large dressing, and he was wearing very large moccasins. He was also sporting the pair of crutches that the doctor had given him.

"Hey, Randy, how are you today?" inquired Rolf. He then turned to the dog. "And how about you, Jack? Are you doing all right too?" All three boys were giving Jack ear scratches and rubs, which he enjoyed immensely.

"Yeah, I'm all right. The doc said that Jack is just bruised up a bit and that he should be fit as a fiddle again in no time."

"Boy, that's good. Um, Randy, we all want to say thank you again for yesterday." Rolf paused and took a deep breath; then he blurted out. "I was wrong about both you and Jack. I'm sorry that I said such mean things. I won't be doing that again for sure." Rolf stuck his hand out to Randy. "Can we be friends?"

Randy gave Rolf a huge smile and pumped his hand. "Sure! We're friends."

"Good!" Rolf said with relief. "Do you think that Jack would be my friend now too?" He stuck his hand out toward the dog to give him another scratch, and to his surprise, Jack lifted his paw up to Rolf's hand. "Why, look at that! He shook my hand as good as anybody! Good boy!" He gave the dog another good ear scratch. "Um, we brought something special for Jack and something for you too. I had the cook save this out. Such a brave dog deserves a reward." Saying that, Rolf pulled out a large paper package that he had brought with him from the car. Inside the brown wrapping was a big meaty beef bone. Rolf offered it to the dog, and Jack took it gently from the boy's hand. All of the boys smiled as they watched him trot off with his prize to his favorite resting spot under the front porch.

"This other package is for you, Randy. Eric, Donald, and I got you a new shirt. It was the least we could do to thank you for saving us from that bull. None of us will ever forget how smart and brave you were." Randy was speechless. He had never thought of himself as being smart or brave before.

"What made you think to wave your shirt at him like that anyways?" Rolf asked.

"Well, the bull, he chases things," Randy blurted the statement out.

"Yeah. Especially us!" Eric quipped.

"Yeah, but, Randy, how did you know that he would go after your shirt?" Donald asked.

"Well, I was going by the pasture one day, and it was really windy, and Mrs. Anderson was right there by the fence, and she was really yelling at the bull. Boy, she was as mad as anything. She was so mad because she had done her wash, and her drawers had blown off the wash line into the pasture. Why, that bull was tossing and stomping them worse than he stomped my shirt. That's how I thought to use it."

The four boys broke out into uproarious laughter at the plight of Mrs. Anderson and her drawers.

When they all finally calmed down, Rolf announced, "Well, we better get these rabbits back to the cook. She said something about having to simmer the rabbits for a good bit of time, so we better get going. Thanks again, Randy, and we will be back to get you later."

Eric had been musing on something, so he finally asked Randy a question. "Say, where did you get Jack from anyways?"

"Um, he just showed up at school one day. He wanted to stay with me, so we came home, and Father let me keep him." Randy looked puzzled.

"Could you call him back out here? I have something that I want to try. I'm not going to hurt him or anything. I just want to see if he knows some tricks."

"All right, Jack, come here, boy." Jack came at Randy's call, and he sat down by his feet.

Eric came and stood next to him and greeted him. Then he said, "Heel," and started walking forward. Jack immediately stood up and began following Eric, staying very close to his side. Eric stopped and said, "Sit," and Jack sat down. Eric said, "Stay," and walked a few steps sway. Jack stayed right where he was told to stay until Eric said, "Come." Jack got up and walked to Eric and looked up to him expectantly. Eric praised the dog and gave him a good ear scratch.

Randy had watched all of this with an open mouth. "How did you get Jack to do all of that?" His surprise was complete.

"My aunt has about ten dogs, all different breeds. They are all purebreds, and she takes them to these dog shows put on by the American Kennel Club all of the time. My father adores his sister, and he didn't want her to travel on her own, so he would send me along to help her with whatever she needed. A couple of her dogs have not only won the best of breed but also the best of show awards. Anyway, when I saw Jack, I thought he might be a purebred, a German shepherd. Now I am sure of it. He's been trained like all of the dogs that are at those shows. He knows all of the commands. I'm just wondering where exactly that he came from."

"A German shepherd? He's just Jack to me." Randy was really puzzled now. "He's been mine for a long time, a couple of months." Randy was now a little stressed.

"If no one has been asking about him or advertised for a lost dog by now, I wouldn't worry about it very much. You're a great guy, Randy, and it's easy to see that Jack belongs with you no matter what." Eric was quick to reassure the boy.

"We had better get going with these rabbits now. Thanks for skinning them and dressing them out for us. My father wants us to come and get you for supper at about five o'clock." Rolf clasped Randy on the shoulder. He stuck his hand to Randy once more. "We'll be back to get you, my friend. Be seeing you later."

Randy smiled as he shook Rolf's hand. "Yup, be seeing you later."

The three boys loaded up into the car and waved out of the windows as they drove off. Randy stood in his driveway, waving back at them. He had a firm hand on Jack's shoulder, and he dropped down and hugged his dog's neck. "I don't care where you came from. You found me, and I found you, and that's all that counts. I will have to tell Father that you are probably a German shepherd, though."

Jack immediately agreed with him and began showering him with wet sloppy licks.

Fourth of July

It had been hot for the past week, and today looked as though it was going to be the same. This was typical weather for Fourth of July, and today the entire town would be celebrating. A town picnic was being set up at the lakeshore, and Abigail and her family were right in the thick of the preparations.

Abigail had been put in charge of the games for the children. Her father, along with a few men from the mill, had constructed a beanbag toss game, and they had also cut some checkerboards and the pieces from wood scraps. Samuel, Jeremiah, Bobby, Jerald, and Randy had all spent an entire day giving the toss game board a clown face. The holes for the eyes, ears, nose, and mouth had been assigned points. The mouth was the largest, so it was worth five points. The big red nose was worth fifteen points; the ears and the eyes were worth ten points each. All of the checkerboards and the round checkers received a coat of red or black paint. The group was proud of their efforts, even though they ended up with almost as much paint on their clothing as was on the articles that they had painted. Abigail, Miriam, and Sarah were charged with sewing colorful bags and filling them with beans for the clown toss game. The other games consisted of jump ropes, burlap bags for the three-legged race, a bat mitten game, and two sets of horseshoes. Mother had rewarded the hardworking little group with a tasty lunch that included apple tarts as a treat. Father had the games delivered to the lakeside for Abigail to set them up and assign volunteers to work them. The best part of the job for the workers is that they would be awarding prizes to the winners. The plan was that every child would win something so all would have a happy day.

At the lakeside, the men had been busy building a dance platform. Everyone was anticipating that Mr. Baer was going to play his accordion so all could enjoy the polka, and Mr. McDonald was going to join him by playing the fiddle. There was talk that there was a secret afoot about another musician. The city council members had worked hard to keep the mystery from being divulged until the dance that was going to be held in the evening.

The banker, Mr. Huffmeister, had arranged for a special treat for everyone who attended the Fourth of July festivities. He had contacted a friend back east who manufactured ice cream machines and had purchased a dozen of them. He planned to use the machines to make ice cream for the entire community. It was his way of thanking his friends and neighbors for welcoming him and his family into their fold. He planned to give two churns away in a special drawing and the other ten as they were considered to be used so they were to be sold for a reduced cost at Mr. Heimlich's mercantile. The proceeds from the sale were to be donated to the church.

All of this had started when he and his family stepped off the train in this quaint Minnesota town. They were met at the station by Mr. Ross, the elderly banker who was now his partner and a group of friendly townsfolk. The Huffmeisters had shipped the major portion of their belongings by train, and it all had arrived a week ahead of them. In anticipation of their arrival, Mr. Ross had the crates transferred from the train station to the house. Mr. Heimlich was surprised when he was told that these same folks who were escorting the family from the train station were staying to help with the unpacking. A grateful Mr. Heimlich quickly began designating which crate was to be placed in each room. The group then opened the crates and not only assembled the beds but also positioned the larger pieces of the furniture at Mrs. Huffmeister's directions. The smaller boxes of belongings were also carried to their assigned rooms and were ready to be unpacked by the family. Because of the assistance of the townsfolk, the Huffmeisters were able to get the bedrooms completely arranged that very first day. Some of the men and women returned the following day to complete setting things up. The men assembled and placed the dining room furniture first; then they moved on into the living room. The women, along with Mrs. Huffmeister, concentrated their efforts in the kitchen, putting all of the cooking equipment to rights. The women then moved to the dining room, getting the china cleaned and displayed. Another group of folks arrived and had stocked the pantry with some staples, and they also brought prepared food to feed the hardworking crowd. Coming from a large city, the Huffmeisters had not expected or experienced this type of welcoming before, and they were grateful for each and every act of kindness. They had planned on having to stay at the hotel for about two weeks, until they could get settled in, but instead they found that they were totally set up and able to move into the house after just two days.

There was a steady stream of people showing up at the lakeside. Children's wild screams and peals of laughter permeated the air. Father had constructed a table and benches of sorts out of scrap lumber that he had in the barn. Getting most of the activities set up, he was able to go and pick up Mother at about eleven o'clock. She had packed a picnic basket with goodies and put the dishware to eat it with in a wooden box. As the adults sat at the picnic table and ate leisurely, the children crammed their food down so they could be first up to play the games. Soon everyone was milling about greeting one another and visiting. It was a great time to socialize and to get caught up on the local news.

Mr. Huffmeister had asked for volunteers to churn the ice cream machines, and plenty of folks stepped forward. The people were fascinated with this novelty, and all wanted to be a part of it. They had watched while the machines had been filled with rich, heavy cream and vanilla. Then the buckets had been sealed and surrounded with ice and salt. Now the churns required a fair amount of churning, which was accomplished by turning the handles. It took time, and as one person got tired, another person took their place. Finally, the frozen confection was ready to serve.

"Everyone! Bring your bowl and a spoon, and we will dish up the ice cream!" Mr. Huffmeister yelled jubilantly.

The crowd lined up as Mr. Huffmeister and the Bernhardts stood at the churns with large spoons and dished up the lovely frozen creation. Some folks had brought strawberries or blueberries and poured them over the ice cream. Others had things like apple pie or cake in their bowls and had the ice cream dished on top of it. Twelve lucky children got the honors of licking the ice cream from the paddles.

"My tongue is so cold!" and "Um, it is so good!" These comments were voiced around sweet, sticky smiles.

After the entire crowd had savored the icy concoction, there was still one churn full left. Mr. Huffmeister called Mr. Janakowski, the iceman, over and spoke softly to him. The old man shook his head in affirmation and took the proffered tin full of ice cream back to his truck and buried it in the ice he had in the back. He was about to step up into his truck and leave when Jeremiah came running up and calling his name. "Hey, Mr. Janakowski, where are you going with that ice cream? Do you think that I could have some?"

"Hey there yourself, Jeremiah. If you really need to know, I am taking it back to my icehouse. Sorry, son, I have orders from Mr. Huffmeister about this ice cream. I am taking it on my rounds tomorrow and am going to give it to the shut-ins who couldn't make it to the festivities."

"Hey, that's great! Can I go on your rounds with you? I sure would like to help."

"That would be fine. I could use the help. I'll be coming by your house about seven in the morning. If you are up and ready to go, I'll pick you up then." Mr. Janakowski wore a huge smile as he tousled Jeremiah's hair. What great fun they were going to have as they passed out the treats to their neighbors, especially the elderly ones. It was probably going to be a very long day. "Well, got to get this stuff back to keep it frozen. Then I'll be back for the dancing and the fireworks." He started his truck and drove off while Jeremiah went to look for his father. He had something important to talk to him about.

Mr. Bernhardt and Mr. Eckhardt got the sack race organized; and Abigail, Sarah, and Miriam were helping the children with the dunking for apples and the beanbag toss. Donations of little toys for prizes would have made the competition fierce, except the girls made sure that each little one that played received a prize, so all went away happy.

"Look, Abigail! Rolf and I won the sack race for our group! We each got a whistle for a prize!" Samuel was acting like a conqueror as he blew his whistle triumphantly. Abigail laughed as she threw an apple at him. It hit him in the chest, but he was able to capture it before it hit the ground. He smiled as he took a huge bite out of it, then scrambled as the juices squirted out and ran down his chin onto his shirt. They all laughed good-naturedly as Sarah threw him a towel to wipe up the mess.

The afternoon was wearing on at a leisurely pace when Mr. Huffmeister got up on the dance platform. "Attention, attention! It is time for the drawing for the ice cream churns! Did everyone put their name into the basket up here? Well, very good. Now I have chosen a special little helper who is going to reach into the basket and draw out the winning names. If you would please do the honors, Little Miss Ellie." Mr. Bernhardt had lifted his little girl up onto the platform. She tentatively smiled at Mr. Huffmeister, and then she reached her hand into the basket, retrieving a slip of paper. "Very good, Miss Ellie. Now can you get another one?"

After handing the banker the second piece of paper, the triumphant and smiling little girl was lifted into her father's arms. She was clutching a little doll that was her reward for a job well done.

Mr. Huffmeister raised his hand to get the crowd's attention. "And the winner of the first churn is Mrs. Anderson." The excited woman ran through the crowd, her voice trilling the entire way to the platform. When she reached it, she was slightly out of breath, her face was red from the exertions, and her hat had fallen askew and was now precariously perched sideways on her thick head of hair. "Um, here you are, dear lady. I hope that you and your family enjoy making ice cream often with this machine."

"Oh, tank you, Mr. Huffmeister. Ya, we will enjoy the ice cream very much. Tank you!" Mrs. Anderson said in her thick Swedish accent. Clutching the churn, she waved to the crowd with her free hand as she made her way back to her husband's side. A heckler raised his voice in the crowd.

"So, Mr. Huffmeister, you reward the family whose bull almost trampled your boy?"

Mr. Huffmeister looked into the crowd in surprise, and then he realized that it was just a good-natured jab. "Oh no, you have it all wrong, sir. I apologized to Mr. Anderson for my son and his friends. Why, they traumatized that poor beast. Here, he was just out frolicking, trying to get a little exercise when the boys jumped into his path and tried to run him down. Now you can't blame the beast if he just couldn't stop himself in time." The crowd let out a tremendous whoop of laughter.

"All right now, we have to get serious here as we have yet another winner to announce. The name of the second winner is Jimmy Ware. Come and get your prize, son."

Jimmy had been standing at the back of the crowd, and when his name was called, his jaw dropped. With a shocked expression on his face, he stumbled his way up to the platform. Folks had nudged him and patted him on the back, saying, "Go get your prize." Mr. Huffmeister handed him the churn with a big smile, and Jimmy grabbed his hand and began pumping it vigorously.

"Thank you, sir! Golly gee, I've never won anything before in my whole life." Jimmy was beaming as he took his prize. He held the churn up over his head as if it was a trophy, waving it back and forth. He turned back to Mr. Huffmeister, shaking his hand again. "Thanks again, sir! My mama had to go on back home, so I'm going to take this to her real quick like." He jumped off the platform and started running through the applauding crowd, whooping and yelling at them, "I won! I won! I won!"

When the crowd finally quieted down, Mr. Huffmeister said laughingly, "I believe that was one happy and excited young man." The crowd again roared with laughter, applauding loudly. Mr. Huffmeister raised his hands for quiet. "The remaining machines will be on display at the mercantile. We can attest to the fact that they are in good working order, and they are priced at a discount as they are considered used equipment. Let me also say that five of the churns have already been sold, so there are just five more left. So don't delay if you desire one of these fine ice cream churns as they are going fast.

"Now I do have one more announcement to make. We are going to start the dancing in about an hour's time. Plus we have a special treat lined up to entertain you. So I suggest that you get rested up so you will be prepared to enjoy tonight's musical performance."

The announcement caused no end of speculation as to just what the entertainment could be. There had been rumors of a surprise leading up to tonight, but the actual truth had not leaked out. With their curiosity totally piqued, the folks scattered to clean their picnic areas and then rest so they could be back in time for the dance to start.

There were also strangers in the crowd. Captain Jolly had been approaching the townsfolk, introducing a tall man in a cowboy suit and hat to them. The stranger was a Mr. King who hailed from Texas. It seems that the Texan and his entourage were traveling the length of the Mississippi River and had hired Captain Jolly and his tugboat for this portion of the trip. The townsfolk had shown the strangers their welcoming spirit by pooling their lunch provisions into a potluck and sharing it with the Texan and the people who were with him. Mr. King was amazed and touched at the town's friendliness and generosity.

The hours passed quickly, and then the folks gathered at the dance platform once again. Mr. Huffmeister was on the platform, along with Mr. Baer with his accordion and Mr. McDonald with his violin, when another man in a kilt and bagpipes came out from behind a small tent that had been erected to one side. He smiled and waved at the folks as he stepped up onto the platform and shook Mr. Huffmeister's hand.

"Ladies and gentlemen, could I have your attention please! I am proud to introduce to you Mr. McDougal. Though he recently joined us from New York City, he originally hails from Ireland, and, of course as many of you know, so did Mrs. Finney here." Mrs. Finney had stepped out of the tent, and she had joined the group on the platform. To the crowd's surprise and delight, she was dressed in traditional Irish costume. "They have consented to entertain us today with music and dance from their home country of Ireland. Please give them a rousing round of applause." He began to exuberantly clap his hands and was joined by the crowd.

"Thank you for your kind welcome. As Mr. Huffmeister said, I am Mr. McDougal, and this lovely creature is Mrs. Finney. I am going to play some traditional Irish melodies on my pipes, and Mrs. Finney is going to perform the dances that go with them."

The bagpipes first gave out a wailing sound, which became harmonious as Mr. McDougal blew air into the bag and his fingers flew over the pipe that resembled a flute. Mrs. Finney had struck a pose with her hands upraised; then her feet fairly flew as she began hopping and twirling in time to the music. The audience got caught up in the beat of the music, and they began clapping in time to its rhythm. When the music stopped, the two performers were met with enthusiastic applause and comments of "Wonderful! Beautiful! More, we want more!"

"Let me play a softer tune, and let Mrs. Finney rest for a wee bit. Then she will demonstrate yet another of our folk dances." With that, Mr. McDougal aired up the bagpipes and played a soft Irish melody. Mrs. Finney had sat to rest on the edge of the platform, and when the music began, she got a faraway look on her face.

A young red-haired lady who was with the group of Texans walked up to the platform. Mr. McDougal had finished with the plaintive song, and she tentatively approached him. "Could you please play that song once more, sir? I would like to sing along if I may?" As he played the tune again, her voice resonated as she sang it in the ancient Gaelic language. When she finished, the crowd again showed their approval as they clapped loudly. "Aye, if I had sang the song thusly in my own country, I would have been locked up. There, it is unlawful to speak in Gaelic."

Mr. McDougal put his hand softly on the woman's shoulder. "Aye, that is the truth. But we are in America now, and, thankfully, those laws do not apply here. We can be proud of our heritage and can practice it boldly. I am Mr. McDougal. And what is your name, lassie?"

"I am proud to meet you, sir. I am Bernadette Lawson, formerly Bernadette O'Brian of Dublin."

Just then Mr. McDonald stepped forward. "Since we have a songstress here, perhaps she would oblige us with another Irish song? Do ye ken 'Danny Boy'?"

The woman laughed gaily. "Of course, it is one of my favorites."

"And if you wouldn't mind, I would be honored if I could join her." Mrs. Finney had risen from her perch at the edge of the platform and stood next to the redhead. The woman smiled and nodded her head. "And if ye two lassies don't mind, I would like to add my baritone to the mix." Mr. McDougal offered to sing with the two ladies.

"Well, this is going to be the best yet for sure!" Mr. McDonald smiled and placed the violin beneath his chin. Lifting his bow, he drew it across the strings, releasing the notes of the song. The women began to sing in clear strong voices as Mr. McDougal's deeper tones added richness. The plaintive song carried out over the crowd. When the trio finished, the audience applauded wildly.

"Now do ye mind if I join ye in the dancing even though I am not in traditional dress?"

Mrs. Finney laughed and grabbed her hand. "Aye, my name is Maureen, and I would be pleased to have a fellow countryman join me."

Mr. McDougal and the ladies performed three more Irish songs and dances before they pleaded exhaustion. The ladies had danced with grace and beauty to the beautiful lilting melodies charming all who gazed on them. They were escorted to a picnic table off to one side and were served lemonade by grateful townsfolk. Bernadette's husband had come to her side, and they all became better acquainted.

In the meantime, Mr. McDonald began playing on his violin. His repertoire included some popular songs and dances, along with more traditional waltzes. The dance platform was filled with participants, and even some of the children were attempting the dance steps on the ground off to the side. It was proof that they had paid attention as they had watched the older children practice the dances for their graduation party in June.

As Mr. McDonald took a break, Mr. Baer stepped up with his accordion. Soon, the air was filled with rousing polka music, and the dancing was jubilant. The little ones' antics as they tried to keep up with the music caused many a mishap as feet and legs tangled, and the children ended in heaps on the ground amid gales of laughter.

After a short break, so everyone could take a well-deserved rest, Mr. McDonald stepped forward with his violin. "Our next dance will be a waltz, so please grab a partner."

Abigail, Sarah, and Miriam had all been chosen to dance at different times. They all brushed at their hair as it was a little mussed after the polkas. And though they had regained their breath, their faces were still rosy from their exertions.

Mr. Huffmeister stood up in front of the crowd. "All right folks, as it is growing dark, this will be the last dance. Then we need to take our positions at the lakefront so we can enjoy the fireworks. Pick your partner." He turned aside to Rolf and giving him a slight push as he whispered in his ear. "You need to ask Sarah to dance with you, son. Go on now before she gets away."

Sarah smiled coquettishly as she consented to dance with Rolf, and he made a show of being the attentive gentleman as they took their position on dance platform. The young couple dipped and twirled to the strains of the music, their performance captivating their neighbor's attention. Caught up in the music and the dance, they didn't realize that the others had stopped dancing and had made a circle around them. The two were surprised when the song finished, and all began applauding. Beaming proudly, Rolf bowed to his prettily blushing partner.

Then an explosion was heard, and the dark sky lit up with an eruption of brilliant colors. Voices in the crowd rang out with ohs and ahs as the folks hurried to the lakeshore to better see the dazzling light display.

Mr. Huffmeister had made sure that the elderly folks of the community had the chance to enjoy the celebration along with the fireworks. He had coordinated efforts with Mrs. Bernhardt, and together they had them supplied with transportation to the event. Those now in attendance along with Mrs. Himmel were her friends Mrs. Rogers and Mr. Marples. The elder Mrs. Bernhardt was also seated with them. Little Ellie had wandered over to the geriatric group, and she had crawled up into her grandmother's lap, clutching her doll.

With her thumb in her mouth, she said, "I'm scared of the loud noise."

Cradling and comforting her, Mrs. Bernhardt whispered in her ear, "After the loud noise is the beautiful display of lights, which is just the opposite of lightning and thunder. So when you hear the clap of noise, you must look for the beauty." Just then there was the thunderous sound of the burst. "Look, my dear, see how wonderful it is!"

Looking up, the child saw the burst of colorful light, and she sat in total enchantment, with her mouth making a perfect *O*. Then she let out a squeal of delight, clapping her little hands with vigor. The next time there was an explosion, rather than ducking her head, she searched the sky with anticipation. When the fireworks performed their magic and began popping and whirling, she laughed with abandoned glee.

Mrs. Roger's sat watching the child with a certain reflective look on her face. "Ah, to see the wonders of the world anew through the eyes of a babe. Now that I think of it, it is the same kind of astonishment that I had of the marvels of heaven. No wonder Jesus so loves the little children. They are so trusting and transparent. They have no guile in them."

The geriatric group drifted into companionable silence and enjoyed the spectral display.

16

Bull-Riding Day

Many people had ended up spending the night at the lakeside, and quite a few of the menfolk had been up before dawn, casting their lines in the lake. Most had gotten lucky, and their stringers boasted the fine walleyes known to be one of the best sport fish in the area.

The entire camp was abuzz with talk of the Texan. When he had heard about the bull chasing the boys, he had pulled Mr. Anderson aside and spent some time talking with him. All were wondering why he would be that interested in the bull. True, many of the local farmers had used the bull for stud service, and their cows had dropped good, hearty calves for beef stock. But the Texan seemed more concerned with the bull's temperament, which didn't seem to make much sense to them. The bull had a mean streak and was known to be territorial. He would run down anyone or anything that entered his pasture. Mr. King arranged with Mr. Anderson to see the bull the following morning, but for exactly what reason, no one knew. He had further piqued their interest when he made an announcement that anyone who cared to could come and observe just what cowboys in Texas did with a temperamental bull.

In any case, out of pure curiosity, the folks began making the trek to Mr. Anderson's farm. Some folks had loaded up in cars, and others just walked the half mile. It was a fine day, and by nine thirty, the fence of the pasture was lined with onlookers. The bull was not used to having so many folks so close to him, and he was trotting the perimeter, stopping periodically to toss his head with its wicked horns, ready to defend his territory if anyone chose to enter it.

There was a small pen built in one corner of the pasture that was next to the road. At ten o'clock straight up, a truck pulled next to it, and the Texan and six cowboys got out of it. As they pulled two barrels off the back of the truck, another cowboy rode up on a horse. Folks recognized that the horse was from a stable located next to the feedstore, but the saddle and tack were like nothing that they had ever seen before. The horse's bridle, reins, and saddle were decorated with medallions made of etched silver that were highly polished, so they glinted like mirrors in the sun. And all of the cowboys were dressed in western garb that included hats, boots, chaps, and wicked-looking spurs. The cowboys swarmed all over the pen, checking it for sturdiness and paying special attention to the hinges and the latch on the gate. It was critical that the hardware was sturdy enough to hold the bull when they penned him.

Mr. Anderson walked up to the Texan, sporting a huge smile, and the two men shook hands. "Seems that we have quite a crowd of onlookers here today. Well, that's good because a crowd is needed for a rodeo to be appreciated." The Texan was pleased at the interest that was shown by the town. "Do you think that we will have any trouble getting that bull into the pen? My boys have heard of this big guy's exploits and are anxious to give him a try. They want to see what he's got in him, to test his meddle as they say."

"Ya, Lars here will just shake dis here bucket of feed, and the bull he will go right in," Mr. Anderson said in his heavy Swedish accent.

With that, Lars took the bucket and began shaking it as he called out, "Come, bully."

The bull was distracted by the large crowd but finally succumbed to the smell of sweet grain emanating from the bucket. The cowboys used some lumber to make the pen somewhat smaller so that the bull could be secured in the enclosed area. The cowboy on the horse entered the pasture while two of the other cowboys brought in the wooden barrels, placing them a short distance apart.

"Look, they have put a heavy leather strap around the bull's middle. I guess they can't put a real saddle on it, but how are they going to stay on?" Samuel was rank with curiosity.

"Guess we are about to find out. That cowboy is getting down on the bull's back. Let's get closer so we can see better." The problem was that a lot of folks had the same idea, so they still ended up a good ways from the pen, but they did maneuver a spot right on the fence.

"Hey, that old bull just tried to jam the cowboy into the rails. He had to get back up, but he's lowering down again." The excitement in Samuel's voice was infectious, and everyone craned their necks toward the gate of the pen.

Suddenly, the gate flew open, and the bull exploded out of the pen. He was twisting and bucking wildly, and the cowboy was hanging on with one hand and had his other hand held high over his head in the air. One more twist, and the cowboy was flying through the air landing on the ground with a thud. The bull turned back toward the downed man, intent on grinding him into the ground when a brightly colored blanket was waved in his face. Shifting toward the offending blanket, he rushed to capture it on his horns. The cowboy who was waving it ran quickly toward one of the barrels, and just as the bull reached him, he dove head first into it.

"Will you look at that? That old bull doesn't know where the cowboy with the blanket got to! He looks just plain dumb!" Samuel was giddy with laughter as the bull was turning in a circle in confusion looking for his prey. "While the bull was chasing the blanket, the rider got up and is safe behind the fence. He's waving his hat to show us that he's not hurt."

The crowd was clapping in appreciation of the cowboy's bravery and skills. It seemed that just being tossed from the back of the critter could cause someone to be hurt, yet the cowboy was up and acted as if nothing had happened. The bull had been loaded into the pen once again, and another cowboy was preparing to ride it.

"All right, Shorty, let's see if you have any better luck than Slim staying on this beast." The Texan was watching the cowboy as he was lowering himself down on the bull's back. "If neither of you can stay on him, then I think we have a real rodeo bull for the circuit."

"All right, boss, I'm ready for my shot. You know that I'm a better rider than Slim, so if I can't ride him, no one can." The cowboy grinned to add punch to his bragging, and the Texan laughed and slapped him heartily on his back. Shorty gave the signal that he was ready, and the gate flew open. Once again, the bull exploded out of the pen. Shorty's ride didn't last any longer than Slim's had. He hit the ground hard and scrambled up running for the fence. The bull was faster this time. He had turned quickly and swung his huge head at the cowboy, just missing him with his vicious horns. The cowboy on the horse rushed up and grabbed Shorty, pulling him up behind him; and the cowboy with the blanket once again waved it in the bull's face, distracting him. This time, after he got to safety inside the barrel, he raised his hat and waved it at the crowd, showing that he too had again escaped from being gored by the bull. The crowd clapped and roared their approval.

"I've never seen anything like this before! Those cowboys sure do know how to work that old bull! I'm going to go and try to talk to one of them to find out how they learned how to do it." Jeremiah scooted off to get closer to the pen.

The bull was captured in the pen once more, and the Texan stood on the fence and waved his hat to get the crowd's attention. "That's all for the show today, folks, and now I want to invite all of you to go back to the lake. My boys and their gals have been cooking all night, and we would be pleased to share some real Texas-style food with you. I believe that we will have enough for all, and we will keep serving it up until it is gone. You have all been so welcoming, sharing your good food and good times with us that we want to give back." With that, he smiled and waved his hat again. Then he got down from the fence and approached Mr. Anderson.

Jeremiah had worked his way to the pen and had sidled up close to the cowboy named Shorty. All set to start his mile-a-minute questions, he was caught up short by Shorty leaning slightly to one side and a releasing a stream of tobacco juice into the dirt. He gazed in fascination at Shorty's face, which sported a large lump on one side of his jaw. All of this so surprised him that the questions he had planned to ask the cowboy just flew out of his head, and all he could do was stare.

Samuel suddenly appeared next to him. "Um, Mr. Shorty, can I ask you some questions?"

Laughing, the cowboy answered, "It's just Shorty. There's no mister about it, no, siree! Just ask away, and if I know the answer, I will spit it out."

"How did you learn how to ride bulls? Do you do it all of the time? You sure knew just what to do with that old bull so that you didn't get tromped on. We all have been scared silly of him, but you guys don't seem to be scared at all."

"Naw, I'm not scared of the brutes, but I do have respect for them. I've been working around beef stock all of my life, and these critters pretty much all think and act the same way. So you learn what makes them tick, and then you use what you have learned to keep from getting hurt by them. You learn how to trick and confuse them until you can get to safety. This guy is wilier than most that I have run in to, but he still fell for the tricks like flapping something in his face and hiding in a barrel. For a big guy, he runs pretty fast, and he also turns on a dime, so we just had to be smarter than him and faster too." All the time that Shorty was talking, he would pause for a moment and squirt out wads of tobacco juice. "Mr. King plans on taking this guy back to Texas and putting him on the rodeo circuit. Only a few bulls have ever been able to throw most riders, and there have been just two that tossed every one that tried to ride them. Me and Slim have been the top riders on the circuit for five years running, and for us getting thrown by this critter shows that he may be the next unrideable bull. He will be a big draw, and all of the bull riders everywhere will want a crack at him. Yup, and Mr. King will stand him at stud as well. Yes, siree, he could become famous in the rodeo circuit."

"For real and for sure?" Jeremiah finally found his voice.

"Yes, siree, partner, for real and for sure!" With that, he let out another healthy stream of spit. Just then, Mr. King called for the cowboys to stow the gear so they could get back to the feedstore. They had an entire steer and a pig that had been smoking in a pit overnight, and they should be finished cooking. They needed to get loaded up and head back to the lake for the picnic. With the incentive of a hearty meal to motivate them, they soon had the equipment loaded in the truck and left in a trail of dust.

As the young boys headed back to the lake, Lars Anderson fell in with them. "Guess what I get to do? Mr. King found out that I had raised the bull from a calf and that I had a way with him, that I could calm him. Well, he asked Da if I could go with and help take him down to his ranch in Texas. He's going to pay me wages plus pay my travel expenses. I've never been out of Minnesota before, and now I'm going to see the whole Mississippi, the ocean, and everything in between!"

The other boys' jaws dropped in amazement at the announcement. Any one of the boys would have jumped at the chance to have such an opportunity handed to them. "How long will you be gone?" Bobby asked with more than a bit of jealousy and longing in his voice. "Don't know for sure, but probably the rest of the summer and then some." Bobby clapped his friend on the back in congratulations, suddenly very happy for his friend. "Well, just don't get lost, because we want you back again, you know!"

The rest of the walk to the lake the conversation was filled with speculations of what all Lars would see and do on the trip and if he would be a cowboy with chaps and all when he got back home.

There was a flurry of activity centered around a group of picnic tables that had been set up under some shade trees by the lakeshore. Some local women were helping the Hispanic women arrange pans of food on the tables and exotic, spicy smells wafted through the air. The local women often lifted the covers of the pans to peer intently at the contents, curious to find out what these strange foods were made of and of course how they tasted. The Hispanic women were proud of their heritage and were glad to share their traditional foods with their newfound friends. The feedstore truck pulled up and was backed up next to one of the empty tables. There were two large washtubs inside that were filled with meat. One of the washtubs contained the beef, and the other one was full of pork. All the meat smelled wonderfully smoky from being cooked in the fire pits.

Finally, all of the food had been spread out and awaited to be served up onto plates. Mr. King and one of the cowboys got up into the back of the truck. The cowboy held up a metal triangle dangling from a chain. With his other hand, he took a metal bar and banged it against the inside of the triangle, and melodious notes rang out loudly.

"Come and get it, my friends!" Mr. King called out with a huge smile.

The local people lined up at the tables, and their plates were filled with exotic foods such as pork tamales, charo, and refried beans; Mexican rice; corn and flour tortillas; stuffed poblano peppers; enchiladas; and a mixture of onions, jalapeno, and tomatoes called Pico de gallo. The pork and beef had been shredded and was served up with a tangy barbeque sauce. The spices that had been used in the foods were strange to their pallets, things like chili powder, cumin, cilantro, and jalapeno and habanero peppers.

"Shorty told me that I will have to get used to the spicy food while I am traveling with them. I guess that a lot of things will be different. Umm, this corn bread has pieces of something green in it. Ow! I just ate a little piece of it, and it burned on my tongue! But it tastes good when you eat the whole bread. I think that I'm going to go over by Shorty and ask just what all of this stuff is." The cowboys had sat down as a group at one of the tables, and Jeremiah had squeezed in on a bench and was sitting in between Shorty and Slim.

Jeremiah had filled his plate with one each of everything and was busily tasting all of the strange foods. Shorty was helping Jeremiah to learn how to pronounce the names of the food and explained what was cooked into in each of them. As Jeremiah was consuming the food on his plate, he noticed that the cowboys were eating some small green peppers that were in baskets on the table. Copying what the cowboys were doing, he reached out and got a pepper. Then he took a bite of his tamale and a big bite of the pepper.

"Ow! Ahhh, ahhh, owie!" Jeremiah had jumped up from the bench, spit out the food, and yelled at the same time. Shorty, realizing what Jeremiah had done, broke out laughing and began pounding the boy of his back. "Here you go, Sonny. Drink up this water, and chew up this piece of bread. It will help to tame the burn. Yup, he sure enough tried one of the jalapenos." Shorty explained to the crowd. The cowboys nodded their heads and began laughing at the poor boy who was gulping water like he had just come out of the desert.

Jeremiah's eyes were running rivers of water, and his mouth felt like it was on fire. "I don't think that I ever want to eat one of those things again!"

"You need to build up to chowing on those peppers. We have been eating them all of our lives, so we are used to them," Slim said as he took a bite of his pepper. "In fact, those peppers are in most of the foods that we have right here. The ladies held back on using them, because they didn't want to make stuff too spicy for ya'll. We like our food to have a little more heat, so we eat peppers to give everything a little kick."

"Well, my mouth has finally cooled down. I like the rest of the food a whole lot, but am staying away from the peppers." Jeremiah was again cleaning his plate but was a little wary of anything that had bits of green in it.

"Here, have you a piece of this here cake. It's a Mexican cake that we have for nearly every occasion. Um, um, good for sure!" Shorty was holding out a plate to Jeremiah that had a hefty piece of white cake on it.

"Is this the tray leeches cake?" Jeremiah asked with trepidation. He slowly took a small bit of it on the fork and put it in his mouth. Thinking about leeches from the lake that were probably used to make the cake made the morsel turn to sawdust in his mouth.

"Yup, and its pronounced *tres leches*, which is Spanish for *three milks*. So it is cake that is topped with three different kinds of milk and frosted with whip cream, so it is really moist." Shorty, Slim, and the others were steadily shoving forkfuls of the cake into their mouths.

"Tray leeches means three milks?" Jeremiah's puzzled look was followed with a heavy sigh of relief. He took a huge bite of the cake, and a smile lit up his face. "Wow, this is really good."

It was Shorty's turn to look puzzled. "What did you think that *tres leches* meant, Sonny?"

"Well, it seems so silly now," Jeremiah said with chagrin. "I just thought, well, we use leeches for fish bait, and well, with all of the other strange foods that you have here . . ." Jeremiah fumbled for words. "Well, I thought that there were trays of leeches in the cake." The words came tumbling out in a rush, and Jeremiah's face was red with embarrassment.

Shorty and the rest of the cowboys burst out in a roar of laughter and began slapping each other on their backs. They were laughing so hard that they held their stomachs as if they thought that they would burst.

When Shorty finally quit laughing enough that he could talk, he said, "Well, we do think that we are pretty tough hombres here for sure, but we aren't so tough that we would eat leeches. But you were willing to eat that cake anyways even when you thought there were leeches in it?" Shorty was shaking his head in puzzlement, thinking that this was one really tough kid.

Jeremiah smiled; then he laughed at himself, along with the rest of the men. Totally relieved, he began shoving the now delicious cake into his mouth, cleaning his plate. "Here you go, Sonny. You need some more leeches if you are going to keep pace with us tough hombres!" Shorty shoved another plate with cake at him, and Jeremiah offered up a huge grin as he took it.

Samuel, Randy, and Bobby came walking up to the group; and they laughed uproariously when they were let in on the joke.

"Now this tough leech-eating hombre is going to have to be the first one to ride the bucking bronco." Shorty was pointing at a barrel that had four large springs attached to it and then was tied up between four trees. A saddle had been strapped to it, and the ground beneath it had a pile of hay that was at least three feet deep.

Jeremiah's eyes grew round as he looked at what Shorty was pointing to. "You want me to ride the barrel? I know how to ride a horse, but I'm not sure I can ride something like that." The group had walked over to barrel, and Jeremiah was viewing the contraption with trepidation.

"Well, Sonny, riding this bronco is going to be different than riding a stable hack. Here, let's give you a boost up into the saddle." Shorty offered his cupped hands, and he lifted Jeremiah up until he was seated firmly in the saddle; then he secured the boys' feet in the stirrups. "Now, you need to hang onto the saddle with one hand and hold your other hand up over your head just like we did this morning with the bull." Shorty took off his hat and handed it to Jeremiah. "Hold on to my hat. It will give you balance. Now hold on tight while we work the ropes. You are about to have the ride of your life."

With that, Shorty and three other cowboys each took ahold of one of the four ropes. "We are going to start slow so you can get the feel of it. This is as close to riding a real bronco that you can have without actually being on a horse. Hang on tight, Sonny. Easy now, boys." Shorty and the cowboys began to gently pull on the ropes, making the barrel swing and jerk.

"Whoa!" Jeremiah called out as he was tossed to and fro. "There you go, Sonny. Raise your hand up and down. Turn and balance. Good! You've got the hang of it. Let's take it up a notch." The cowboys began pulling the ropes a little harder and faster. To his credit, Jeremiah was holding on while he was being jerked and bounced. Suddenly, his body was twisted and tossed, and he flew out of the saddle. The pile of hay broke his fall, giving him a soft landing.

"Wow!" Jeremiah said as he shook his head to clear it. Shorty lifted him up and was looking him over. "Seems that nothing is broken. Are you all right, Sonny?"

"I'm not hurt. Just a little dizzy is all. Did I do good?"

"Yup, you had a fine ride," Shorty said with pride. He picked up his hat, dusted it off, and stuck it on his head again.

The demonstration had drawn a crowd, and others were asking if they could also have a turn. The cowboys were busy for a couple of hours, giving rides to any and all who wished to have a turn at the bucking bronco. Not only the children, but even some of the local men gave the ride a try. It gave them a deeper understanding and a new respect for the cowboys and the tough job that they had.

As the day was finally coming to an end, the cowboys brought out a fiddle, their guitars, and the prairie musical staple, a harmonica. They started out playing and singing traditional mariachi music. The Hispanic women had changed into brightly colored dresses, and as they performed their traditional dances, they enhanced the beat of the music with canastas that they wore on their fingers. The crowd was charmed, and some of the local women and girls tried the dance steps that the Hispanic women made look so effortless. Then the cowboys changed the tempo and began singing cowboy ballads. The night was filled with the songs of the prairie and life on the range. Songs such as "The Yellow Rose of Texas," "Buffalo Gals," "Bury Me Not on the Lone Prairie," and "Clementine." The day ended on their plaintive musical notes.

17

The County Fair

Jeremiah and his father had been up since before dawn as they had promised to help Mr. Boggs with loading a pumpkin into his truck. Jeremiah had been puzzled as to why anyone would need help loading a pumpkin until he had seen it for himself. It was a monster!

"How much do you think that it weighs?" Jeremiah said as he watched his father and Mr. Boggs wrapping straps around the huge squash.

"Not sure, Sonny, but I can't wait to see the look on Mr. Graf's face when he lays eyes on it," Mr. Boggs said with a chuckle. "He has been trying for years to find out what I use on my garden to make the vegetables grow. I have had many a laugh when he has grilled me, trying to trip me up and reveal my secrets."

"All right, it's time to hoist it up. Then we will back the truck up and put it down on the pallet. I'll work the hoist as you two keep it steady." Father and Jeremiah were ready to work the chain. The pumpkin rose slowly, and then Mr. Boggs carefully backed up the truck squarely, positioning a pallet beneath the gourd. The pumpkin was carefully lowered, and Father and Mr. Boggs used straps to secure it to the pallet so it wouldn't shift as it was transported.

"Very good! Thank you so much for your help. This is much better than last year when I tried to use a come-along to load that one. That proved to be a total disaster. All right, let's go and get this registered." Dropping the car off at the house for Mother to use,

Father got into the truck, and the three began the slow ride to the fairgrounds.

Abigail had just finished up her chores, and when she entered the kitchen, she found her mother cleaning up. Abigail noticed that her mother's face was somewhat flushed, and she was distractedly muttering to herself. She was a little puzzled as she had not seen her mother in such a state before.

"Abigail"—she turned with a start—"your oatmeal and toast is there on the table. Did you check the gate to the chicken pen to make sure it is secure? I don't want to have to chase the beasts when we return this evening."

"Yes, Mother, the gate is secure." Abigail gave her mother a hug; then she sat down and hurriedly ate her meal. She brought the dishes to the sink, and as her mother washed them, she dried them and stored them away.

"Well, I guess it is time that we head out now." Mother nervously hung up her apron and put her hat on. She then picked up a bundle from the sideboard and caressed it, lightly smoothing the material. She called out to her mother-in-law. "Mother, we are loaded up and are ready to go." Then she turned back to Abigail. "Oh, I do hope that Mrs. Himmel is at the judge's booth to check me in. She was the main person that encouraged me to make this quilt, and I do want her to be pleased with my efforts."

"Here I am, my dear. Sorry to cause a delay, but I couldn't find my glasses. But now they are safely tucked into my purse." The elderly woman made her apologies and headed out the door to the car.

Abigail had only had glances of the quilt and had seen other bits and pieces as Mother had worked on the appliques in the evenings. Mother had even done all of the hand quilting by herself using a frame that she had set up in the spare room. In order to keep it a complete surprise and also to keep it clean, she had kept the quilt covered so that no one could peek. Finally, she had also sworn the family to total secrecy about it. Abigail was not to even speak about it to their quilting bee friends. All of this secrecy had kept Abigail's curiosity piqued, but she had honored her mother's wishes.

"We will stop and get Sarah first, and then we'll pick up Miriam. Here, I want to give you this. It is a little something for you to do whatever you want to with. Yes, I know that you have money of your own from your soapmaking, and I am so very proud of you for that. But you have been such a tremendous help doing extra chores this last year while I worked on this quilt that I want to treat you." With that, she gave Abigail a smile and a hug. "Would you please get that basket over there? I have some sandwiches packed in it, though I am sure that we will all be feasting on funnel cakes and buttered popcorn too. After all, those treats are a fair tradition."

"Thank you, Mother, and if it's all right with you, I would like to share this with Sarah and Miriam. I'm sure that there will be something special that will catch our eye, and now we will be able to buy it. But, frankly, I am dying of curiosity to see the quilt."

"Well, we must not waste another moment then. Come." They both wore huge smiles on their faces as they joined Grandmother in the car.

At the fairgrounds, Mr. Boggs pulled his truck up next to the last display booth and parked it. As the three got out of the truck, Mr. Boggs took a moment to check that the tarp was still secure, hiding the secret within. As all was well, Mr. Boggs retrieved his basket of vegetables, and the trio ambled over to the check-in booth. Mr. Graf took his position as an official very seriously, and he was sitting there, appearing much like a real judge holding court. Other folks who had arrived earlier and had registered were busy displaying their vegetable contributions in their assigned spaces. Mr. Boggs and Mr. Eckhardt greeted their friends with smiles and waves as they traversed to the judge's booth.

"Good morning to you, Mr. Graf. I see that you have already been busy checking in the contestants. I'm running a little late today as I had a task that I required help with. Mr. Eckhardt and Jeremiah were good enough to assist me this morning," Mr. Boggs explained with a smile.

"Good morning! I see that you have a basket of vegetables there, and I assume that you want to register them. We can certainly do that and get you set up with a booth. Is this all that you have this year?"

Mr. Boggs had an impressive number of entries in the basket, but Mr. Graf felt that he was holding back.

"I do have a bit more, but it's back in the truck."

"Well, carry it on up here, and we can fix you right up."

"There is a slight problem with doing that. Walk on down to the truck with us. It's right here at the end of the stalls."

Mr. Graf gave Mr. Boggs a speculative look, and it appeared as though he was going to argue. Finally, he just bobbed his head. "All right, let's go have a look-see."

They got to the end of the stalls, and Mr. Eckhardt and Jeremiah jumped up onto the back of the truck and began untying some ropes, loosening the tarp.

"All right, Boggs, just what did you drag me down here for?"

Mr. Boggs just pointed up at the bed of the truck. Mr. Graf's face held a smirk until he shifted his eyes and spied what had been covered by the tarp. His mouth turned into a perfect *O*, and he let loose a whoosh of breath. "Well, I'll be jiggered! That is the biggest pumpkin that I have ever laid eyes on!"

"Yup, it's a big one, all right. But I think the one I had last year was even bigger. It's a shame that I never got it here for the judging, though. It got busted up when I tried to load it up with a come-along. Yup, when it fell off that ramp and broke, it clinched my gizzard for about a half an hour or so. Then I prayed and asked the good Lord what was to be done. I ended up giving that pumpkin away to Mrs. Himmel and Mrs. Ware. They were pleased as punch to get it too. After they cooked it on down, both of them told me that they put up enough jars of pumpkin to make pies for an entire year. To show their appreciation, they were kind enough to grace me with a bit of it baked into pumpkin pie too. Though things did come to a good end, I decided to enlist help loading this one up this year." Mr. Boggs chuckled as he explained.

Mr. Graf was in deep thought, stroking his chin. "This is the largest pumpkin we have ever had entered here, and I'm pretty sure that it will take the blue ribbon hands down. Could we just cover it back up for now? I have an idea, but I need to talk to the other officials about it. Can you come back right after lunch? And in the meantime, you can go ahead and take this last booth here and set up your display of the other things that you brought."

"All right, I'll get it all set up, and then we wanted to take a gander at the livestock exhibits. We'll be back right after lunch like you said," Mr. Boggs said in agreement.

Mother parked the car under a tree where it would be shaded. As they planned to eat lunch together later, they left the picnic basket on the backseat. Entering the fairgrounds, all the trio was carrying was the quilt.

"Oh, I'm so nervous. Mrs. Crawley's quilts are always exquisite. She has taken the blue ribbon for the last five years, so I don't think that I have a prayer of winning that. But, hopefully, it will at least place." Mother was nervously smoothing her skirt and touching her hat. The tent set aside for the homemaking exhibits was just ahead. "Well, here goes nothing."

As they stepped through the door, they spied Mrs. Himmel sitting at the judge's table. She saw them too and beckoned them over. "Oh, thank goodness," Mother said under her breath.

"Good morning, ladies. I have been waiting for you. I can't wait to see your contribution to this exhibit. Mrs. Crawley registered her quilt about fifteen minutes ago, and as usual, it is a fine piece of work. She did a most-difficult pattern, the five-pointed star, and every stitch is absolutely perfect. But, my dear, I have an inkling from the few things that you shared with me this past year, that your quilt is going to be most exciting. Are you ready to submit it for our viewing pleasure now?" Her eyes were twinkling merrily in anticipation.

Mother took a deep breath and let it out. "Well, it's now or never, and I have worked too hard for it to be never. Besides, I have put so much of myself into this quilt that I feel as though I am sharing a part of my life. Even if it doesn't win a ribbon, it has already won my heart." Then she smiled as she unwrapped her package.

As she began unfolding it, Abigail took the bottom edge and gently straightened it down the table as Mother held the opposite edge and Mrs. Himmel supported it on one side. The picture that emerged caused Abigail's breath to catch in her throat. It was their front gate with the trellis and all of the flowers in the garden. Each flower looked so real it was as if you could cut them from their stems and make a fresh bouquet. There were the climbing roses that grew up the sides of the trellis and spilled over it. And there were the hollyhocks that grew tall enough to peek over the fence. Closer to the ground were the snapdragons, lily of the valley, and Mother's personal favorite, her lady's slippers. Each flower and leaf was appliqued, and the petals of the flowers had been slightly stuffed, so they were three-dimensional. The sky area was of a light-blue material, and the quilting lines replicated a soft breeze blowing across. Mother had also made pillow shams that appeared to be soft clouds. Added to the beauty of the flowers was the charm of the small animals and insects that inhabited the garden. There was a fat bumblebee that was hanging from the blade of a lady's slipper. A butterfly was fluttering over a hollyhock blossom. And there was a red ladybug crawling up the stem of a rose as it was being watch by a blue jay that had alighted on the trellis. And, lastly, there was a rabbit that was peeking out through the leaves near the gate. Details such as eyes, noses, feathers, and even dewdrops had been added by the use of embroidery.

"Oh, Mrs. Eckhardt, this is exquisite! All of the flowers look so real it is as if you can smell them. I have never seen anything so beautiful. Your hand stitching is perfect, and the way you used stuffing makes the flowers seem so real. I see that you followed my idea of fading some colors and dying them darker in other areas of the material to add dimension. I am amazed at the detail that you used in fashioning this quilt. I'm also glad that I am not on the judging committee, as then no one can say that our friendship swayed the vote in your favor. I believe that you are going to get that blue ribbon, and it is going to be on your own merit."

"Oh my, I'm not sure about the ribbon, but I do thank you for your praise and support. This quilt is destined for Abigail's hope chest." Mother smiled as she squeezed Abigail's arm.

"Oh, Mother, really? You're giving the quilt to me?" Abigail's eyes filled with unshed tears as she looked into her mother's face. "It's so beautiful, and you've worked so hard on it. Are you sure that you don't want to keep it for yourself?"

Mrs. Eckhardt reached up and gently cupped Abigail's face. "For a time now, I have wanted to make you something special for your hope chest, something that was unique to your childhood memories. You are growing up and will be marrying and perhaps even leaving someday. I hope that this quilt will remind you of your roots and those who loved you first."

The two stood for some moments just smiling and looking into one another's faces. Mrs. Himmel was touched by the love and affection that the mother and daughter displayed, and she was honored to have witnessed it.

Mr. Boggs and his two friends found themselves in the livestock exhibit.

"Hey, there's Mr. Larson's calf." Jeremiah stuck out his hand to it, and the little calf gave it a good licking. Jeremiah giggled at its antics. "It's a Guernsey, isn't it? She's a real looker, isn't she?"

They wandered from the bovine area, ending up by the chicken pens. Someone had set up an incubator, and a couple of the eggs in it showed evidence that a few of the chicks had been diligently working to escape from their shells. "Look, there are a couple of shells that are cracked. Yup, those little ones will be out scratching for feed in a couple of hours." Mr. Boggs observed.

The next few cages held some very strange-looking fowl. "Look! Those chickens are wearing hats! It almost looks like Easter Sunday at church. And those look like they are wearing fluffy skirts." Jeremiah let out a giggle at the comparison, and Mr. Boggs and Father laughed right along with him.

"Yes, son, Mrs. Anderson has started raising some very different breeds of birds since Mr. Anderson sold off the bull. In fact, Lars brought a special gift for his parents from Texas, and it inspired Mrs. Anderson to breed other exotic birds too."

Suddenly, the air was split by a loud shrill call, almost like a scream.

"What was that?" Jeremiah was looking wildly around the exhibit area. "It sounded like it came from the other end of the building." Jeremiah took off running while Mr. Boggs and Father followed at a more leisurely pace. At the farthest end of the building just outside the door was a large pen that was fully covered with wire to keep its occupants from flying away. Inside the cage was a type of bird that Jeremiah had only seen in books.

"Father, is that a peacock? It's just beautiful! Just look at how long its tail is! Look! It's opening up! Wow! Look at that!"

"Yes, Jeremiah, that's a peacock, all right. Lars Anderson brought them back from Texas for his parents. Actually, they were a gift to the Andersons from Mr. King. That male is truly magnificent. The brown mousy-colored ones over there are the females. I hear that they have not bred yet, but the Andersons have high hopes. I understand that the birds are tasty when they are roasted up, and there is a big market back east for the feathers. Many ladies use them to decorate their hats." Mr. Bernhardt had learned quite a bit about the birds from Lars. Lars had learned what he could about the birds from the breeder in Texas because he wanted his mother to be successful at breeding and raising them too.

"Hum, I may have to take a hand at raising them myself. I have a friend who may take a fancy to those feathers. It would take a good while to raise them, so I may have to just buy some of the feathers first." Mr. Boggs was stroking his chin as he watched the male strut around in his full glory. He pictured his friend the chief when he presented him with some of the fine feathers.

It was noontime, and Mr. Bernhardt went to the car to fetch the basket of sandwiches. The family, along with Mr. Boggs, had secured a picnic table in the shade of a tree to sit at while they ate. The girls had visited the stand that sold funnel cakes, and they had bought enough to make a fine dessert for everyone.

Everyone ate and shared their stories of the morning, of all the new and strange things that they had seen and of the neighbors that they had greeted.

"So, Mother, did you get your quilt registered?" Father asked with a soft smile.

"Yes, I did. Mrs. Himmel was very forthcoming with her praise, but then I expected it from her."

"But, Mother, she was not the only one complimenting your quilt. I was standing a bit away from it admiring another quilt, but it was your quilt that they were talking about the most. I even over-heard them talking that it should be awarded the blue ribbon."

"Well, ah, it is up to the judges and not the general public to determine the winning quilt, though I do have to admit that I would be very gratified if it did take the blue ribbon. And it also makes me glad that others think so highly of my quilt. I have seen the other quilts, and they too show very fine workmanship. I am pleased to wait on the judges to make the final decision." A small contented smile played on Mother's lips.

After the picnic basket had been stowed in the car, once again the group scattered. The ladies all went to view the housekeeping exhibits, and the menfolk went to find Mr. Graf. When they got to the judges' booth, members of the judging committee were waiting for Mr. Boggs.

"Mr. Boggs, would you please show us this enormous pump-kin of yours? We have to admit that you certainly have piqued our curiosity." Mr. Huffmeister and Mr. Heimlich were both anxious to see the pumpkin, not quite believing it could really be as large as Mr. Graf had portrayed it.

"Follow me, gentleman." Mr. Boggs stepped out and began walking toward his truck. "I assure you that Mr. Graf has not exag-gerated in the least." As the party reached the truck, Mr. Eckhardt and Jeremiah again jumped up onto the back of it and peeled back the tarp, exposing the pumpkin.

"Oh my!" Mr. Huffmeister exclaimed. "It certainly is a huge pumpkin! How did you ever grow such a monster? It is magnificent!"

"I can't give away my secrets of gardening, but I do have a con-fession to make." He paused for a dramatic effect. "I cannot register it for competition. I confess that it is not a pure pumpkin. It has been crossbred with other squash and gourds for it to grow to this size."

"Well, that certainly puts another light on things. Thank you for being so honest and forthcoming. It does make things fair for the other competitors. Mr. Graf had suggested an idea that now I think applies even better to this situation. Let me present it to you, and you can decide if it will work for you."

"Shoot!" Mr. Boggs was burning up about what idea that Mr. Graf could come up with.

"We are thinking about having a contest 'Guess the weight of the pumpkin'! We can sell chances, and the one who guesses the closest to the actual weight wins the pot. The guesses will be posted, and on the last afternoon of the fair, we will take the pumpkin to the feedstore to weigh it on the scale and announce the winner. What do you think of the idea?"

"Hum, I think that it's a grand idea. Let's get it rolling!" Mr. Boggs was more than happy with the contest idea. He even offered to work in the judges' booth to sell and document the chances. It was a good way to show off his pumpkin and yet still be fair to the other competitors who were also his friends and neighbors.

The fair continued on for the rest of the week, and on the last day, the pumpkin was being taken to the feedstore for the weigh-in. It seemed that the entire town was in the procession that was following the pumpkin through town effectively making an impromptu parade. Chances had been sold for a quarter a piece, and the pot had grown to an unprecedented thirty dollars. The weight was to be calculated to the pound and ounces, and the excitement was high.

The truck pulled up to the scales, and there were plenty of hands to help move it from the truck and onto the scales. The face of the scale was covered, and the weight was not to be revealed until the judges had the posting board displayed for all to see.

"Are we ready, gentlemen? All right, Mr. Boggs, you have the honor of uncovering the scale." It was as if the entire crowd was holding its breath. Mr. Boggs reached up and pulled the cloth from the scale. "And the winner is, two hundred ten pounds and four ounces. That ticket was sold to Tucker Ware! Come on up here, Tucker, and get your prize!" Mr. Huffmeister called out.

Little Tucker was so excited that while he was running up to the scale he tripped and almost fell flat on his face. He was caught by the patrons in the crowd before he smashed into the ground. "Lookee here, you could light a torch from the brilliant smile on this young man's face! Congratulations, young man." Mr. Huffmeister thumped the boy roundly on his shoulders, almost knocking him down while he handed him his money prize.

The day and the fair came to an end. Mr. Boggs left with his enormous pumpkin planning to cut it up and make deliveries of it to some of the fine ladies the next day. The Eckhardts had loaded up into their car, worn out from all of the excitement and festivities. Mrs. Eckhardt sat in the front seat. She held the quilt on her lap with the blue ribbon clutched securely in her other hand. She smiled contentedly at her family.

18

Gone Fishing

It was turning out to be a special summer for Jeremiah. He was going fishing again, and he was up and ready for Mr. Boggs when he arrived. They loaded up the fishing poles and, this time, the camping gear too and pulled out onto the road.

"I could hardly wait for the sun to come up because I was so excited to go fishing again. And we will be camping overnight too. Do you think that we will make a good haul? Will the eagles still be there?"

Jeremiah was almost bouncing as Mr. Boggs calmly steered the aging truck and puffed on his pipe. He just gave Jeremiah his non-committal "Hum."

The day before when Samuel had heard about the fishing trip, he had started questioning Jeremiah about just what was under that tarp in Mr. Boggs's truck. Jeremiah had proven to his father that he could keep Mr. Boggs's secret. He answered his brother, "Oh, it's just some fishing gear and stuff that he doesn't want to get wet." Then he muddled the situation by doing his mile-a-minute dialogue. "Why, we caught so many fish last time that we shared them with Mrs. Himmel and Mr. Marples. And I saw a huge eagle with a fish in its talons. And then there was a beaver in the lake, and we saw some trees that it had gnawed on." By the time he slowed down, Samuel had totally forgotten that he had asked a question and that Jeremiah had not answered it. As Jeremiah gave out a big sigh of relief, he felt a hand on his shoulder. He turned and looked up into his father's face. He was smiling, and he gave Jeremiah's shoulder a big squeeze. Jeremiah smiled back, and without a word, they both turned back to their chore of weeding the garden.

Jeremiah spent a good portion of his time once again lying on the seat and gazing up at the clouds. This time, Mr. Boggs joined him in the game, and together they saw many amazing things. Mr. Boggs surprised Jeremiah when he pointed out the fire-breathing dragon. A dragon was a new concept to the boy. "I've never seen even a picture of a dragon before. How big are they? Are they fierce?" Mr. Boggs promised to borrow him a book that he had about dragons but only if Jeremiah's father approved. Jeremiah made a mental note to ask his father's permission the very first thing when they returned home from fishing.

By midmorning, they had reached the lakeshore. The two worked together to unload the truck; then Jeremiah went to gather firewood. Meanwhile, Mr. Boggs took a chain and attached it to a bar at the rear of the truck. He then used it to pull several large logs to the fire pit area. "These are going to make some fine seating for us. Make sure you get a good pile of wood, so we will have plenty. We will want the fire to burn all night to keep the chill off." When the camping preparations were finished, they grabbed their fishing poles and settled in to fish for a couple of hours.

Jeremiah had shot some inquiring looks at Mr. Boggs. He seemed to have some kind of a secret and was acting kind of mysterious. Well, Jeremiah would just have to wait and see how things played out. There was a good breeze that caused small white caps on the lake. This had the walleyes biting, and they had pretty well filled up one line with the fine fish already. They had each eaten a sandwich at noon, washing it down with the lemonade that Mrs. Eckhardt had sent. And some of the sugar cookies had been consumed in between baiting the hooks and adding another fresh catch on the stringer. Jeremiah's stomach let out a decidedly loud rumble, causing him to giggle.

"I think that it is high time to stop and prepare us some supper. I'm ready to get some of those fish we caught to roasting on some sticks and consume those delicious victuals that your mother packed in the basket. What do you think, Jeremiah?" Mr. Boggs said with a twinkle in his eye. "Could you make a trip to the spring and fill the water jugs for us first?"

"Oh, yes, sir! It won't take me no time at all to fetch us some water. I'm ready for some of that apple pie that Mother packed. We can have the biscuits and jam for breakfast with the bacon and eggs. Then there are some cherry turnovers to have on the way home, too. Mother thought of everything!" Jeremiah's stomach let out another loud rumble in anticipation. Laughing aloud, he grabbed both water jugs and sprinted off toward the spring.

When he reached the spring, he rinsed his hands well; then he cupped them and filled them with the fresh cool water and slaked his thirst. He then began filling the first jug. The day was beautiful, and the breeze from the lake felt wonderfully cool. He got the first jug filled and prepared to do the same with the second one when he looked back toward the camp. He saw that another vehicle was there and that Mr. Boggs was talking to someone. It was too far for him to make out who it was, so as soon as the jugs were full, he hefted both of them and made for the camp. As he got closer, he recognized that the other person was Mr. McDougal. The Fourth of July celebration had been a huge success where Jeremiah had first seen Mr. McDougal and his bagpipes.

Mr. McDougal had come to America from Ireland about a year ago. He had landed first in New York City, and it was there that he had met and made friends with Mr. Finney, Bobby's father. Five years earlier, Mr. Finney had left his wife and son in Minnesota and had traveled back to New York City, planning on using his skills as a boxer to earn money. His dream was to get enough money to buy a farm, but it had taken much longer than he thought it would. The fight one fateful night featured a boxer who had won every fight that he had been in, so the betting was fierce. A substantial prize was offered to any fighter who could best him, and Mr. Finney was sure that he was the man to do it. By adding that prize money to what he already had, he would finally have enough to pay down on the farm of his dreams. Early in the bout, Finney had taken a rough beating, but in the end, he managed to land an uppercut that had laid his opponent out cold. He and his friend Mr. McDougal had planned to meet up at a local bar to celebrate his victory, but McDougal had not shown. Finney celebrated anyway, bragging about the fight and the prize he had won. After he had more than a couple of drinks, he left the bar to go to his boardinghouse. A band of ruffians followed him and overtook him as he was entering his room. The group fell on him, beating him severely. They not only took the prize money, but they also found his hidden stash. In a last desperate attempt to hold onto the money, he rushed one of the men, knocking him down. That was when another of the men turned on him and bashed him in the head with a length of wood.

Mr. McDougal had finally made it to the bar, and then he went out looking for his friend. When he found Finney in his room, the man was barely hanging onto life. With his last breath, Finney asked McDougal to go to Minnesota, to Bobby and his mother, and tell them that he was sorry, that he had tried and almost made it. He had another goodly sum of money along with his father's watch that he had hidden away separately that the ruffians had not found, and it was all that he had to leave to them. Honoring his friend's last request, Mr. McDougal sent the money to the widow through a bank; then he traveled by train to Minnesota to tell them the final words of Mr. Finney and to deliver the watch to them. After fulfilling his duty to his friend, he decided not to return to New York but to stay in Minnesota.

When Jeremiah got near the camp, Mr. McDougal gave him a wave in greeting. "Well, hello there, Jeremiah. And aren't you lads just enjoying a fine day of fishing. Do ye mind if I be joining you? Mr. Boggs says that the fish are fighting with each other to get at the worms on your hooks. Here, let me help you with those jugs, me fine young lads."

Jeremiah smiled at Mr. McDougal's Irish brogue and the two put the water jugs in the bed of the truck. "We were going to have our supper soon. We're going to get some of the fish roasting and Mother sent some good things to eat, too. We have plenty."

"Aye and I have brought a bit to add to the bounty. Mr. Boggs and I have planned a little surprise for ye a wee bit later. For now I was hoping that we would have time for a quick dip in this lovely little lake. I do enjoy the clear water to wash the days dust off."

"Hum, I agree. As you can see, I believe that a little swim before supper is a good idea. Get your trunks on, my boy, and we'll see if we can out swim those fish." Mr. Boggs had already donned his trunks and was pulling some towels from a box in the truck.

It didn't take long for Jeremiah to get changed, and he yelled joyously as he charged for the lake. "Whoopee!" He ran into the water, and when it was deep enough, he dove beneath the surface. He bobbed up a few yards from where he had disappeared waving and laughing.

"Aye, you had better be careful, me laddie, or I will mistake you for a fish and hook you!" Mr. McDougal and Mr. Boggs were both laughing as they enjoyed the antics of the boy. The two older men got caught up in his exuberance and hurried to join him in the cool water. Jeremiah dove once again to see if he could reach the bottom of the lake. The water was so clear that it seemed that it was only a few feet deep, but in diving, he realized that it was much deeper. He saw a movement out of the corner of his eye, and turning, he saw that it was a very large fish. And it looked like it had something in its mouth. Jeremiah raced to the surface and came out sputtering, "Mr. Boggs, Mr. Boggs! I was diving down to the bottom of the lake, and I think that I saw that big fish of yours. I think it had a hook in its mouth and everything!" Jeremiah was very excited.

Mr. Boggs let out a good laugh. "Well, son, it could be that you did see him. If no one has hooked him yet, then he could still be in the lake."

"We will have to delay fishing for a bit here. We should have some company joining us soon. Aye, there they are now and just in time for supper too. Up there, take a look up at the escarpment." Mr. McDougal was gesturing toward the end of the lake.

"Indians! Those are Indians up there!" Jeremiah's jaw had dropped, leaving his mouth hanging wide open. "I wonder what they want."

"Why, those are the Chippewa Indians that I invited to join us. I believe that there are plenty of fish, and I'm sure that they have brought more things to eat. Aye, they are a friendly and curious bunch. I am hoping to go back to their village and learn some more about them," Mr. McDougal stated.

"I have been blessed to be a friend of the chief for many years. Frankly, the Indians were residents here for a very long time before we showed up and started to settle this land. Yup, Jeremiah, your father is a friend of the chief also. In fact, he asked me to deliver a gift to the chief, and he wants you present it to him." Mr. Boggs chuckled at the surprised look on Jeremiah's face.

The swimmers had gotten out of the lake and dried themselves by the time the Indian party arrived. The chief warmly greeted his old-time friend Mr. Boggs. He then greeted Mr. McDougal and Jeremiah. Everyone walked to the fire and sat down on the logs that Mr. Boggs had placed there. Three other male Indians joined them, stretching out on the ground close to the chief. The three female Indians in the group had taken a stringer of the fish and cleaned them and threaded them on sticks, putting them over the fire to roast. Then they began preparing other foods that they had brought with them. Soon the feast was ready. Mr. McDougal had stopped at the town bakery and had brought bread and cookies and added them to the spread.

After they all had eaten their fill, the women cleaned up the camp while the men all chose a place to relax around the campfire. Mr. Boggs had gone to his truck and brought back a package and placed it by his feet. When the group had fully settled, he spoke softly to the chief and gestured to Jeremiah, motioning him to come forward. He then placed the package in the boy's hands and urged him toward the elderly Indian.

The chief looked very intently at Jeremiah's face. Then as if he was satisfied at what he had seen, he beckoned Jeremiah to come closer. Jeremiah was somewhat disconcerted by the fierce expression on the Indian's face, but he bravely moved closer as he was asked. Then the chief spoke. "You look very much like your father. He has been a very good friend to me for many years."

Jeremiah gulped. "Thank you, sir. He has sent a gift for you." He lifted the package and handed it to the chief. The Indian took the package and nodded his head. There were actually two packages, so he opened the smaller one first. It contained a pipe made from very dark-brown wood. The stem and the bowl had been intricately carved with vines and leaves. The second package contained a large pouch of tobacco.

"Um." The Indian grunted. "This is a very fine gift. I see his choice of wood, the black maple in it, and I see the work of Mr. Marples in the carving of the pipe. Tell your father that I thank him for it." With that, he took the pipe and packed it with tobacco. Jeremiah turned quickly and retrieved a burning twig from the fire and handed it to the chief. Smiling, the old man took the proffered twig and lit the pipe. He then began puffing on it contentedly.

In the meantime, Mr. McDougal had gone to his car and had brought out a large wooden box. He set it on one of the logs they were using for seating and then opened the latches, gently lifting out what was inside.

"Why, those are your bagpipes." Jeremiah was curious as he had not seen the box before.

"Aye, this is the reason that we have guests this evening. Why, I brought me pipes all the way from Ireland with me, I did. Me uncle wanted them, but I just could not part with them. You were there when I played them on the Fourth of July. The chief here and his party have traveled a long way today to hear me play them."

The sun had slowly begun to set. The breeze had finally died down, and there was a chill in the night air. Mr. Boggs threw some more wood on the fire, and the group drew closer to take advantage of the heat that it gave off.

Mr. McDougal took one of the wooden pieces attached to the bag and lifted it to his lips, took a big breath, and blew into it. The bag gave out a wailing sound at first, and then it began issuing a harmonious melody. The sounds wafted out across the lake, lightly echoing off the escarpment. The entire group sat enraptured by the music. Some of the songs were soft and lilting, and others made

Jeremiah feel like he wanted to jump up and dance. Mr. McDougal played five songs, then stated that he needed to take a break.

"Aye, it takes a wee bit of breath to work me pipes. After I rest, I'll play some more."

Jeremiah approached Mr. McDougal. "May I touch the bagpipes?"

"Aye, but ye must be careful with them. If they would need any repair, I would have to send them back to Ireland. As of yet, there is no one in America who can repair them. A man is supposed to be coming from Ireland and setting up a repair shop sometime in the next few years, but it has not come about yet."

"Wow. Is it hard to learn how to play them? The music is so pretty. How long have you been playing them? "Jeremiah peppered him with questions.

"Hold on, me lad! I can only answer one question at a time." Mr. McDougal was laughing as he tousled Jeremiah's hair. "I have been playing the pipes since I was a young lad. It takes a fair bit of time to learn them, about five years to be sure. Then ye must put in many, many hours of practice to get really good at it. I also had to memorize the ballads as there is no sheet music for our traditional folk songs. It has been a lifelong labor of love for me. The pipes are me heritage and a tie to me country."

Mr. Boggs took the opportunity during the break to pass around the sugar cookies. The women especially seemed to enjoy the thin sweet treat. The chief had motioned Mr. McDougal over to him and was speaking to him softly. Mr. McDougal gave the chief a nod; then he picked up his pipes again and began playing once again. The songs he played were mournful and sad. He said that they were songs of his homeland, of war and strife. Then he played a marching song saying that it was a century-old traditional song played when the men were going into battle. And finally he ended with a song that Jeremiah knew well. It was "Amazing Grace" as he had heard Mr. McDougal play it before. The music was richer and deeper than when it was played on the piano. The only instrument that could match it was an organ, and their church did not have one. The notes that emanated from the pipes seemed to make the very air vibrate and hum. Jeremiah and Mr. Boggs sang along softly, but the words seemed to hold more meaning when they were rendered along with the music from the bagpipes.

"You remember that I played this song very last on the Fourth of July, don't ye, laddie?"

"Yes, sir, but it seems somehow that it was even more beautiful here."

Jeremiah watched Mr. McDougal as he put his bagpipes gently back into their carrying case and latched it. "Those pipes really are something. I've never heard music so pretty before except maybe when someone plays the fiddle. Thanks for playing for us tonight."

"Why you are more than welcome, me young laddie. I'm glad that you accompanied Mr. Boggs here for a fishing trip. I sometimes come out here to the lake to practice on the pipes. You see, they are rather loud, and they can wail a wee bit. I can play as much as I want to out here as there aren't any neighbors to disturb. At least that is what I first thought. Then one of the Indians heard me practicing here a little while back, and he asked if the chief could come and hear the 'the singing bag with many legs.' I was more than happy to oblige him, and we set the date to meet here tonight on the first full moon. You see, I have really wanted to visit with the Indians in their village and to learn about their culture. I also wanted an opportunity to share my faith in the Lord with them. And now the chief has invited me to come back to their village with them, so it seems that it is all worked out."

"How long are you going to stay with them?" Jeremiah asked.

"Oh, a couple of weeks I believe. The chief's aunt, who is now a very elderly woman, heard pipes played many years ago. She very much desires to hear the pipes again before she dies. So, to that end, I am going to visit the village."

Knowing that the walleyes were usually best caught at night, the men all got their fishing gear out and baited their hooks. They fished in companionable silence, talking only when someone got a bite, which turned out to be pretty often. After they had all fished their fill, they bedded down to get some sleep. Sometime before dawn, the Indians and Mr. McDougal slipped off to journey to the Indian camp.

When Mr. Boggs and Jeremiah arose just before dawn, they found that the party had left.

"They are gone already, and I didn't hear a thing!" Jeremiah exclaimed.

"Hum, that's their way, son. That's also why I'm mighty glad that the Indians are my friends and not my enemy." Mr. Boggs's statement had the ring of truth to it. "Well, let's see if we can fill our stringers yet this morning, and then we will head on back."

The walleyes were hungry, and they had filled one stringer in no time with a good start on the second one. Now the sun was slowly making its entrance in the east, painting the clouds a soft shade of pink against a charcoal-gray sky.

"We got us some fine fish, don't we, Mr. Boggs? This is the best fishing hole ever! I do get some good ones at the dam sometimes, but I have to throw some back because they are too small. I haven't had to throw back but a few here. I do like fishing with you, Mr. Boggs. Thank you for bringing me with you," Jeremiah chirped happily.

"Well, son, I enjoy fishing with you too." Mr. Boggs was puffing softly on his pipe.

"Do you think that we . . . whoa!" Jeremiah was suddenly holding onto his pole with both hands. His line was taut, and then it began jerking wildly from side to side.

"Hold onto that pole real good, son. I believe that the hook is set well, and I hope that the line is strong enough not to break. I think you got yourself a big one here, and if you do, you got a real fight on your hands." Mr. Boggs was now puffing fiercely on his pipe.

"Yes, sir! Boy, it sure is pulling hard. Do you think it is the big one?" Jeremiah's eyes were shining, and he was almost squealing with excitement.

"Well, it may not be that big one, but it seems to be good sized. You are going to have to work it, play it, and wear it down." Mr. Boggs voice was soft as he worked to encourage and to calm the boy. "You may be at this for an hour or so. He will not give up easily."

Jeremiah tried twice to land the fish, but each time he got it close to shore, the fish rallied, almost jerking the pole out of his hands. Finally, the fish tired, and Jeremiah worked it to the shore once again. This time, Mr. Boggs was able to throw some netting over the fish, and together, the man and the boy were able to pull the fish out of the water.

"My, my, my, son, it is the big one at that!" He let out a slow whistle. "All this time and it still has my old hook in its mouth," Mr. Boggs said as he was untangling the flopping fish from the net.

"Look at him! He's huge!" Jeremiah was winded from lifting the heavy fish on to the shore but was still doing a wiggly dance of excitement. "Can we measure it now?"

"To be sure, we are! Let's muscle it up onto the truck and put him up to the measuring stick. I knew long ago when he got away from me that he was already a big fish. Well, he's had a chance to grow some since then, and it appears that he did a mighty fine job of it."

Struggling not to drag him, the two got the fish to the truck and up into the back end of it. "Hum, I am glad that I attached the yard-stick to the tailgate. It makes it easier to get a proper measurement. Yup, it's as I thought. He's a full thirty inches long."

"Thirty inches! Wow! Thirty inches!" Jeremiah exclaimed over again in surprise.

"Yup, we need to register him at the feedstore to get him in the record books. I kind of hate that as we will have to give the name of the lake he was caught in. My fishing hole will no longer be a secret, but it is for a good cause. I will have to learn how to share now, won't I?" Mr. Boggs said with a twinkle in his eye. "I am right proud of you, son. You worked hard landing this fish, and you deserve the recognition. Now let's get this camp broken down and get on into the feedstore. We will stop and get your father to go with us to get this big boy registered."

The two got their equipment loaded, and the camp tidied up in record time, and they were soon on the road heading back home. They traveled in companionable silence. Mr. Boggs's thoughts were centered on how much he enjoyed the company of this young boy.

The boy's zest for life and boundless energy brought much joy to the old man. He planned to approach his friend Mr. Eckhardt and speak to him about something that was very important to him. As he was childless and no longer had any living relatives, he had determined that he was going to make Jeremiah his heir. The house and farm was small, but the land was rich. To him, it was like he was leaving it all to his little brother, and the thought of this boy making it his home brought the old man a sense of peace and contentment.

19

Boat Trip

They were really going! The girls were beside themselves with excitement. It was all that they could think about as they sat on Sarah's porch attempting to work on some crocheting. All of the girls were making doilies that they were going to add to their hope chests.

"So we are leaving on Friday morning. I'm so glad that all of our parents are allowing us to go. Mother was so surprised when Mrs. Himmel arranged for us to stay at her sister-in-law's house. She lives in Minneapolis, and she told our Mrs. Himmel that she is thrilled to have us stay with her for a few days. She is looking forward to having young people in the house again." Abigail was so excited that she just gushed. "She wants to make sure that we get to see as many of the sights in the Twin Cities as possible, so she asked if we would consider staying for at least five days. Oh, it is going to be so marvelous!"

"I know. My mother said the same thing. It is a plan that both of the Mrs. Himmels thought up. It seems that our Mrs. Himmel has been impressed with our visits, and now they want to do a kindness back. It is something about having us 'do the town.'" Sarah was all smiles. "Oh, it is going to be so much fun!"

"Mother told me that I have to bring a gift for our hostess. I'm bringing some rose soap. What are you two bringing?" Abigail had wrapped three bars of the soap that had turned out the best. The rose petals and bits of greenery she had imbedded in the bars peeked out from the milky-white soap, making a beautiful pattern. The soap also gave off a deep rose aroma from the rose oil that she used when she prepared it.

"I'm bringing one of my prettiest candles. It has red berries and pine needles in it and it smells of mulberry." Sarah had sculpted the sides of the pillar candle with the hot knife that they use to open the honeycombs. When she applied the heated knife to the sides of the candle, the wax draped down the sides, and it appeared to have ruffles. It was a new technique that she had been working on, and the candles she had brought to the mercantile had flown off the shelf. "I'm sure that she will like it." Sarah was so happy with her contribution.

Miriam sighed happily. "I'm bringing her a box with an embroidered petit point rose on the lid. It is the prettiest needlework that I have ever done. Mother loves it so much that I am making her one for Christmas."

"Mother is also looking forward to doing some shopping. Mrs. Acres has told her about some specialty shops that carry some things that are hard to find. She had asked Mother if she would mind looking for some specific things for her. Of course, Mother is more than happy to oblige her," Abigail said.

The girls were giddy with excitement as they spent an enjoyable couple of hours together talking about what they would need to pack for the trip and speculating about everything that they would be seeing. Just as they were finishing up for the day, Samuel came running up, he was out of breath, and his face was red with exertion.

"Abigail, you need to come home right away. Grandmother took a fall in the garden and has gotten hurt. Father and Mother are taking her to Dr. Holliday's office right now." His voice was filled with stress and concern.

Mrs. Bernhardt had just stepped out onto the porch as the girls had wanted to show off their crochet work to her. "Oh, Abigail, be sure to call me right away when you get any news. I will call and start the prayer chain. I will also be bringing a meal over for your supper tonight."

"Thank you, Mrs. Bernhardt. I promise to call you as soon as I know anything." She turned to her friends. Both of them gave her a

quick hug. "Go, hurry and get home. I'll be there later with Mother."
Sarah comforted her friend.

"I'll try to come too. I'm sure that Mother will want to send
some kind of food. I'll be praying for you all." Miriam gave her friend
a soft smile, remembering her own sweet grandmother.

As it turned out, Grandmother had a sprained ankle from trip-
ping over a trowel she had forgotten that she had laid on the ground.
"I feel so foolish." She admonished for a third time in less than an
hour.

Mrs. Eckhardt let out a soft sigh as she laid an ice pack on
the older woman's affected ankle. "Mother, please stop stressing over
this. I too have tripped over garden tools more times than I care to
remember. I am just so grateful that you are all right. I think that
your pride is hurt worse than your poor ankle."

"I'm sorry, my dear, my whining is causing you stress. You are
right. I need to take my lumps with better grace and try to see God's
will in this." Suddenly, she let out a cheery chuckle. "Oh my, I had
not thought of this. Why, Mrs. Acres taking the girls to the Twin
Cities is indeed an act of providence. I do believe that Captain Jolly is
sweet on her. What an opportunity this could be for them to explore
a relationship without the stress of actual dating."

"Why, Mother, I had not thought of that. I was just grateful that
she was willing to chaperone the girls on the trip." At this thought,
she too let out a chuckle. "I have no fear that she and the captain
will be circumspect and that they will see to the girl's safety. Oh, now
this whole thing is giving me a shiver of delight. I would have never
thought of playing matchmaker, but now I can see the Lord's hand
in this."

Friday morning dawned bright and clear, and the group was at
the dock early. "All right, my pretties, walk the gang plank, and come
aboard my humble vessel. I will do my best to see to your comforts."
He gave a theatrical bow as he ushered the group onto the boat.
"I can see that we are going to have fair weather for the trip so we
can enjoy the river sights along the way. Your trunks and bags have
already been delivered to your stateroom. Now if you would please
allow me to escort you so that you may make whatever preparations

that may be needed. Then we will meet again on the deck so that I may give you a tour and then impress you with some light refreshments that I have had prepared for you."

The girls emitted twitters and giggles at his performance. "Why, thank you, kind sir, for your thoughtfulness." Mrs. Acres smiled and played along with his grandiose manners.

Abigail leaned over and whispered in Sarah's ear, "I think that I see a spark there. What do you think?"

"Hum, it will certainly be something to keep an eye on. Mother gave me a heads-up as she also thinks that there may be something between these two. I, for one, certainly hope that there is. In fact, I think that it is just grand!" Sarah giggled at the thought.

It became a game for the girls to encourage the captain's attentions by including him in their circle so that he and Mrs. Acres were thrown together. Their motives were innocent. In fact, they considered it their duty to give these two every opportunity to explore a relationship. Being young and full of fantasy, they had already begun to plan the wedding from the dress to the banquet. Their dear chaperone would have blushed if they would have shared their thoughts with her. The young ladies got caught up in their harmless dreams of romance.

They made the trip to the Twin Cities without incident, and Mrs. Himmel had arranged for her chauffeur to be at the wharf to meet them. Mrs. Acres and the girls happily piled into the car, while the captain had their luggage loaded onto a separate truck. The chauffer conveyed an invitation from Mrs. Himmel for the captain to come for dinner. He accepted the offer with aplomb and waved the group good-bye saying that he would be joining them soon.

The group had another surprise when they reached Mrs. Himmel's home. Not only was it a mansion; it was the largest one in the area. The grounds were extensive with magnificent gardens that surrounded a tennis court and an indoor pool. The group was escorted to their room so they could settle in and refresh themselves. The room had a very high ceiling, and it was equipped with two unusual bunk beds. The ladders leading up to the upper beds were actually curved staircases, and the beds were framed like boxes and then draped with curtains. When the curtains were closed, they provided complete privacy. The entire idea was modeled after poster beds that were so popular in Europe.

"It seems that this room was set up for you, girls, and I have the adjoining room." Mrs. Acres had peeked into that room, and she was very pleased as it was just as bright and cheerful. Just then the head housekeeper walked in.

"Hello! I am Mrs. Waller, the housekeeper here. Your belongings should be here shortly, and Hannah here will assist you to unpack. She is assigned to you to help you in any way that is needed. She not only will help you with your wardrobe, but she is also very talented at arranging hair. Ah, your luggage has arrived." Two men brought the suitcases into the room, and then they left. "The girls can choose which of the bunk beds that they wish to sleep in. Mrs. Himmel had these beds built when the relatives brought their children with them to visit. The boys all wanted to stay in the same room together, so this was an obvious solution. Is this arraignment acceptable to you?"

"Oh my, yes, this is so wonderful. I can speak for the girls in saying that we can hardly wait to thank Mrs. Himmel in person. We are all very touched by her thoughtfulness and generosity." Mrs. Acres was smiling softly as she gazed at the girls for affirmation.

"I'm glad to hear you say that, Mrs. Acres." Mrs. Waller let out a jolly laugh. "Wonderful! I will convey your message to Mrs. Himmel, and she looks forward to seeing all of you at five sharp for dinner."

Hannah proved to be a wonderfully joyous person and not only helped the girls to refresh their dresses, but she also arranged their hair and added ribbons. At just before five o'clock, the group was ready to go down for dinner.

"Does everyone have their gift ready? Good. Then it is time to go on down." Mrs. Acres smiled at the girls and ushered them out of the room. "All of you look absolutely lovely."

Mrs. Himmel rose to greet them as they entered the parlor. She was bright and cheerful, and her entire demeanor exuded hospitality and true warmth. Everyone was soon at ease and chatting comfortably. She was surprised and touched when everyone presented their gifts to her. She was amazed that she was in such talented company, and she asked each person to explain about how they had made their gift. "Well, they are all exquisite, and I thank you for thinking so highly of me. Oh, here is Captain Jolly. Now we can all go on into dinner and make our plans."

The girls were hard put to fall asleep that night. They were very excited for they were going to the Barnum and Bailey Circus in the morning. It seemed that the travel manager for the circus, a Mr. Farnum, was a good friend of Mrs. Himmel's, and every time the circus came to town, Mr. Farnum had her bring a group of friends for a backstage tour. As she had a previous engagement, she had asked Captain Jolly if he could escort them until she was able to join them. He assured her that he was more than happy to oblige her. Abigail noticed that Mrs. Acres's gaze would settle on the captain and that she smiled more frequently that evening.

"We are going to see everything up close including the elephants, plus the lions and tigers too! Oh, the boys are going to be so jealous when we get back home." Abigail was excited to see it all, but she was also softhearted. She did wish that her brothers were here for this. "Well, I guess that they will have adventures without me also, so I will keep a diary like I did at camp so that I remember everything and share it all with them."

When they got to the circus grounds, they were greeted warmly by Mr. Farnum. "My, Mrs. Himmel has certainly sent a bonny group of beauties this time. She did advise me that she will be joining us later. Come, it is my pleasure to escort you and introduce you the members of our troupe. We will start with the clowns and the acrobats, and we will finish with the animals. The lions will be in their cages, but I have planned for all to have a ride on the elephants."

The girls had been dazzled by the acrobats when they had seen firsthand how they practiced for their parts in the show. While they practiced, they used safety ropes and nets until they were secure in the execution of their show tricks. It was apparent that they had to be very strong and well versed in each trick before they would perform it in the show. Then the clowns had totally charmed the group by including them in their antics of magically producing paper flowers and throwing buckets full of paper over them. But the elephant ride topped everything. It was bittersweet for Abigail as all she could think about was how much that the boys would have enjoyed being with them.

The circus parade was ready to start when Mrs. Himmel joined them in the box seating area set aside for her and her guests. She had brought someone along with her and was surprised when the girls rushed up and greeted the man.

"Why, Reverend Arnold, it is so good to see you again." Abigail smiled widely.

"Oh good, you all know each other already. Where did you meet?" Mrs. Himmel was curious.

"Why, we attended a wonderful tent meeting where Reverend Arnold officiated. We met a missionary from Africa, and there was also an African who had just become an ordained minister. The whole evening was filled with surprises and revelations, and it certainly changed my way of thinking about the mission field. It especially made an impact on my brother, Randy." Sarah was almost sparkling while she related the story.

"Later, when we attended summer camp, the African minister's daughter, Benah, was there. She is amazing, and she became a very special friend to all of us." Sarah had turned toward Abigail and Miriam as she said this, and they were shaking their heads in agreement.

"Well, young lady, we need to take our seats, and I do believe that we have a special surprise in store for all of you." The reverend smiled cryptically and motioned the group to their chairs. Suddenly, a group led by Mr. Farnum approached the box. The girls had been preoccupied with getting settled into their chairs when they looked up in surprise at the sound of someone calling out their names.

"Abigail, Sarah, Miriam, it is so good to see all of you! So, Father, this was your surprise for me! I could not have asked for anything more wonderful than to see my friends again!" Benah had rushed up to the girls, and they were all hugging one another in unadulterated joy coupled with high-pitched squeals of delight.

The adults watched with pleased smiles at the display of happiness exuded by the young ladies. Benah gave her father a huge smile, plus a high-spirited hug of appreciation. Reverend Uhmah laughed, hugging his daughter in return, and then he turned to address the girls. "I am honored to meet the young ladies that befriended my daughter at camp earlier this summer. I am glad for this opportunity to thank all of you in person as you not only welcomed her, you reached out and embraced her. I see now just why she loves you so very so much, and therefore so do I."

Mr. Farnum interrupted the group as he waved his hand toward the chairs, urging the group to be seated. But the girls couldn't contain their joy, and even after they were seated, they continued to reach out and hold one another's hands. Their happiness was shining out from their faces.

The circus parade began with the calliope out in the lead, followed by the colorful clowns with their ponies and dogs performing their tricks and antics to the delight of the crowd. Then came the beautiful white horses with their acrobatic riders. The riders first stood upright on the horses' backs; then they would disappear under the horse, only to come up on the opposite side and stand upright again on the galloping horse's back. The crowd was cheering and clapping in appreciation at the control and artistry of the tricks.

The clowns were delighting the crowd with their hilarious pranks in the first of three rings. The horses had paraded into the third ring, continuing with their magnificent tricks. This left the center ring vacant.

The curtain parted once again at the far end of the show arena where the largest attraction of the circus was prepared to enter. The crowd was on their feet, clapping and roaring in excited anticipation. They weren't disappointed, as in walked the elephants bedecked in all of their finery. The pachyderms were lined up single file, and as expected, they began their grand procession around the arena. Suddenly, the lead elephant stopped in her tracks. She began swaying from side to side; her gaze concentrated on the side of the tent where Mrs. Himmel and the group were sitting. Despite the urgings of the handler, she was refusing to move; in fact, she was ignoring the handler's commands completely. Suddenly, the elephant lifted her trunk high and let out an earsplitting trumpet blast.

The reverend Uhmah had been speaking with Mrs. Himmel when his head swiveled at the sound. He appeared puzzled as he stared toward the elephant. Being the show master, Mr. Farnum was flustered at the interruption of the performance. "You all will have to excuse me, as I must go and attend to this situation."

Reverend Uhmah reached out and put his hand on the man's arm to stop him. "Wait. I can't believe it! I know this elephant. Look, she has a scar along the side of her trunk. She sustained that injury when she came between me and a very hungry lion. Her heroic actions saved my life that day. Yes, it is! It is Tanoo from my child-hood. Watch!" With that, he stripped off his suit jacket, vest, and tie, along with his shoes and socks. Then he leaped over the side of the seating box and advanced toward the elephant with his arms upraised. At the top of his lungs, he began calling out to the ele-phant. "Tanoo! Tanoo!" He followed this with some more words in his native language.

The elephant lifted her trunk once again, trumpeting in answer. Then she started out at a run toward Reverend Uhmah, with her handler trying his best but failing to control the animal. The rev-erend had stopped and again called out the name Tanoo. Then he dropped to his knees and bowed to the ground right in the elephant's path. Everyone in the tent watched in horror believing that the man was going to be trampled by the enormous beast. But to the crowd's amazement, the elephant ran up to the man and stopped directly in front of him. She then ever so gracefully knelt down on bended knees and bowed to the man. Then both man and elephant stood up at the same time facing one another. The elephant gently tipped her head down to him so that he could place his forehead against hers. He reached up a hand and began stoking the side of her face. She, in turn, wrapped her trunk around him, lifting him up and cradling him in the crook that had formed. Man and beast, long-lost friends, had found one another again.

The reverend finally lifted his tear-stained face, and he saw that Mr. Farnum and the handler were standing to one side, watching the tender display.

"This is Tanoo. I found her as a baby when her mother had been killed for her ivory tusks. She was so starved that, for many weeks, I did not know if she would live. As she healed, we became inseparable, enjoying many happy years together. Then one day, when a lion attacked me, Tanoo fought it off, saving my life. In the fray, she sustained a gash on her trunk, and my leg was severely broken, requiring me to be in traction for many weeks. While I was recuperating, Tanoo disappeared. I later found out that she had been stolen, and though I searched diligently, I never found her. I always wondered what had become of her." Reverend Uhmah's voice was soft as he shared the story.

Mr. Farnum turned quickly to the handler. "This has given me an idea. Go and do the show with the other elephants for now." Then he turned back to Reverend Uhmah.

"Sir, your story is very compelling, and I would like to share it with the crowd. Della here has been highly trained to do many tricks. They are quite simple and only require a little agility. Would you be willing to perform with her?"

"Why, yes, I would be glad to do so. I believe that Tanoo remembers some tricks that we used to do together, and with your permission, we can do those also."

When Mr. Farnum shared the reverend's story with the crowd, they were totally charmed. And then they were further delighted with the performance put on by the reverend and his elephant. They especially enjoyed the fact that they had been privy to the joyful and touching reunion of man and beast.

The afternoon came to an end all too soon as Benah and her father had to leave that very evening. They were to travel by train to New York City, where Reverend Uhmah had many commitments yet to fulfill. Then, one week later, they were to board an ocean liner to sail back to Africa. The girls were just thrilled that they'd had the chance to meet again and to share such a wonderful time. They parted with promises to keep in touch and spoke of hopes of seeing one another again someday.

Five fun-filled days later, the wonderfully happy but exhausted little group sat on the deck of Captain Jolly's boat, reminiscing about the outings that they had enjoyed. Mrs. Himmel had also treated them to a live performance of a Shakespeare play at the theater coupled with a dinner out afterward at a fine restaurant. On three of the days, Mrs. Acres had led them on shopping jaunts where they visited wonderful little shops followed with lunch at quaint tearooms. Then Captain Jolly had escorted them downtown to see the bustling city for themselves, and at the last, he took them for a picnic at Minnehaha Falls with a visit to the zoo. Mrs. Himmel had supplied the girls with swimsuits, and they spent every free evenings enjoying her private swimming pool. It was such a novelty to them to swim in something other than a lake.

"I have filled so many pages in my journal that I am going to have to buy another one! We have had just so many adventures and seen so many things that it has been hard for me to find the time to write it all down!" Abigail smiled at the two adults who were relaxing in the two large deck chairs. "There is just no way that I can thank the both of you and of course both of the Mrs. Himmels too." The other two girls were quick to chime in and add their heartfelt gratitude.

"I don't know about the captain here, but I have thoroughly enjoyed spending time with you three young ladies. I too have had my world expanded by the adventures that we have had on this trip."

The captain smiled hugely and reached out and gently patted Mrs. Acres's arm. "I can't remember when I have enjoyed traveling so much and have had the pleasure of such charming company."

Suddenly, Abigail stood up pointing toward the shore. "Otters! Come look! Oh, aren't they just adorable?" With that, she grabbed Sarah's and Miriam's arms, effectually dragging them over to the boat's railing. As the other girls got caught up watching the charming creatures playing on the shore, she serendipitously looked back at the two adults who were still sitting side by side in their chairs. Mrs. Acres had placed her hand over the captains, and they were talking together quietly. The captain's eyes seemed to be twinkling, and Mrs. Acres's face was fused with a soft glow. Abigail turned back to the otters so she would not be caught intruding on their private moment. But the glance caused a slight tightness in her chest, awakening an unfamiliar longing within her. With mature insight, she realized that what she had just witnessed was newfound love. She had observed the same occasional tender looks that had passed between her parents, and now it was clear to her what a wonderful relationship they shared. Their marriage was built on mutual respect and deep abiding love, and of course it was all grounded in their love of the Lord. Oh yes, she would have much to talk to her mother about when she got home.

20

A Wedding and a Funeral

It was going to be a beautiful fall day. The robins had already begun to disappear flying south to a warmer climate, and the Canadian geese would not be far behind them. The days were getting shorter, and the temperatures were cooler in the mornings. The leaves were still green; but they appeared faded, dusty, and dowdy.

Abigail was beside herself with giddiness. The captain and Mrs. Acres were getting married, and Mrs. Acres had chosen her to be her maid of honor. Both Sarah and Miriam were thrilled to act as bridesmaids. Randy was chosen to be the best man with Samuel and Bobby as the groomsmen. Mrs. Bernhardt was the matron of honor. With Mrs. Acres having two best friends, the choice would have been difficult, except that Mrs. Eckhardt had begged off as her mother had been frail since she hurt her ankle; and she really wanted to concentrate on her and the other elderly who would be attending the wedding.

The ceremony was going to be at the Lutheran church, with the reception being held at the lakeside. The captain's friends Mr. McDougal, Mr. McDonald, and Mr. Baer were providing the music, and the dance floor had been assembled to accommodate the participants.

The girls were all wearing flower-print dresses, but they had made matching moss-green pinafores to cover them. This was topped with matching white capes embellished with white braid.

Mrs. Bernhardt's dress was made from the same green material as the girls, and she also had a white cape. The boys were going to be wearing three piece suits and string ties. What a beautiful wedding party they were going to be.

The town was using the wedding reception as a huge social gathering, and to that end, all intended to make contributions to the wedding banquet. Captain Jolly had contracted Mr. Heineken to make his homemade beer. His family had mastered the art of brewing beer back in the Netherlands, and he continued his passion for making the beer when he settled in Minnesota, much to the delight of the town folk. Though it was still prohibition, his brew was the highlight at many of their celebrations. The sheriff only asked that they refrain from imbibing until he left so he could claim ignorance of the infraction. Mr. Bernhardt contributed a large smoked honey ham, and Mr. Boggs had caught and smoked fish. The local ladies were all bringing covered dishes of vegetables and other local delicacies. And, of course, there was going to be a beautiful wedding cake made by the local bakery. The captain had become enchanted with the English wedding tradition of serving iced fruit cake, which was beautifully decorated with marzipan fruits that appeared almost real.

Mrs. Bernhardt, Mrs. Himmel, and Mrs. Acres had emptied their flower beds of blooms. The flowers were not only used to make the bridal bouquets and boutonnieres but were also dispersed in the greenery that bedecked the interior of the church. It was going to be a beautiful and joyous celebration!

Randy was so excited. Captain Jolly had asked him to be the best man. He was glad that he had his good suit that he had worn to the graduation dance in June. In preparation, Mother had sent him to the barbershop for a haircut so he would look sharp. But Randy did have one other concern. During the ceremony, he was to take the ring from his pocket and hand it to the captain when he asked him for it.

"It's all right, Randy. I will give you the ring just before my bride comes down the aisle. Then you will just need to hand it back to me when I ask you for it. See, it is simple. I know that you will do a fine job." The captain smiled and patted him reassuringly on his shoulder.

Randy did not want to leave anything to chance, so he went through his father's toolbox and found a washer that he thought was about the same size as the ring. Each night, for an entire week, before he went to bed, he would put his suit jacket on and stand in front of the mirror. Then he would solemnly reach into his pocket and take the washer out and place it on the dresser as if he was placing it in the captain's hand. He repeated the ritual at least five times each night until he was satisfied that he did it perfectly. Then he would hang his suit coat back up in the closet and go to bed dreaming about the big day.

Mrs. Bernhardt and the three girls hurried up the porch steps, chatting gaily. Mrs. Acres met them at the door with a cheery greeting and a bright smile.

"Oh my! Don't you all just look so very lovely! You girls each resemble a beautiful bloom from my garden just as I pictured that you would."

"We want to use some of the green ribbon in our hair. We learned how to fix it up when we went to the Twin Cities." Miriam's eyes were shining bright, and she fairly bubbled.

"Oh yes, that is a wonderful idea. Here, I made some tea and cookies to nibble on. At least I hope to be able to nibble a bit. I feel so foolish as I can't remember when I have been so nervous. I mean, after all, this is not the first time that I have married."

Mrs. Bernhardt burst out in laughter. "Well, it's certainly the first time for you to marry the captain. You are a bride, and therefore you have a right to be nervous. Let's nibble a bit. Then we will get you into this beautiful dress."

The dress was fashioned from rich cream-colored materials. The bodice was constructed in two layers with the strapless under bodice made of the heavier material. Topping it was a layer of a cream-colored sheer material that was pleated in the front from the neckline to the waist. This had a choker-type collar and long sleeves that where puffed and ended in long French cuffs that were fastened with a row of covered buttons. The collar and the cuffs were embellished with heavily reworked lace. The full skirt ended just below the knee and was nipped in at the waist. A thick creamy ribbon was used as a belt, and it was tied in the back in a large full bow.

Instead of a traditional veil, Mrs. Acres had a hat made by a milliner friend who owned a shop in Minneapolis. The woman had taken the creamy material and folded and tucked it in a diamond pattern, and she used it to cover a simple pillbox-type hat. To this, she had added a net veil that came just to the chin. She had embellished the netting by attaching small pearls to it. Mrs. Acres then used more of the pearls as accents that bedecked the braids of her deep-auburn hair. The last finishing touches were white high heels and white gloves.

Mrs. Bernhardt finished dressing Mrs. Acres's hair into two elegant French braids, which she had worked along each side of her head, ending in a twisted bun at the nape of her neck. As she was adding the pearls, the three girls had finished fixing their hair also. Their eyes went wide when Mrs. Acres stood up and adjusted her dress.

"Why, Mrs. Acres! You are so beautiful! I mean, you have always been beautiful, but today you are especially so!" Abigail gushed.

"Yes, dear, you are truly exquisite! Here, take a look in the mirror." Mrs. Bernhardt gently turned her friend until she fully faced the cheval mirror in the corner of the room.

As the woman slowly raised her head to see her reflection, her eyes widened in surprise. "Oh my, is that really me? Why, I guess that I do clean up pretty good. It is your talent working with hair that has made the difference here." Then she began to giggle.

Giggling along with her, Mrs. Bernhardt gave her friend a hug. "You are so silly, my dear! Oh, I hope that the captain realizes what a lucky man he is."

"Well, if we don't get to the church on time, he may never know," Mrs. Acres joked as she gathered the flower bouquets into a basket. "There is just one more thing that we have to do before we leave. Come, my friends, let's pray together."

The two women and young ladies held hands in a circle and bowed their heads.

The church was fairly bursting at the seams. To accommodate the crowd who could not fit into the building, the windows had been opened so that the folks could still watch and hear the ceremony inside. The crowd was amiable as they were all friends and neighbors, and they took advantage of the opportunity to catch up on all of the "news."

Mrs. Bernhardt drove up into the church yard and was surprised at how many folks were outside the church. They were guided to a parking spot that had been reserved just for the bride and groom as Mr. Bernhardt was going to chauffer the couple to the reception and then to the boat afterward so they could begin their honeymoon. The crowd was happy to see the bride's arrival as they knew that the ceremony would be starting soon. The ladies were greeted and exclaimed over and then ushered up onto the porch where they took their positions.

"I believe that the bride has arrived. Ladies and gentlemen, take your places, please, and we will begin." Reverend Arden organized the groom and his party into their proper order; then he waved to Mrs. Talent at the piano to start the processional march.

On cue, Mrs. Bernhardt entered the church and began her slow saunter down the center aisle of the church. Suddenly, the captain turned to Randy and handed him the ring. "It will be just as I said. Just give me the ring when I ask for it. Buck up, son. Everything is going to be just fine." The captain smiled and patted him lightly on the shoulder.

Randy had been somewhat nervous before this event, but now his anxiety reached a bit higher level. To his chagrin, he had begun sweating. When he swiped his hands on his pants to dry them, he looked up and into his mother's face. She gave him a reassuring smile and a nod, and it steadied him.

Then the music swelled, and he knew that the bride was on her way. He looked up to see Mrs. Acres being escorted down the aisle by Mr. Heimlich. Only this was not as Randy had ever seen Mrs. Acres before. Gone was the beekeeping attire. Instead, she was a vision in her cream-colored dress carrying her bouquet. He saw that her gaze was focused on the captain's face and that she seemed to be glowing.

When they reached the front, Mr. Heimlich gently lifted the veil from her face and kissed her lightly on her cheek. Then he put her hands into the captain's.

The ceremony was progressing, and the time came for the captain to put the ring on the bride's finger. He put his hand out toward Randy, and as he had done every night for the past week, he reached into his pocket and pulled it out, placing it into the captain's hand. The captain looked down and got a puzzled expression on his face.

Confused, Randy looked at the captain's hand, and to his horror, he saw that what he had put in his hand was not the ring but the washer. Panicking, Randy whispered a "Sorry," and quickly reached back into the pocket to retrieve the ring. But in his panic, Randy had made a fist around the ring, and his hand would not come back out no matter how hard he pulled. Finally, he gave it a tremendous yank. Well, his arm flew upward with the force, and the ring sailed up and out of Randy's hand, arcing upward into the overhead rafters.

The entire bridal party broke out into laughter as Randy stood rooted to the spot and blushing a deep red. Mr. Heimlich and Randy's father hurried up from the front pew. His father put his hand on Randy's shoulder. "It's all right, son. I saw where it went, and we will lift you up so that you can get it. Are you ready?"

Randy shook his head in affirmation. Each man grabbed one of Randy's legs and lifted him straight up under the rafter where the ring had disappeared. Randy felt around for a moment, and in relief, he called out, "I got it! I got it!" Randy tried to give the ring to the captain, but he curled Randy's fingers up around the ring. Looking directly into Randy's face with a smile, he said, "Everything is just fine, son. You need to hold it as you have a task that you need to finish."

When the parishioners had regained their solemnity, Reverend Arden repeated some of the ceremony and then again asked for the ring. This time, Randy put the ring safely into the captain's hand, and the ceremony progressed to its conclusion. The wedding party exited the church with the bride and groom being inundated with a rice shower, as was traditional. Then the entire crowd loaded up into their vehicles and proceeded to the lakeshore for the reception.

Some of the ladies from the church had opted to forego the ceremony so they could prepare the food tables for the reception. That way, when the bride and groom arrived, they could immediately cut the cake so that the feast could be consumed and the dancing could begin.

The captain and Mrs. Jolly observed that Randy was hanging back from the festivities as he was taking quite a ribbing for the episode with the ring. He had his head down and was shuffling his feet as the two gently pulled him aside. The captain put his arm around Randy's shoulders, and Mrs. Jolly took his hand in hers. "Randy, we want you to know that the episode with the ring was the best thing that could have happened. We wanted our wedding to be so joyful and memorable that everyone who attended would never forget it. Your part with the ring did exactly that. It was the grandest joke ever played on us, the best ever! So when anyone says that you tossed the ring, you just tell them, 'Yup, I sure did, didn't I!' Then just laugh at yourself right along with them."

"You mean you're not mad at me?" Randy mumbled.

The captain lifted Randy's head, and he looked directly into Randy's eyes. "Far from it, son. In fact, we are both so very proud of you. You finished a task when you could have run off instead. That was a very manly thing to do. Now we want you to see the humor in this and be a sport about it."

"Okay, so long as you're not mad at me, then I will laugh too!"

With Randy finally being mollified, they shared smiles and a group hug. Then the couple was called to the dance floor to begin that part of the festivities.

The girls had all taken their turns to dance with the groom and were standing back sipping some of the punch that had been supplied. Abigail spotted the group of elderly that had been ensconced in large rockers off under a tree. "Look, there's Mr. Ware talking with Mrs. Rogers. Father says since his accident he has been visiting her almost every week. He comes to church every Sunday and has been there to help out for projects too. He gathered all of the greenery used to decorate the church today. He couldn't climb the ladder, but he handed all of the branches to my father to hang up. Jimmy says that life at home is so different now. His mother and father don't argue anymore, and his father is involved in everything that they do. Mr. Ware does things like helping to fold the laundry, cooking, reading to them. and playing games. He has really changed since the accident."

"Yeah, I ran into Tucker at the mercantile, and he told me that he takes them all fishing quite a bit too. He helps the little ones to bait their lines, and then when they land a fish, he puts them on the stringer for them praising them for a job well done. He's a totally different man, and it has made a big impact on the family," Sarah shared.

Abigail grew somewhat somber and gave out a sigh. "Father noticed the change in him too. He told me that good things can come out of bad experiences and that this just proves him right. Mrs. Himmel is still paying him his full wages, but Mr. Ware really wants to come back to work. Father has found him something that he can do while he is still healing, so Mr. Ware will be working again starting next week. He is really happy about it."

Randy was munching on a plate full of food and was watching while the bride and groom made the rounds of their guests. Right then they had stopped to talk to Mrs. Rogers. The three had spoken for a bit; then they had bowed their heads in prayer. In awe, Randy saw that an angel was standing next to them. He blinked his eyes to see if it would disappear, but it was still there. He was so surprised that he almost fell over. When he heard the captain say amen, suddenly, the angel was gone. Randy felt a hand on his shoulder, and he looked up into Mr. Ware's face.

"You saw him too, didn't you?" Randy shook his head in affirmation. "He was the one who held the logs back from crushing my head that day at the mill. Mrs. Rogers and I have spoken about him many times. He was with her years ago when she while she was lying in the freezing water. There is a reason he is here today that will be revealed to us soon. Go and talk to Mrs. Rogers about seeing him. She will want to know. Well, I need to get back to my sweet little Janie. Oh yes, and I want to thank you for helping her with her math problems. Using her dolls and their clothing to teach her how to add and subtract was absolutely genius." As Randy watched Mr. Wares retreating back, his mouth dropped open in amazement. He had not been accused of being a genius before.

A few minutes later, Randy approached Mrs. Rogers and sat down on the ground next to her. She appeared to be dozing but without opening her eyes she greeted the young man.

"Well, son, you have certainly had an exciting day, haven't you?"

"Yes, ma'am, I have. The captain and Mrs. Acres—ah, I mean Mrs. Jolly—weren't mad at me at all about the ring. They think that it was a fine joke. Whew! Now I can laugh about it too." Randy gave a sigh of relief.

Mrs. Rogers opened her eyes and chuckled. "My goodness, yes, son, it gives them great joy to have such a joke played on them. You did just fine, boy, and you finished your task. That shows a lot of character. Now what did you really come over here to talk about?"

"I saw the angel. He was here when you were praying. Mr. Ware saw him too."

Mrs. Rogers looked intently into Randy's eyes. "How do you know the angel, son?"

"When I was first born, I was really sick. I was so hot, and I couldn't drink my momma's milk. She cried and cried. She and Daddy prayed and prayed, and then the angel came and touched my head. Then I could eat. That's how I know him."

"Ah, then their prayers were answered. That is a wonderful story. Thank you for sharing it with me. I know that your mother and father would like to know about this also. Would you please make sure that your share about the angel with them?" Mrs. Rogers closed her eyes again. "They are going to have the fireworks soon. You need to find a good spot to see them from. First, give an old woman a kiss, though."

Randy dutifully kissed her on her cheek; then he ran off toward the lakeshore.

Mrs. Rogers sat in bemusement, and she smiled at Zachariah as he arrived at her side. He began arranging the blankets that covered his mother, tucking them in around her. "Are you warm enough,

Mother? Do I need to find you another blanket? Or are you too tired to stay and watch the fireworks? I could take you home if you'd like."

The old woman looked up at her son with a twinkle in her eye. "What? And have you miss an opportunity to share a romantic snuggle with sweet little Susan? That young lady thinks that the sun rises and sets on you. How could I not approve of someone who holds my son in such high esteem? No, son, I will be fine here sharing the moment with my friends." Her eyes became distant. "Night is falling soon enough, and to cut the day short would be a tragedy."

Zachariah leaned to kiss her on her cheek, and she reached up and gently stroked his. He looked deeply into her eyes. "I am so blessed to have a mother such as you."

"Pshaw! Go on now." But she watched him as he walked out of sight, and she lifted a prayer for him and the lovely girl whom he went to find.

The fireworks had just finished, and the captain and his bride were saying their last good-byes. Mrs. Eckhardt, along with her husband, was loading the elders into their neighbors' cars to be escorted back home when she noticed that Randy was sitting quietly next to Mrs. Rogers. Zachariah walked up to his mother's chair and softly called out to her. With a tear-stained face, Randy looked up at him.

"The angel, he came and got her a little bit ago."

With surprise, Zachariah got down on his knees and called out. "Mother? Oh, Mother!" Then he reached out and took her cooling hand and brought it to his chest, bowing his head over it. He quietly began to weep.

The others heard the anguish in his voice and rushed to his side.

Mrs. Jolly stooped down, and she gazed at Mrs. Roger's. "Oh, my dear, dear friend. You have finally gone home again." She turned and looked up at her husband. "We will have to postpone our trip, dear."

"Oh no!" Zachariah softly interjected. "Mother would not want you to do that. I believe that it took all she had to stay here this entire day in honor of you two. She would not want you to postpone your honeymoon." He turned back and looked at his mother. "We will lay her body to rest as we celebrate her finally going home again. It is how she would want it."

The following day was the wake, and the day after that it was a somber yet joyous crowd that gathered at the graveside. Each of her friends had an anecdote that they shared about how Mrs. Rogers had touched their lives, thereby enriching theirs. After that, as was the custom, each person said good-bye as they tossed a handful of dirt onto the casket that had been lowered into the hole. Back at the house, the group talked quietly as they comforted one another.

Randy found Zachariah talking with Mr. Huffmeister, and he shifted nervously from foot to foot until Zachariah noticed him. Zachariah put his arm around Randy's shoulder. "I take so much comfort in that Randy was with my mother when she passed, that she was not alone. He also told me that an angel came to get her. Isn't that right, son?"

"Yes, sir. She wanted me to tell you something else too. I forgot until right now. I'm sorry. But I don't know what she was saying. Oh, darn, I'm getting it all messed up." Randy was almost stuttering in his confusion.

"All right now, just slow down and tell us what you do remember." Zachariah gave him a smile and a little hug in reassurance.

"She said something about a legacy. What's a legacy anyways? But she said that it is under a black rock on the north side of the well." The words fairly rushed out of Randy's mouth. "There, I did it. I said it just like she told me to."

"What? Over these later years, Mother did talk about a legacy left by Grandfather and the old colored man, but then she always became upset because she couldn't remember where it was they had supposedly hidden it. I always thought that it was just some confused ramblings on her part, a leftover from her injuries from the accident. I never put any stock in it."

Mr. Huffmeister's expression was pensive as he rubbed his chin. "Hum, it must have been pretty important to your mother for her to leave this specific information with Randy with instructions to relay it to you. This well, it is the one out back, is it not? I think that it deserves a look, don't you?"

"It certainly is a puzzle. All right, let's go take a look." Zachariah called out to Mr. Bernhardt and Mr. Eckhardt to come along with them.

Zachariah explained the story to the two other men as they trooped out to the north side of the well. Sure enough, there was a black rock built into the wall about three rows down. One of the men hurried to the toolshed and brought back a shovel and a crow bar.

The men slowly began removing the rocks that were stacked above the black one. It was hard going because the stones had been well set, and they had been together for a long time. When Zachariah put the pry bar under the black stone and applied pressure, the stone suddenly began to give way. Zachariah dropped the pry bar and lifted the black stone, revealing that the stone beneath it had been hollowed out, leaving an indentation that contained a small leather pouch. He worked the drawstring of the pouch loose and tipped the bag. Then he stared down quizzically at the contents that dropped into his hand.

"Rocks? I don't understand." Zachariah was gently rolling them around in his hand.

"Do you mind? I would like a closer look at them." Mr. Huffmeister was holding his hand out. Zachariah shrugged and handed them over. Mr. Huffmeister began rolling them around in his hand also. "In New York, I have a friend who is a jeweler who specializes in fine gems, mainly diamonds. Sometimes, when he got a shipment of them from South Africa, he would invite me over and teach me gemology. I am not an expert by any means, but I did learn a little about diamonds and how to grade them. Though these are still uncut, they are very large, and I can also tell that they are of very fine quality and clarity."

From the shocked expression on Zachariah's face, he could tell that the young man had no idea just what he had here.

"Zachariah, if you would like to take these to my friend in New York to get an appraisal and even perhaps to sell them to him, I would be glad to write you a letter of introduction. He is a fair and honest man and would do well by you."

Zachariah was still somewhat dazed, but he immediately saw the wisdom in it.

"Yes, yes. I believe that is what I should do. Thank you, sir, for your offer of assistance. If you had not been here and recognized them, I may have just put them in a drawer and forgotten about them. So you think that they may be valuable?"

"Humph!" Mr. Huffmeister seemed to almost choke. "My dear young man, if these are as fine as I think they are, you are now a wealthy man."

Later that day, when the Bernhardts got home, the elders each got a cup of tea and were sipping it on the front porch. Randy had changed from his suit and climbed up onto the porch swing next to them. He let out a sigh and looked over at them.

"Mother, Father, I have something very important to talk to you about. It's about Mrs. Rogers and her angel. Well, she told me that I had to tell you that he's my angel too."

Mr. Bernhardt looked at the boy and nodded his head. "Son, after all that has happened these last few days, I am inclined to believe anything that you have to say. Now I think that it is time for you to share the entire story with us."

ABOUT THE AUTHOR

Hannah Lynn Grace is a freelance and historical fiction writer whose narratives are loosely based on family stories that have been passed down through the generations.

Hannah lived in Minnesota for over twenty years during her childhood and young adult years, both in the cities and on the farm. She now makes her home in East Texas with her two cats, a small garden, and a large back porch that overlooks towering pine trees where she dreams and spawns more escapades of adventure for all her growing number of extraordinary but everyday characters.

She is also a mother of two grown daughters, a grandmother of five, and a great-grandmother of one.

Courage Rises from the Ashes is her debut novel.

CPSIA information can be obtained
at www.ICGtesting.com
Printed in the USA
FFOW02n2144281217
44291366-43869FF